THE FINISHING SCHOOL

Also by Joanna Goodman

Harmony
You Made Me Love You
Belle of the Bayou

THE FINISHING SCHOOL

A Novel

JOANNA GOODMAN

HARPER

NEW YORK • LONDON • TORONTO • SYDNEY

HarperCollins
PUBLISHERS
Since 1817

This is a work of fiction. Names, characters, places, and incidents are products of the author's imagination or are used fictitiously and are not to be construed as real. Any resemblance to actual events, locales, organizations, or persons, living or dead, is entirely coincidental.

FIRST EDITION

Designed by Leydiana Rodriguez

Library of Congress Cataloging-in-Publication Data has been applied for.

ISBN 978-0-06-246558-0 (pbk.)

17 18 19 20 21 LSC 10 9 8 7 6 5 4 3 2 1

For Miguel, Jessie & Luke, who are everything.

"Of the not very many ways known of shedding one's body, falling, falling, falling is the supreme method, but you have to select your sill or ledge very carefully so as not to hurt yourself or others."

—*Vladimir Nabokov*

"I love you, even if there isn't any me, or any love, or even any life."

—*Zelda Fitzgerald*

THE FINISHING SCHOOL

I want you to know the story of how you came to be and to understand why I had to do what I did. I know that some of the things I did were crazy. Some people thought I went too far, that I became unhinged. At times, I did, too. But no matter how strange or surreal it seemed, there was, for me, a perverse logic to it.

I'm here to tell you it was worth it. You were worth it. And I would do it all over again if faced with the same choice. I challenge any woman in my shoes to walk away from the fortuitous opportunity that was presented to me, or to opt for defeat when a solution so miraculously landed in my lap.

I never saw myself as the kind of person who would stop at nothing to get what I wanted, but this last year has proved that's exactly who I am. I found within myself a selfishness and a relentlessness I did not know I had. Those traits are not always a bad thing, especially for someone like me. Someone who rarely staked a claim.

You brought that out in me; my desire for you prevailed over all else, including that need to please everyone and be approved of and always do the reasonable thing. Nothing about how I wound up here was reasonable. Nothing about your story to this point aligns with the woman I thought I was. You summoned me to fight, to do the inconceivable and be utterly dauntless about my ambition. Funny, the harder I fought—not just for you, but also for the truth—the more I began to like myself.

Turns out I'm not so different from Cressida after all. You have your life because of it.

CHAPTER 1

TORONTO—September 2015

Lille is dead.

Kersti rereads the letter, which arrived inside an innocuous envelope from her agent, Rona Sharpe. She tore it open, anticipating the usual royalty statement with Rona's familiar *for your records* scribbled at the top. But inside that envelope there was another letter, still in its sealed envelope. It was addressed to Kersti Kussk-Wax, c/o Rona Sharpe Literary Agency. There was a Connecticut postmark and the name Robertson printed on the back flap.

Kersti opened it and read the square yellow Post-it stuck to the letter, which was from Lille's mother.

> *Kersti, we found this letter on Lille's computer after she died. I had forgotten about it until I received an invitation to the Lycée's 100th Anniversary. Lille's letter is unfinished, but it may be of interest to you. Best, Jaqueline Robertson*

Kersti's mouth went dry. *After she died?* She unfolded the letter, her fingertips tingling. After all these years of silence, a letter? It made no sense.

Dear Kersti,

Mwah mwah mwah. Three kisses for old times' sake. I know it's been a long time, but I've been following your writing career and I've read your last two books and I'm so happy for you. My favorite was *Moonset over Tallinn*. (I tried to order *The Ski Maker's Daughter*, but it doesn't seem to exist.)

I won't get to read your next one. I'm going to die soon.

After I graduated from the Lycée (I stayed to complete the year . . . where else could I go?) I was accepted at Brown, and managed to get a degree in Psychology. I briefly entertained the possibility of becoming a Jungian analyst. Ha! In the end, I decided I couldn't risk further undermining the already fragile mental stability of my future potential clients. So I took some photography courses. I love photography. I even had a show at a small gallery in Williamsburg back in '99, but my confidence wasn't up for all that scrutiny—having my work displayed on the walls for people to judge. I even felt unworthy of the positive attention. Nothing sold. I wasn't very good anyway and continued to pursue it only as a hobby.

I've had an underwhelming life, even by my own standards. There was more I could have accomplished—there's actually a fairly sharp intellect in this warped brain—but my desires and ideas never seemed to match my output.

Fear. That was my problem. I've always felt like a child cowering in a corner. Oddly enough, the one thing I did not fear was death. I feared not being liked; not being good enough; not being worthy; not being respected; not being beautiful; not being happy or useful or productive; I feared being exposed, being abandoned, being seen, being judged, being rejected.

But I never feared death. (Good thing, it turns out.) Do you remember that book *The Secret* that came out a few years ago? Everyone was talking about the Law of Attraction and how you could manifest whatever you wanted in life just by thinking about it—but also that you could manifest whatever you *didn't* want just by thinking about it. The whole concept was oversimplified and exploited, but not without its truths. I believe the fear inside me eventually turned into a tumor and settled in my breast. Stage 4, at the time of my diagnosis. Seventeen lymph nodes infected. That's a lot of fear.

The process of dying stirs up a lot of shit, Kerst. I'm not intending this to be a confession, but I've kept a lot of stuff to myself over the years. I wonder if I should have shared it, at least with a shrink. I imagine that all the crap I've kept to myself lives inside that tumor. (Have you ever read the story "Hairball" by Margaret Atwood? After the main character has a tumor surgically removed, she stores it in formaldehyde, keeps it on her mantelpiece, and calls it "Hairball.") That's how I picture my tumors (I've got lots of them now—in my bones, my liver, my spine).

I know this is a cliché of the dying person, but certain things in particular still haunt me:

1. I don't believe Cressida "fell" by accident.
2. There's something incriminating in the Helvetians ledger. I think Deirdre has it (if not, where is it?).
3. I wonder if Magnus saw anything (I saw him leaving Huber House that night).
4. I wish I'd spoken up sooner
5.

The letter ends abruptly. Obviously, Lille had more to say. Maybe she got too sick; maybe she wrestled with how much more to confess and then died before a satisfactory answer ever revealed itself.

Kersti realizes she's still standing at her desk and collapses heavily into the chair.

Lille is dead.

She sits with that for a moment, a feeling of trepidation pulsing inside her. She hasn't seen Lille in almost twenty years, so it's not like there's a physical void, but there's definitely a heavy-heartedness, a crush of dread that has more to do with Kersti's recollection of that entire era; of what happened to them that forever expunged their freer, more hopeful selves.

Lille was a strange, acutely empathic girl whose awkwardness and discomfort in the world was a palpable thing. Her sensitivity was an affliction, like an exposed nerve. Certain people dying young are not a surprise. Lille's death, though tragic, is one of those unshocking deaths. She always possessed a certain sadness of spirit, a weary resignation about life that probably could not be sustained deep into old age.

Cressida was the opposite. She was life itself. She was beauty, vitality, and possibility all breathed into an exquisite physical form. She was the embodiment of power, inner and outer. She was unforgettable, her impact no less potent in her absence.

They're both gone now and Kersti's long-repressed grief over Cressida's accident is starting to fester and rise to the surface. She can feel it in her chest, her throat, her head. As she folds up the letter and shoves it in her top drawer—as though hiding it can keep the truth from encroaching on her life—Kersti already knows that hearing about Lille's death so soon after being invited back to the Lycée will be the inevitable catalyst that forces her to face the tsunami of grief and guilt she's been holding back since the age of eighteen.

The invitation to the hundredth birthday gala is hanging on the magnetic board above her desk. She glances at it now, still undecided about whether or not to attend. Her years in Switzerland were the best of her life; the way they came to an end, the worst.

You are invited to celebrate our 100th birthday on
June 11, 2016, at the Lycée International Suisse.
1005 Lausanne, Switzerland.

Inside the envelope there was also a letter.

Dear Kersti,

In 1916, the Lycée opened its doors to a handful of students seeking the highest standard of education in the world. Since that time, we've been accredited by the European Council of International Schools and become one of a group of schools to be officially recognized by the Swiss Confederation. In 1925, our day school became co-ed and although we are proud of the great many achievements of our male alumni, as part of our centennial celebrations, we have selected "One Hundred Women of the Lycée" to represent the last century of our success in grooming young girls to reach their full potential and become thriving citizens of the world.

In 2016, the Lycée Internationale Suisse will celebrate its 100th birthday. We are delighted to inform you that you have been selected as one of our "One Hundred Women of the Lycée" for your outstanding achievements in the Literary Arts. We invite you to be one of the keynote speakers at our 100th Birthday Garden Party on Saturday June 11th, 2016 . . .

What would Cressida have thought of Kersti being chosen one of the One Hundred Women of the Lycée? She probably would have made Kersti feel like an idiot for feeling flattered.

When Kersti first got back from Lausanne after the accident, it was hard not to think about Cressida all the time. She became so depressed and reclusive she finally had to make the purposeful decision to *not go there anymore*. From that point on, she stopped living in the memories—the good, the bad and the surreal; stopped visiting that dark, deep place in her mind and forged ahead with her life. That meant she had to ignore all the unanswered questions that had been left dangling, which became easier and easier to do over the years. And yet here it is, that sleeping beast, gently waking after all this time, claws extended, determined to pull her back there. She's not surprised. It takes outrageous arrogance to think one can successfully outrun the past, and Kersti has never been that arrogant. Cressida was, but not Kersti.

She opens her desk drawer and removes Lille's letter again. She rereads it, finding herself stuck at the part about Magnus. *I saw him leaving Huber House that night . . .*

Lille's letter is a welcome distraction from her last, tense conversation with Jay. She gets up, leaving the letter on her desk, and goes downstairs to the basement, where she drags a box marked LYCEE out of the storage closet. In it, she's saved report cards, photo albums, yearbooks, and a shoe box full of tokens and mementos—a coaster for Bière Cardinal . . . *moment d'amitié;* programs from the Fête des Vendanges in Morges and the 1989 Holiday on Ice at the Palais de Beaulieu; lift tickets from every ski trip she ever went on, from Thyon to Gstaad; placemats from Niffenager's Brasserie (they called it Niffy's) and from Café le Petit Pont Bessières (they called it 2,50's, the price of a chope); her medals from the Vaud

Volleyball Championships; an artsy black-and-white photo of the Molecular Structure; a paper menu from Chez Mario, which has a strong mildew smell; and a handful of photo-booth photos—Kersti and Cressida, Kersti and Lille, Cress and Raf; Lille and Alison; Kersti and Noa. All six of them. Serious, silly, smiling, tongues out, kissing, fake tans, frost-and-tipped hair, the nineties.

The sharp stab of nostalgia is piercing. She hasn't allowed herself to do this in almost two decades. Still, she kept everything. She was happy there, truly herself.

The yearbook is unsigned by her friends. She left Switzerland before it was handed out to the students and it had to be mailed to her. Her "Bequeaths" aren't even included. Neither are Cressida's or Lille's. She reads Noa and Rafaella's Bequeaths and what surprises her now is that they were able to bounce back so quickly after the accident and compose their lighthearted summations of the school year. *I bequeath my tweezers to Komiko; raw brownies to Ali; the third-floor bathroom to the "Helvetians of '94."*

Strange, given that one of their best friends had mysteriously plunged from her fourth-floor balcony just weeks before the end of the school year. Kersti had a much harder time recovering. Maybe she never did. Not just from the accident, but from the friendship itself. Going through the yearbook again, Kersti can't help being transported back to that phase of her life that was both so brief and so deeply impressive. There she is in Stratford-upon-Avon, in Basel, at the Christmas Torchlight Descent, at Villars, Verbier, Chateau-d'Oex—

"Kerst?"

She looks up, disoriented. Jay is standing at the bottom of the stairs, looking disheveled and sleepy. He must have fallen asleep on the couch. She feels far away from him tonight, not just because of everything that's been going on between them—the stress, the arguing, the tension—but because her mind is in the past.

He looks older to her at this moment, as if she's looking at him through the eyes of her teenage self. He's just turned forty and has a wreath of silver in his dark hair, some lines indented in his forehead, which was as smooth as a candle's surface just a year or two ago. But she's being hard on him. She's in that kind of a mood. He's handsome and well preserved; he makes an effort. If not for the silver wreath and the newish forehead lines, he doesn't look a day over thirty-five. Plus he's got a formidable upper body—broad shoulders, slim waist, great abs—that can be attributed to the flour- and sugar-free diet he embarked on after his thirty-ninth birthday.

He takes a step toward her, but keeps his distance. "What's going on?" he asks, running a hand through his hair.

"My friend died," Kersti says, closing the yearbook.

"Who?"

"Someone from the Lycée. She had cancer."

"Shit. That's young."

Not as young as seventeen, Kersti thinks, remembering something Mme. Hamidou once told her about Cressida. "Cressida is too brilliant to waste her talents on an ordinary life," she'd said in a portentous voice. "She has a great destiny, which someday she'll share with the world."

Kersti had always believed that to be true. Everyone did. And Cressida *was* destined for something far bigger and more unimaginable than the rest of them. Her great destiny turned out to be tragedy.

"I might go back to Lausanne in the spring," she tells Jay. "For that hundredth birthday thing."

CHAPTER 2

LAUSANNE—September 1994

Kersti and her mother arrive at the train station in Lausanne on a brilliant September morning. The air is muggy when they step out of the Gare. Most of her luggage was shipped to the school ahead of time so she only has one suitcase to manage. Facing the McDonald's across the street, Kersti's first impression of Switzerland is that it looks just like Toronto. It's nothing like all those pictures of green valleys and pristine lakes and snowcapped mountains. It's traffic, fast food, sour faces rushing to work. It could be any generic city, which bothers Kersti because what's the point of coming all this way?

Her mother hails a taxi. Kersti gets in and slumps against the window while her mother drones on about the fondue she used to have at some café in Place St. François. Her mother went to school at the Lycée when she was young and always wanted her daughters to have the same experience. The "privilege" has fallen to Kersti because her sisters didn't have the grades to earn the Legacy Scholarship. Kersti had the grades, though not the inclination; but being her mother's last hope, she didn't have much say in the matter. Everyone thinks it's some marvelous gift but the truth, Kersti knows, is that her parents are sending her away because they're exhausted.

Kersti's mother was forty-five when she had Kersti, which makes her the age of most kids' grandmothers. She's got faded blue eyes and her pale blond hair has yellowed over the years, like discolored paper. She's still slim, but her angles and lines are softening into old age. Kersti has always resented having older parents. From an early age, it was obvious to her that their energy and enthusiasm had been used up raising her three older sisters; she could sense they were tired and a little disinterested. Shipping her off to boarding school feels more like they're giving up than bestowing a privilege.

"After you settle in," her mother chirps, her Estonian accent even more grating than usual, "we'll walk down to Place St. François for a hot chocolate and a ramequin. You haven't had hot chocolate until you've had one here."

Kersti continues to stare out the window, remembering bits and pieces from the dozens of Lausanne brochures her mother gave her before they left. The city is built on the southern slope of the Swiss plateau, she recalls, rising up from the lakeshore at Ouchy. As the taxi climbs the steep cobblestone streets, a dramatic panorama of the Alps comes into view and the city begins to look distinctly more European than it did down by the train station.

Her new school is in a suburban section of Lausanne, set back from the street, enclosed by a black wrought-iron gate and hidden behind a fortress of leafy trees. Kersti notices the black bars on the windows and can't help comparing the school to an eighteenth-century women's prison. She can't believe this is where she will be for the next four years.

There are half a dozen buildings that make up the campus, the two largest connected by an enclosed footbridge. All the buildings are white with carved green dormer windows and red-tile roofs.

A sign at the entrance announces LYCÉE INTERNATIONALE SUISSE. *BIENVENUE.*

Kersti hauls her suitcase inside Huber House, which her mother tells her is the main building that houses both the dining room on the first floor and the dorms on the second, third, and fourth. The other houses are Frei, Chateau, and Lashwood.

Inside Huber House, it's dark and drafty, shabby. It reminds Kersti of the Estonian House back home. Everywhere is dark wood—the long dining tables, the chairs, the floors and ceilings, the crown moldings, the stairwell and banister. The drapes are dark green velvet, puddled on the floor. A carved plaque in the foyer proclaims the school's founding mission statement: *Preparing Young Women to Become Citizens of the World since 1915.* The corridor smells of beef stew and cigarette smoke.

"Ah, the smoking," her mother says, with a nostalgic sigh. "I miss Europe." Her big complaint about Canada is that no one smokes anymore.

A small, dark-haired woman wearing a red blazer with dwarfing shoulder pads, a matching red pencil skirt, and bright white Reeboks greets them in the foyer. She looks somewhere between forty-five and fifty-five, but it's hard to tell. She isn't very attractive—her hair is cut in a blunt, mannish style, very unflattering, as though she did it herself with kitchen scissors—but there's something warm about her brown eyes. Or maybe it's the way she smiles, like she's absolutely thrilled to see you.

"I'm Madame Hamidou," she says, giving Kersti a hard handshake. "Welcome to the Lycée and to Huber House. I'm your housemother."

She has a wiry, athletic body that she propels up the stairs, taking two at a time in her pristine running shoes. "You'll be in good shape by the end of the year," she calls down to them. Kersti can't figure out her accent. She speaks perfect English with only the faintest trace of something European—possibly French or German. "Here's your room," she announces, throwing open the door. "Your roommate is Cressida. She's a returning student so she can show you the ropes."

"When did she start?" Kersti's mother wants to know. "I was here from fourth grade until I graduated."

"Cressida's been here since second grade."

Second grade? Kersti looks at her mother in a new light of gratitude for not having shipped her overseas at the age of seven.

"The welcome luncheon is at twelve fifteen," Hamidou says. "Students only."

Kersti steps into the room and looks around. It's weird and old-fashioned; nothing matches. There are two single beds side by side, with tall brass headboards and matching comforters in a 1960s gold paisley design. The furniture is of a heavy oak—a bedside table between the beds, two twin desks, a bookcase, two behemoth dressers. There's a garish carpet with a design of brown, mustard, and rust medallions, faded floral wallpaper in pinks and greens, dingy eyelet curtains in the windows, and a porcelain pedestal sink in the corner that may have been here since the school was built in 1916.

"Is this what forty thousand dollars buys?" Kersti asks, going over to the bed and touching the disgusting comforter. She knows what a year at the Lycée costs because she overheard her father complaining about it. He didn't want to send Kersti here even on a scholarship, but her mother can be extremely forceful.

"Wait till you sleep under it," her mother says, unzipping Kersti's suitcase. "It's filled with goose down."

Kersti would be happy with her old polyester quilt from home.

She wanted to go to a regular high school in Toronto and have her own room with her own things. She doesn't need to ski the Alps and sleep under goose down or learn French to make her well-rounded. She opens the large bay windows overlooking the back of the school grounds and here at last is the postcard she's envisioned—clusters of red-tiled roofs and church spires descending into shimmering, opalescent Lake Geneva, which stretches out toward France and the majestic Alps.

"That's Evian over there," her mother says. "Isn't it breathtaking? I remember the day I arrived. . . ."

Kersti tunes her mother out. The view is nice. It smells good, too. Like clean laundry. But it's not home.

At lunch they serve thick brown stew and strange noodles that look like fried white worms. Nice warm rolls, hot chocolate, and kiwi. Kersti eats in silence, seated beside a giant German girl with a crude bowl haircut, clothes from the seventies, and a strong body odor that wafts across the table. According to the sticker on her chest, her name is Angela Zumpt. The smell is so pungent Kersti can't turn her head in that general direction without feeling queasy.

The teacher at the head of Kersti's table is Mrs. Fithern. She has curly brown hair and slightly buck, overlapping front teeth. She tells them she's from England and asks them where they're from, what grade they're going into, and how they like Switzerland. Kersti is grateful to be halfway down the table so she doesn't have to answer. She isn't like the rest of these girls. She's only here because she got some obscure scholarship.

Her roommate doesn't turn up for the welcome lunch, nor is she there when Kersti's mother drops her off after dinner. Curfew is ten. *Ten!* Kersti hasn't gone to bed at ten since third grade. She sits by herself in her new room, staring out at the Alps, feeling completely alone. She already misses her mother. How does a mother just drop her child off in another country and leave, she wonders? How did all the mothers of all these orphans do it?

Kersti imagines the kind of mother she'll be to her own children. Loving, nurturing, fun, present. She will never ship them overseas. She'll be hands-on, devoted; she'll *want* to be with them. And she'll have them before she's thirty, too, so she can be full of energy and enthusiasm. Eila will be her first daughter, Elise her second. She doesn't like anything for a boy yet, but she probably won't have boys anyway.

Close to ten, Mme. Hamidou sticks her head into the room and interrupts Kersti's fantasizing. "Cressida will be here tomorrow," she says. "It gets better, love."

Hamidou turns out the lights and closes the door behind her. Kersti can hear her running downstairs to the lounge, one floor below. She can smell the smoke from Mme. Hamidou's cigarettes. She closes her eyes and lies down, succumbing to the jet lag. She sleeps like a baby under the fluffy down duvet with the fresh Swiss air blowing in from the open dormer window.

The next morning, Kersti comes back from the shower to find her roommate, Cressida Strauss, unpacking a box of books. Kersti's breath catches; she's never seen anyone like her.

"Hi," she says, shoving a handful of books in the bookcase.

Kersti is wrapped in a towel, naked except for her flip-flops and a streak of blood on her shin from where she cut herself shaving. Cressida is wearing a chambray Polo button-down tucked into faded Levi's, with riding boots, completely casual. But on *her* . . . She looks like she's just ridden in on her horse, fresh-cheeked and wind-blown, posing for a Ralph Lauren ad. Her suitcases and a number of boxes are piled on the floor at her feet.

"I'm Cressida," she says, as ordinary as can be. But she's far from ordinary. She has a beautiful, unruly mane of hair, spiraling out in all directions. Her head is just slightly too big for her slender body, but she's dazzling, with pale green eyes, exquisitely long lashes, and a prominent, arched brow. Kersti is literally awestruck by her perfect pink complexion, no doubt from all that good clean Swiss air. Her posture, her height, her long legs—all of it together a masterpiece of teenage magnificence.

Staring at her, practically with her mouth agape, Kersti hates, worships, and wants to *be* her in one sweeping, exhilarating moment. She feels suddenly dwarfed in her presence, diffused. Cressida is on a whole other level of beauty. She's in another realm.

"Where are you from?" Cressida asks, shoving books onto the shelf.

"Canada."

"With a name like Kersti Kuusk?"

"My parents are Estonian but I grew up in Toronto."

"Great. No language barrier. My last roommate was from Japan. Didn't speak a word of English."

Kersti can't help noticing the books she's lining up in their communal bookcase: *Ulysses, The Wings of the Dove, To the Lighthouse, The Sound and the Fury, Tender Is the Night.*

"Do you want to go get a chope?" Cressida asks, Dostoevsky's *The Idiot* in her hand.

"What's a chope?"

Cressida smiles. Gorgeous teeth, gleaming white, straight.

They go up the street to the Café le Petit Pont Bessières, a fluorescent-lit saloon full of old Swiss men drinking beer for breakfast. Cressida orders two chopes, which are barrel-shaped steins of Cardinal beer. "Welcome to Switzerland," she says, clanking her mug against Kersti's. "What do you think so far?"

"The students seem kind of strange," Kersti says. "Everyone smokes and speaks a bunch of languages and wears shoulder pads in their sweatshirts."

From what she gathered at yesterday's luncheon, most of the kids at the Lycée have grown up in European boarding schools. Their parents are princes, princesses, famous designers, actors, oil barons in the Middle East. "I like the name Cressida," Kersti says. "I've never heard it before."

"My mother is a Shakespeare buff," Cressida explains. "Of course she had to name me after one of the most obscure and misunderstood of all his plays."

She waits a beat and, realizing Kersti has no idea what she's talking about, says, "Cressida was a traitor, the archetype of female duplicity. She betrayed her supposed true love Troilus, a Trojan, and aligned with the Greeks. And then she was basically forgotten."

"My name means 'follower of Christ,' which is ironic since my parents are both atheist."

Cressida laughs and Kersti feels a sudden crushing desire to impress her new roommate, to hear that laugh again and again.

"So what's your story?" Cressida asks her.

"I don't think I have one."

"If you're here, you've got one."

Kersti thinks about it for a moment. She feels unsure of herself, more than the usual low hum of insecurity. The beer is making her queasy. Everything is whirling—her mind, the room, her sense of balance.

Cressida hands her a cigarette from her pack of Marlboro Lights.

"I don't—"

"Right." Cressida lights one for herself. "Give it some time," she says confidently. "Smoking is like breathing here. I started at twelve."

"My parents are European. They both smoke."

Cressida exhales perfect smoke donuts above Kersti's head. "You met Claudine?"

"Who?"

"Madame Hamidou. Our mother-away-from-home."

"Yes. She seems nice."

"What does your dad do?" Cressida asks her, jumping from one question to the next.

"He owns a travel agency."

Cressida raises an eyebrow.

"I'm here on scholarship," Kersti says.

Cressida tips her head and fixes her aquamarine eyes on Kersti, as clear and brilliant as two perfectly round gemstones.

"My mother is an Old Girl," Kersti explains. "Her parents had money, but they cut her off when she moved to Canada with my dad."

"That's romantic."

Nothing about her parents' marriage strikes Kersti as romantic. It's true Anni Lepp came from a fairly affluent family—by Estonian standards—and gave it all up to be with Kersti's father, Paavo, but having grown up in their home, under the dark cloud of their mismatched union, Kersti can only describe her mother's decision as impractical and misguided. Romantic, *never.*

Anni was from the Old Town of Tallinn, the daughter of a successful architect. She claims to have had a good childhood. They lived in a modern house facing a vast pine forest and her fondest memory is of putting on her cross-country skis inside the house every morning, and then skiing down the stairs right into the woods. When she was nine, her father sent her to school in Switzerland. It was 1944 and he wanted her to be safe and also to have better opportunities than she would have had in a poor country like

Estonia. She ended up staying there almost a decade. Her father also sent his money to Switzerland, stashing it there for safekeeping during the war, which is how he managed to hang on to it when most people lost everything. When she graduated from the Lycée, her parents sent her to Canada to live with second cousins, always hoping she would have a better life than Estonia could offer.

Paavo was a poor working-class guy from Kalamaja in Northern Tallinn. He was not educated and had no obvious skills or ambition. He worked on the assembly line at the cross-country ski factory. In 1948, when he was eighteen, he went to Canada on the SS *Walnut*—a boat full of Baltic refugees fleeing the Soviet invasion. Paavo had nothing of real substance to offer a girl like Anni Lepp, but he was extremely handsome and charismatic, and she fell in love with him at an Estonian Youth Club dance. He'd already been in Canada five years but was still doing odd jobs in factories. He hadn't managed to build anything.

Her parents were furious. All their hard work and sacrifice to ensure a good life for their daughter had led Anni to a blue-collar Estonian barely eking out a living. When she married him, they cut her off.

Four decades later, Kersti's parents have the kind of terrible marriage that is marred not by vicious fighting, but by frequent, long, punishing silences.

"Does she ever regret it?" Cressida asks Kersti.

"Marrying my dad?"

"Sacrificing the family money."

"We don't talk about that stuff."

"Parents rarely do," Cressida says. "They're too afraid to let us know they make mistakes. God forbid we would ever find out they're human."

"What are your parents like?" Kersti asks her. "How come they sent you here when you were so young?"

"It was the best thing for me," Cressida says, as though she's said it a million times before and believes it. It's a canned response, even Kersti can tell. "My mother's a stage actress and my father is a producer. She's British and he's back and forth between L.A. and New York all the time. They're never in the same city for very long. They felt boarding school would give me the most stability."

"Did it?"

"Oh, sure."

Kersti can't tell if she's being serious.

"What difference does it make if I'm here on my own, or if they're fucking me up in closer proximity?" she says rhetorically. "It all evens out in the end."

She finishes her chope and flags the waiter, who doesn't seem to care how old they are.

"Do you do this every Sunday morning?" Kersti asks her.

"And Saturdays after lunch."

"Is there anything else to do?"

"Besides skiing? Sometimes we go to Ouchy, down by the lake."

The waiter brings over the chope and Cressida speaks to him in perfect, melodic French. They laugh and he pats her shoulder affectionately.

"What else can you tell me about Kersti Kuusk?"

Kersti wants to tell her something dramatic and shocking that will impress her, but she doesn't have much in her arsenal. Her father drinks too much. Whose doesn't? She's a virgin. It's the usual adolescent alienation and sense of impending doom. "I'm pretty ordinary."

"You must have some little juicy secret."

"My family's nickname for me is Ônnetus," Kersti offers.

"Which means?"

"Accident," Kersti replies. "My mom got pregnant with me after her tubes were tied, seven years after what was supposed to be her last kid. I don't really get along with any of them."

"Didn't they adore you and smother you? Isn't it always like that when the baby of the family comes along late?"

"Not in my family. They were pretty indifferent to me. It's kind of like I'm not a real Kuusk because I wasn't supposed to *be*. I think that's the real reason they sent me here. They don't have the energy to parent me."

"I knew you had a story," Cressida says triumphantly.

"I don't think about it much."

"That's a lie. I bet you think about it a lot."

Cressida is right. Kersti does think about it a lot. Cressida already understands that about her, which is really quite thrilling. No one has ever gotten her before, or for that matter, really seen her and accepted her anyway. Cressida doesn't seem to give a shit about Kersti's lack of credentials, or who she has to pretend to be for the world, or what she looks like, or her silly bravado. She's dug her hands right inside Kersti and she's feeling around in there, looking for something she can get hold of, something dirty and real she can grasp. That's what she's really interested in—the gory truth—which is utterly freeing.

"What about you?" Kersti says. "What's your story?"

"It's only our first date," Cressida answers, smiling. "Too soon for my dark secret."

Kersti suspects Cressida has more than just one.

CHAPTER 3

TORONTO—September 2015

The view through Dr. Gliberman's picture window on the eighteenth floor looks like a grainy black-and-white photograph. Sheets of rain against the glass blur the Toronto skyline, completely obscuring the CN Tower. Kersti is distracted today. Lausanne's been on her mind, whether or not to go back. And Lille has, too. Ever since Kersti got Lille's letter, she's felt uneasy. The new information that Magnus Foley was at Huber House the night Cressida fell has been niggling at her. Did Lille want her to do something? Is that why she wrote her? And if so, what?

"Kersti?"

Her gaze drifts away from the window and over to the baby pictures on Dr. Gliberman's Wall of Success. *Thank you for making our dreams come true! We will be forever grateful, Dr. G! Introducing Kiley and Kiera! Introducing Jack, Sam, & Mason!* Singles, twins, triplets. The cards on the wall seem to be multiplying as fast as the infertile couples around her. She wants her own card up there on the wall. *Introducing Eila!* She's had the name picked out since age six, her first year at Estonian summer camp.

"You've got a few options," Dr. Gliberman says. Kersti's head snaps back and she regards him with her usual blend of reverence and desperation. Gliberman is self-important and abrasively arrogant, but he has a reputation for getting even the most hopelessly infertile couples pregnant. His desk is cluttered with framed pictures of his own five children, who mock Kersti whenever she sits across from him.

Behind his head, there's a life-size poster of a woman breastfeeding her baby. The mother and baby both have milk mustaches, and beneath them, the slogan: GOT BREAST MILK?

"I don't recommend more IVF, Kersti. You've already done six cycles and you're just not producing good-quality eggs. In fact, your eggs in this last cycle were the quality of a woman in her midfifties."

Kersti lets out a soft gasp and looks down at her feet, ashamed. She's only thirty-five. Jay reaches for her hand and she can't help but think about all the promise of their wedding day. She'd felt utterly triumphant walking down the aisle toward him, so damn handsome in his black tux and white Converse. She believed then that only good things lay ahead for them, the fulfillment of every wish and dream.

Jay had just quit his job and was about to open his own ad agency when he showed up at Kuusk Tours, where Kersti was working for her father, looking to book one last trip before his new business swallowed his freedom. The moment he walked through the door, Kersti was taken. He had dark hair that fell to his jawline, brown eyes that kind of winked at her without actually winking, and a smile that made her feel like a jelly fish. He was wearing a suit with Converse running shoes and had a computer bag slung across his chest. He could have been a college student or a stockbroker, but he was exactly Kersti's type. She knew right away with a sinking feeling that she was with the wrong guy. What had been only a nagging suspicion about her current boyfriend of four years, Aleks Rummo, the beloved Estonian camp sweetheart whom her parents had practically chosen for her, was now a sickening, irrevocable fact.

Jay ended up buying a plane ticket to Stockholm that day and, thinking she was Scandinavian, asking Kersti out on a date. Lucky for her, he wasn't too disappointed when he found out she was Estonian and by the time he got back from his Scandinavian holiday, Kersti had already broken up with Aleks.

In the years that followed, life began to unfold in delightfully unexpected ways. Jay proposed and Kersti started taking creative writing courses at a local college. After their wedding, which was officiated by an Asian Unitarian minister—a reasonable compromise, given that Jay is Jewish and Kersti is an emphatically nonreligious Lutheran descended from a long line of nonbelievers—Kersti took time off from Kuusk Tours and, with Jay's moral and financial support, began to work on her first novel. The marriage was in a renaissance. Jay's agency was thriving. She was writing. They bought a house.

And then one day they looked at each other and they both knew. It was time. They were ready for a baby. She remembers the excitement of deciding on their timeline. How naïve she'd been, thinking she could *choose* the timing of her pregnancy. But those first few months of trying were wonderful. Sex everywhere, all the time. Lying upside down with her legs in the air, believing *this was it.* "I think we just made a baby," she would giggle. "I *feel* it."

When nothing happened, panic set in. It was fertility monitors and thermometers and increasing anxiety, until it all culminated with a grim diagnosis of blocked tubes. Not technically blocked—which would have been simpler to fix—but *closed*. Or, as her ob-gyn put it, deformed. The ob-gyn drew a picture of normal tubes, and then Kersti's, which looked like a pair of boxing gloves. Still, her doctor was optimistic. Kersti was a perfect candidate for IVF. She was only in her early thirties and everything else was in perfect working order.

Thus began their long journey here, and what is starting to feel like the end of the road. One last chance to please her old-world Estonian parents. Motherhood surely would make her less of an outsider in her family; at least that's what she keeps telling herself.

"I think it's time to explore other options," Dr. Gliberman says. "I don't want to risk another miscarriage—"

Jay turns to her abruptly. "We could go on that cruise in the Baltic Sea," he says, sounding way too excited for the situation at hand. "The *Baltic Beauty,* the one that goes to Copenhagen and Oslo and Russia. And then we could even pop over to Tallinn for a few weeks—"

"A cruise?" she says, astonished. "Instead of becoming *parents*?"

"We talked about our life getting back to normal if this cycle didn't work. Dr. Gliberman is telling us it's over—"

"I haven't said it's over," Dr. Gliberman interrupts. "I *can* get you pregnant."

"We've given this everything we've got," Jay says, grabbing her hand with urgency. "We can see the world together. Let's move on, Kerst. Let's put our life back together—"

Kersti looks over at Dr. Gliberman. "How can you get me pregnant?" she asks him.

"With an egg donor."

Jay jumps up. "We're not using a donor," he says.

"Jay, just listen—"

"I never signed on for this," he mutters. "I'm done." He runs a hand through his hair. "I'll be waiting outside."

When they're alone, Kersti folds her hands in her lap and looks at Dr. Gliberman as though nothing has happened. "What are the next steps?"

After the appointment, Kersti goes home by herself and Jay goes back to work. She heads up the front walk to her house, bending once to inhale the sweet scent of her stargazer lilies, which are still blooming happily in the sun and completely indifferent to her self-pity. She loves her garden, especially now, wet and lush, carpeted with soaking grass. The thrips are swarming the sunflowers, burrowing holes in their leaves, their fringed wings propelled by the post-thunderstorm gusts. The neighborhood is otherwise still. Life goes on, she thinks. All around her, life goes on, and she's slightly buoyed by the reminder.

Inside, the foyer is light and open, flooded by sunlight; a mirrored Venetian pedestal table sparkles beneath an admittedly ostentatious crystal chandelier. The walls are Cloud White, the wood floors and stairwells stained almost black, the three fireplaces carved white marble. Kersti likes her spaces simple, soft, and clean. The only bright color is found in their art—bold, bright pieces personally selected for them by their art dealer at the Bau-Xi Gallery. She drops her bag on the table and goes into the kitchen to make lunch. She pulls out the pot of leftover *nogesesupp*, sets it on the stove, and then retrieves the hard-boiled eggs she prepared this morning. She stirs the soup, tastes it with a wooden spoon, adds salt, and tastes it again. Sunlight is streaming in through the kitchen window, softly lighting the six eggs that are perfectly arranged in the glass bowl. Like a painting, she thinks, ladling soup into a ceramic bowl. She crumbles one hard-boiled egg over the bowl, places it on a tray with some sourdough bread and the day's mail, and heads upstairs to her office.

Her office is a small oasis that occupies its own wing at the end of the second-floor hallway. It's got sloped ceilings and wood beams and the wall-to-wall bookcase Kersti always dreamed of having when she used to fantasize about writing for a living. Today, her laptop sits open on her desk, the words from the first chapter of her next stalled effort ridiculing her. The three novels in her bookcase with her name printed on the spine do nothing to silence that voice in her head that shrieks: *You're not a real writer! You suck! You're going to humiliate yourself with this one!*

Her first short story was published by the *Tundra Peregrine Literary Review,* a prestigious though obscure Northwest Territories magazine, while she was still at Humber. With her creative writing professor's guidance and encouragement, she decided to turn that story into a novel. Three hundred and seventeen pages later, when she was just twenty-six, *The Ski-Maker's Daughter* was published by Snapping Turtle Press, a small publisher out of Nova Scotia, to decent reviews. The novel, which sold about twelve copies and was quickly removed from the shelves of Indigo and Chapters bookstores, vanished from the literary landscape as though it had never existed. But its publication helped Kersti land a fairly prominent Toronto agent named Rona Sharpe, who was instrumental in getting her next book, *Moonset Over Tallinn,* published in Canada and the United States by one of the big publishing houses.

The love story of an Estonian refugee and his beautiful Russian lover, *Moonset Over Tallinn* sold an astonishing hundred thousand copies in Canada alone, making it a surprise bestseller. Kersti was not yet thirty, which added to the PR frenzy around the book's success. She was nominated for all sorts of literary awards, including the prestigious Luba Shishbaum Prize for best writer under thirty, which she did not win. There were a lot of accolades at that time for being the Most Promising Writer Under Thirty, or the Most Promising Canadian Woman Writer Under Thirty, or the Most Promising Historical Women's Fiction Writer Under Thirty. The only thing that did not happen for her before thirty was having a kid.

Her third novel generated respectable sales and brought forth another round of literary prize nominations, although again no actual prizes. And no sign of her parents' approval, either. "Another corny saga about star-crossed Estonian refugees?" her father said. At least she was solidifying her own literary niche, in no danger of being challenged by another better writer under thirty. She dominated the Estonian refugee market.

It doesn't seem likely at this point that she will be able to please her parents, not even if she wins a Nobel Prize for literature. What would have made them happy is if she had married an Estonian and been able to breed.

She opens her desk drawer and takes out the letter from Lille. She notices a newspaper clipping in the envelope and realizes Mrs. Robertson also included Lille's obituary.

After a long battle with cancer . . .

Lille would never have "battled" cancer. She didn't battle anything or anyone. She succumbed. Cressida was the one who fought. She fought for what she wanted, fought against what she didn't want, fought for the sake of fighting. Which was what made the fall so shocking. Whether she was drunk and indifferent or suicidal, Kersti always felt the falling implied she'd given up.

One of Kersti's last memories of Cressida is of her floating across the grass in the moonlight to meet one of her lovers, daring to snatch the freedom she believed she was owed. How can you know everything is about to change? You can't, of course. Kersti had no premonition. That night, she was angry with Cressida. She felt betrayed.

Cressida had changed by then. It was obvious to Kersti and the rest of their inner circle that the more selfish, self-centered side of her was now fully in command. Their friendship had become something of a love/hate roller coaster. Cressida had a way of always drawing Kersti back in, but that night, as Kersti watched Cressida escape from the school grounds, she wasn't sure she could be there for her much longer.

The next morning, when Mme. Hamidou told Kersti what had happened to her roommate, Kersti was paralyzed with guilt. She'd contemplated the possibility of abandoning Cressida that very night. In the end, it was Cressida who abandoned her.

The days that followed the accident are still quite hazy. Kersti remembers Mme. Hamidou sitting down with her on the front steps of Frei House. It was dusk, the same day Cressida's body was found. The ambulance and police were long gone and an eerie silence had fallen over the school. Hamidou had given her a sedative that morning and even though it was almost dark, Kersti was still groggy. Hamidou handed Kersti a cigarette and lit it, and then lit one for herself. "Take a deep breath," she said. Her voice was shaky, but it was also soothing. Kersti tried to focus on it in order to feel calmer.

"Did she go out last night, *mon amour*?" Hamidou was looking at Kersti expectantly with her warm brown eyes. "Do you know if she snuck out?"

Kersti nodded.

"Where did she go?"

"I don't know," Kersti lied, not sure if Hamidou believed her.

Hamidou put her arm around Kersti and held her. She loved Cressida, too, had practically raised her. She was a mother to all the motherless boarding school girls in her care.

The police asked Kersti questions. Did she know where Cressida had gone last night? Who she had gone to meet? Had she heard any noises? Fighting? Kersti's answer was always the same. *No, no, no, no.* Had she confided in Kersti about being depressed? Had she been suicidal? Had she fought with anyone?

No, no, no.

They searched her room for a note but found nothing. It soon came out that she'd been very drunk. A bottle of vodka had been found. Her blood alcohol level came back .26. Word spread through the Lycée that Cressida had been wasted and accidentally fallen from the fourth floor. There was little time for speculation before the school closed ranks and put an end to the entire unpleasant matter. The fall was declared an accident, which was confirmed by the police investigation. Any other possibility was bad for business. And the Lycée was a business, first and foremost.

The next thing Kersti remembers, her mother was in Lausanne, standing in the middle of her room, helping her pack. She may have tried to persuade Kersti to stay and finish out senior year, but Kersti refused. She had to get away.

The memories of school she's tried to keep close to the surface are the lovely, sentimental ones—flinging open her window every morning to look out at Lake Geneva; train rides through perfect green pastures and snowy mountains; afternoons lingering in cafés, sipping hot chocolate, nibbling pastries and gossiping with her best friends. Nights out on cobblestone streets with European socialites or dancing in discotheques with royalty. But that wonderful life tucked away in the Alps also had a sinister underbelly, which culminated with Cressida's beautiful body broken on the concrete. In the end, that image edged out all the rest, no matter how hard Kersti has tried to blot it out.

She has a few spoonfuls of soup and then turns back to her novel. The voice in her head attacks immediately. *How many Estonian Harlequin romances can you write?*

She quickly abandons the chapter she's been working on and googles an egg donor website, losing herself in an endless parade of potential donors. One after another, the fertile, vibrant twenty-somethings smile back at her, their youth and properly functioning reproductive parts making her feel a little more useless with every click.

"What stinks?" Jay calls from downstairs, startling her.

"Boiled eggs!" she answers, closing the donor website and returning her novel to the screen. "There's Nogesesupp on the stove!"

Moments later, Jay appears in the doorway, holding a bowl of soup. He sits down on the chaise longue and balances the bowl on his lap. "I'm sorry about today, babe," he says. "I just . . . I freaked out."

"It was a lot to take in."

"Can we just take a few days and not talk about it?"

Kersti purses her lips and nods. She doesn't bother telling him she's already been researching possible donors. Somewhere along the way, this became *her* crusade. It wasn't always this way. When they first found out she had deformed fallopian tubes, Jay pulled her into his arms at the clinic and declared, "We *will* have a child. We'll do whatever it takes. We're *partners*."

"Soup's delicious," he says, filling the silence.

She reaches for the letter from Lille. "Can I show you something?" she asks him, wanting to change the subject. "I got this letter from Lille. The Lycée friend who just died."

He takes the letter and reads out loud:

. . . certain things in particular still haunt me:

1. I don't believe Cressida "fell" by accident.
2. There's something incriminating in the Helvetians ledger. I think Deirdre has it (if not, where is it?).
3. I wonder if Magnus saw anything (I saw him leaving Huber House that night).
4. I wish I'd spoken up sooner.

"She never finished it," Jay says, looking up at her.

"What should I do?" she asks him.

"What can you do?"

"I'm not sure. But I feel like I let Cressida down."

"How?"

"I moved on. I never questioned anything. I just assumed it happened the way they said, that she was drunk and she fell—"

"Did you really?"

"I don't know anymore," Kersti says. "But I think Lille knew something she never got to tell us."

"What's that ledger she's talking about?"

"It belonged to some Lycée girls who were expelled in the seventies," Kersti explains, not wanting to elaborate. "Cressida was obsessed with it. I never knew why."

"Was Cressida the suicide type?" Jay asks her.

Kersti thinks about it for a moment and realizes she's always known the answer. "No," she says. "She could be dark, but she was never hopeless or depressed. She always had an idea or a plan. I never thought it was suicide."

Charlie and I are going to travel through Europe this summer.

That's what Cressida told Kersti the night before she fell and she'd seemed genuinely excited about it.

"Maybe Lille thought someone pushed her," Jay suggests.

"Maybe."

"You never talk about what happened in Switzerland," he says.

"It was another lifetime."

"Your best friend fell off her balcony and you left school before finishing. Hardly insignificant. I've always felt a bit shut out of your past."

Kersti shrugs, not sure what to say. "I told you. I didn't want to dredge it up. I wanted to forget about it and move on."

"Did you?"

"I guess not."

"What about this Magnus guy? Can you talk to him?"

"I don't know—"

"What about Deirdre? Could she have that ledger? Obviously this was your friend's dying wish, for you to find out what happened to Cressida. You could probably use the distraction—"

And there it is. Kersti bites her lip. He wants her to find something to occupy her time so she'll stop pressuring him about an egg donor. "I don't know where the ledger is," she mutters.

"What are the Helvetians?"

"It was a secret society at the Lycée. It was banned after those girls were expelled, long before I got there. I have no idea what any of it has to do with Cressida," she says. "Anyway. I should get back to writing."

She looks purposefully at her laptop, but they both know she hasn't been writing.

"Sounds like you might have the makings of a good mystery novel here," Jay says. "Maybe it would be cathartic to write about what happened to you at the Lycée. Maybe you could look at it as research for your next—"

"Maybe," she says, gritting her teeth. And even though she's annoyed with his suggestion, she can already feel the familiar stir of that feral writer inside her getting wind of fresh prey.

Jay stands up, collects the tray with her cold, unfinished soup, and forces a smile. "I'll let you get back to your work."

Kersti doesn't respond, but after he's gone she stares disapprovingly at her laptop, hating every word of the opening paragraph of her latest Estonian novel. She feels no spark for *The Jewel of Reval*.

In spite of how angry she is with Jay, his idea to explore what happened to her in Switzerland is not a bad one. Baby or no baby, she already feels that creative twinge in her gut, the spark that typically informs which direction she's going to go with a book.

CHAPTER 4

LAUSANNE—February 1995

Ten p.m. on a freezing cold Saturday night. All six of them stumble inside Huber House, the door slamming behind them. Curfew. The foyer is warm. They're giggling and shushing one another. Six drunk girls, stomping their snowy boots on the mat, removing their hats and mittens, unzipping their coats. Alison Rumsky, Lille Robertson, Noa Vandroogenbroeck, Rafaella Schwartz, and Cressida and Kersti.

They clomp upstairs, tracking snow and slush on every step, doing a poor job of being quiet. Kersti and Cressida are holding hands. Kersti is very drunk and still buzzing from her flirtation with Magnus Foley. Cressida yanks her backward, making it impossible for them to get up to the third floor.

"*Shhhhh!*" Alison hisses. "Hamidou's going to come out."

Kersti and Alison are on the volleyball team together. Kersti is a setter, Alison the star hitter. She's from Vancouver—one of the few other Canadians at the Lycée—and has an open, friendly way about her. She has red hair, golden freckles on pink skin, and a tall, ultralean body that serves her well as captain of both the basketball and volleyball teams, as well as on the slopes. She's the school's superstar athlete, Coach Mahler's protégé.

Mahler himself was the silver and bronze medalist respectively at the 1948 and '52 Winter Olympics for bobsled. He's been coaching at the Lycée since the late fifties and some say he still wears the same uniform he wore back then—a snug-fitting undershirt, high-waisted shorts, and tube socks pulled up to his knees. Like many teachers of his generation, he's never embraced political correctness in his coaching style. He often refers to the girls as twits and spinsters and *schwachköpfe*—which means imbecile, but sounds slightly less offensive in German—and thus he somehow manages to get away with it. In spite of that, he's well liked. He's ferociously competitive and his winning record over the past three decades no doubt gives him sway with Harzenmoser and Bueche. After all, great sports teams attract an excellent caliber of students.

Even though she's usually second setter, Kersti enjoys being part of a sports team. It makes her feel even more woven into the fabric of the Lycée's world.

"One more floor," Lille encourages, and they stare up at that last flight as though it's the Monte Rosa. Cressida and Kersti double over laughing, clutching each other, tears streaming down their frostbitten cheeks.

"Sh-sh-sh!" Rafaella says, spraying saliva. She has the room next door to Kersti and Cressida. She's the daughter of a painter from New York and a European prince. Her godfather is Tom Jones. She has a tendency to weave these whopping fibs with equally fantastical truths so that no one is ever really sure which is which. But her mother *is* famous and her father is in fact a prince, though Kersti isn't sure from which country.

"I need a smoke," Cressida says, reaching inside her coat pocket.

"Me, too," Noa agrees, reaching into the pocket of her parka. She smokes horrible-smelling, hand-rolled cigarettes. Her father sends the tobacco from Rotterdam.

"Wait till we're in the bathroom," Lille says, having enough good sense not to let them light up in the stairwell. There's supposed to be no smoking in the building, except for in the teacher's lounge and the TV room on the main floor. But Mme. Hamidou is a smoker herself and turns a blind eye to it. The one thing she doesn't allow is smoking in the dorm rooms, even though she smokes in hers. It's a fire hazard, she says, with all those flammable polyester fabrics.

Mme. Hamidou is a good housemother. She's fair and funny, and possesses just the right balance of strictness and kindness. She runs Huber House virtually independent of the rest of the school, which speaks more to the laissez-faire attitude of the Lycée's owner, Mme. Harzenmoser, and its principal, M. Bueche. The Lycée is a family business. It was founded by the heir to a pharmaceutical empire in the Upper Rhine Valley, Philipp Harzenmoser, when he was twenty-five. He married a much younger woman—one of the Lycée's cooking teachers—and promoted her to vice principal, a position she held, alongside her husband, until the mid-sixties. They had one daughter, Françoise, to whom leadership of the school eventually passed in 1966.

Françoise Harzenmoser never married and over the years has become more of a figurehead than a director. She lives on campus in a charming chalet, and is frequently spotted tending to an enchanting garden of purple bellflowers, lupines, Alpine rock jasmine, and potted petunias. She's a tall, white-haired woman who cuts an imposing figure, but she is utterly benign on campus. The real leader—or principal and CEO, as he's known—is her business partner, M. Bueche, an elegant man in his late forties with wavy black hair, a coiled mustache, and a triangle of silk scarf always poking out of the breast pocket of his jacket. There's something slightly sinister about M. Bueche, like one of those cartoon characters who twirl their mustache while laughing maniacally. There's a certain insincerity about him—his too white teeth, his intricately coiffed hair, the silk handkerchiefs, the airs. But the man cannot be faulted for his devotion to the Lycée.

M. Bueche is the one who controls the school, and its mission is to make money, something he's achieved by attracting new and prominent students every year. He's obsessed with the Lycée's reputation, a word one might hear M. Bueche utter hundreds of times each day. He's much less concerned with discipline than he is with profits, which are generated largely from the obscene fees students pay for laundry services, dining fees, mandatory monthly travel expenses, books, extracurricular activities, and uniforms, all automatically billed to the parents.

"Guys, come on," Lille pleads, looking nervous. "The whole stairwell stinks of smoke. Hamidou's going to wake up."

Lille has a fragile quality about her. She comes across as being much weirder and more damaged than the others. She has a series of peculiar grooming quirks, which she thinks improve her appearance but actually draw attention to it. She has an obsession with the width of her nose and draws black lines down the bridge of it to make it look narrow. She also cakes her face with white translucent powder and bleaches her long blond hair until it's white and brittle, after which she teases it out. Between the crazy hair and the white face and the black lines, she's like a mad wraith in designer clothes. Cressida calls her a sad soul.

Upstairs in the third-floor bathroom, they finally land in a tangled heap of coats and scarves and wet boots. Kersti lies flat on her back on the cold tile floor, staring up at the cracking brown ceiling. She's happy. Happy because of Magnus's attention earlier at the Brasserie, happy to be here now. She loves her strange new friends, loves being away from her family and their relentless in-your-face Estonian-ness, and most of all, loves her independence. And it all began right here, in this derelict bathroom on the third floor of Huber House, with its rusty toilets and damp musty smell of mothball and mold. Harzenmoser and Bueche are supposed to renovate it, but so far they haven't found it necessary to put their francs toward modern plumbing. Most of the girls shower in the second-floor bathroom and use this one for middle-of-the-night peeing and smoking.

The first gathering of their little circle took place organically on a Saturday night in the fall. Cressida and Kersti went to sneak a smoke and discovered the other four girls already sitting cross-legged in a circle. Rafaella was drinking from a plastic bottle of Evian. She passed it to Cressida and Cressida had a swig. When she made the slightest grimace, Kersti knew it wasn't water. Then she passed it to Kersti and Kersti drank from it and gagged. It was straight vodka, burning hot in her chest. She handed it back to Rafaella.

"Noa was just telling us about her brother," Lille said. It was September and they were all still getting to know one another.

"He was kidnapped," Noa told them matter-of-factly. She was from one of the wealthiest families in Holland. "That's why my parents sent me here. They figured I'd be safer in Switzerland."

"Is he okay now?" Kersti asked her.

"They killed him," Noa said, expertly rolling tobacco into a thin paper. "My father paid the ransom but it didn't matter."

None of them said anything for a while. They passed around the vodka and watched smoke fill the room. Alison stood up to breathe with her head out the window.

"We all have our shit," Noa said, tilting her head up and releasing a cloud of smoke into the air.

"My mother and I communicated by easel my whole life," Rafaella offered.

"By easel?"

"She worked and traveled so much, she decided to set up one of her easels outside my bedroom with a giant pad of paper. I'd wake up in the morning and there would be a note. *Have a good day at school. I'm going to Monaco for the weekend.* And then at night I'd scribble back to her. *I got an A on my test. I have a cold. So-and-so pulled my hair in class. Blah blah blah.*"

Alison abruptly shut the window. "I masturbate every single day."

The others fell absolutely silent.

"I'm not sure if other girls do that or what," she went on. "Or if I'm, like, not normal. But I think about it constantly. Every minute. In class, doing sports. Except for when I'm skiing, that's when my mind is clear."

"Maybe it's because you've never had a boyfriend," Lille said.

"Maybe. Do you think something's wrong with me?"

The other girls were watching her, mouths slightly agape. Kersti was hoping she would be able to look at Alison from that point on and not picture her masturbating.

"Because most of the time, if you look at me and I seem preoccupied, that's probably what I'm thinking about."

No one said anything for a long time. And then, like a cork popping, they all burst out laughing. Alison smiled and relaxed. Kersti was grateful for the levity.

"What about you, Lille?" Cressida said, turning her attention to the nervous little creature beside her.

"I was conceived in Lille, France, on my parents' honeymoon," she divulged, accepting her turn in the circle. "My dad lives in Oman and my mother splits her time between a pied-à-terre in

Paris and our farmhouse in Westport. Mother doesn't let me have friends over if the crystal chandeliers aren't polished or if her hair hasn't been professionally blown out." She looked up at the others through her curtain of bleached hair and said, "And I hate the word *nipple*."

Everyone laughed.

"Your turn," Noa said to Kersti.

"She's got a complex because she's poor," Rafaella answered for her.

"I'm middle class," Kersti corrected, embarrassed.

"Same thing," Rafaella remarked.

"It's not the same thing," Cressida said sharply. "And who gives a shit? You have no perspective, Rafaella. You don't know anything about the real world."

"You can't be poor and go to the Lycée anyway," Lille said.

"I'm here on the Legacy Scholarship," Kersti admitted, her face hot with shame. "My dad has a travel agency and we live in a regular house. Not an estate, or a pied-à-terre, or a villa. Just a regular old house with shag carpets and forty-year-old wallpaper. I've never traveled, I don't have my own bank account or credit card—"

And she was basically pretending to belong, but she left that part out.

"None of that shit matters," Cressida said, speaking more to the other girls. "I love that you aren't like the rest of us, Kersti. You're probably the most normal, grounded one here."

"Definitely more normal than Alison," Noa joked.

Kersti felt the shame leaving her body. She sat up a little straighter, was able to look them all in the eye and own her place in their group. She looked at Cressida, surging with relief. Cressida had defended her to the others, stood up for her in a way no one else ever had before. And in doing that, Cressida had established how the others would treat Kersti from then on. By not judging her, she'd made it okay for everyone to accept her. Kersti would never forget that. She felt in that moment that she could finally be herself.

"What about you, Cressida?" Rafaella said. "What's your deal?"

Everyone in the circle looked at Cressida.

"My chauffeur used to make me give him blow jobs," she said.

The other girls looked down at the floor. Kersti was stunned. But then, with a mischievous smirk, Cressida said, "Just kidding."

Kersti pinched her and they were all laughing and then all of a sudden Angela Zumpt shoved her head inside the bathroom. "I can hear you in my room!" she snapped, her face red. The smell of her body odor quickly filled the bathroom, cutting through all the smoke.

"Close the door!" Rafaella said, covering her nose.

"Be quiet or I go to Madame Hamidou," Angela threatened.

Angela Zumpt's hygiene was already a state of emergency at the Lycée. One morning, Kersti and Cressida were roused from sleep by a shriek of laughter on the second floor. They went downstairs to check on the commotion and discovered a cluster of girls standing in front of Angela's room. Her door was covered with yellow police tape and a crudely handmade sign of skull and crossbones with the word QUARANTINED above it.

"Here," Nastia Panagakos said, handing Kersti a clipboard. "Sign our petition to force Angela to bathe or be suspended."

The other girls standing outside Angela's room started chanting, "Bathe! Bathe! Bathe! Bathe!" Kersti was reminded of her family's chanting around the bonfire at the festival of St. John.

Angela's door opened and she popped out, looking confused. She took it all in, almost in slow motion, her eyes blinking, her mouth half open. First the police tape, then the sign Scotch-taped to her door. "Vass iss mean *quarantine*?" she asked, staring blankly at her tormentors. She wasn't very bright. She was in the Econome program, which meant she was learning how to iron, sew, can fruit, and fold linens for her future. There were only a handful of girls left in the program—it was outrageously outdated—and most of them were from Japan.

"Iss mean you stink!" Nastia told her. "Everyone is going to sign that petition, so why don't you just have a goddamn shower?"

"*I'm* not going to sign it," Cressida said defiantly, shocking the rest of them. And then she strode heroically across the landing. In one swift movement, she ripped the yellow police tape off Angela's door and crumpled it into a big ball, which she dropped at her feet. "Leave her alone."

Someone at the other end of the hall whipped a stick of deodorant at Angela. It smacked her in the forehead, leaving a purplish mark, and then landed on the floor with a bounce.

The other girls whooped and laughed. "Bull's-eye!" someone yelled.

"Who threw that?" It was Mme. Hamidou. She had appeared midway up the stairs.

The girls' chanting tapered off into contrite mumbling. Angela's pale oblong face was blank, but her eyes were filling with glassy tears.

"Madame," Nastia said, mounting her defense, "Angela doesn't shower or wear deodorant. I've tried speaking to her nicely, but she doesn't care. It's not fair to the rest of us—"

Mme. Hamidou looked from Angela to Nastia, her lips pursed into a taut thread. She picked up the deodorant and tucked it into the pocket of her robe. "Miss Zumpt," she said, "Komm mit mir." They disappeared inside Angela's room, closing the door behind them.

With the show over, everyone retreated. Cressida said nothing, but she seemed upset. Kersti was impressed once again by her unexpected compassion for Angela Zumpt. A girl like Angela was utterly beneath Cressida, not even worthy of her kindness, yet she'd jumped in to protect her, ripped the sign off her door, showed her solidarity for no apparent reason. Just as she had done for Kersti. She had a good heart beneath her beautiful surface, which made Kersti love her all the more.

Since then, these girls have become Kersti's best friends, each one special in her own way. Beautiful, brilliant, fractured. There's a palpable brokenness in each one of them, a lonely interior life or a penchant for drama. Kersti occasionally tries to figure out her place in the group, but all she can come up with is that she's their mascot for Reality.

Alison immediately opens the window again, letting in a rush of frigid air.

"Close the fecken window!" Noa cries. "It's minus a thousand out there."

"I have a game tomorrow," Alison says. "I'll close it if you Eurotrash put out your butts."

No one does.

"Did you see Magnus tonight?" Rafaella says. Magnus Foley attends the day school and lives with his uncle a few blocks from the Lycée. He has spiky blond hair and blue eyes, both the gift of phenomenal genes from his Swedish mother and Irish, music producer father. He lives in Malibu during the summer, where he spends his time surfing and playing guitar. He's smart and sarcastic, too, which, if you put it all together, basically makes him perfect.

"I love his new haircut," Noa says, sucking on her misshapen hand-rolled cigarette.

"He still likes Cress," Lille reminds them. "There's no hope for any of you."

Kersti is stung but doesn't say anything. She likes Magnus, too. Has quietly liked him since their first math class together. And she thought, given how he always talks to her in class and how he looked at her all night tonight, that he might like her back.

"Magnus is not my type," Cressida says, and Kersti is secretly overjoyed. She was sure he'd been staring at her most of the night at the Brasserie. "I like someone else anyway."

"Who?"

Before Cressida can answer, the door flies open and Mme. Harzenmoser appears. Lille lets out a soft gasp and they all drop their cigarettes in the toilet.

CHAPTER 5

TORONTO—October 2015

Kersti is lying on her bed with her laptop on her chest. She opens the link that Dr. Gliberman emailed her with information about a new donor agency in Minnesota and, after scrolling through the potential donors—most of them blond, rosy, and descended from Vikings—she actually starts to feel excited. She stops at one she really likes, a twenty-four-year-old with white-blond hair and prerequisite blue eyes, a perfectly shaped oval face, a straight nose with a slightly upturned tip, and full lips. No feature that would be jarringly different from Kersti's, if the child was to look like her real mother.

The donor is wearing a tank top and shorts in her photo, her skin sun-kissed. Her hands are on her hips and her expression is one of self-satisfaction, as though she's just finished running a marathon or climbing a rock or producing a shitload of viable eggs. An overachieving reproductive savior, that's what she is.

Kersti saves the profile and shoots an email to Dr. Gliberman. *I found her.* Finally, this is one she can show Jay with confidence. She grabs her laptop and runs downstairs to Jay's office. He's sitting at his desk, sifting through contact sheets from a recent photo shoot, surrounded by all the things that make him Jay. His framed ADCC Scarlett Letter Award for best ad agency 2009; a signed poster of George Lois's 1969 *Esquire* cover with Andy Warhol drowning in a can of Campbell's tomato soup; Lois's book *Damn Good Advice*.

"Look at her," Kersti says, opening her laptop.

"You're finally agreeing to a ménage-à-trois?"

"She's a donor, Jay."

His mood instantly changes and she can feel his shoulders tensing in her arms.

"You've been doing this behind my back?" he says.

"No. I'm just . . . I wanted to start."

"Egg donation is illegal in Canada, by the way. Did you know that?"

"This agency is in Minnesota," she explains. "They have an arrangement with Gliberman's clinic. We would fly our donor in for the procedure. He's the only doctor in Toronto with a donor program—"

"We agreed to not talk about it for a while."

"I just wanted to check out some profiles," Kersti said. "Look how beautiful she is."

"It wouldn't even be yours. Not by blood."

"You sound like my father."

"You've officially become *that* woman."

"What woman?"

"The desperate, obsessed woman who has to have a baby to feel okay about herself. You swore you'd never become her."

Kersti takes a step back, reeling.

"Remember the contract?" he flares, opening one of his desk drawers. "Here! I kept it!"

He pulls out a piece of paper and waves it in her face. She wrote it not long after their first IVF cycle failed. She wanted to start another cycle right away, but Jay was reluctant. She decided to persuade him the best way she knew how. One night, when he was reading in bed, she sauntered in wearing fishnet stockings, black Manolo pumps, and a sheer white baby-doll trimmed with black lace. There was a piece of paper between her teeth. She approached the bed and straddled him. He pulled the paper out of her mouth.

"I know when we started this journey I swore I wouldn't become one of those self-pitying, baby-obsessed freaks," she said. "And I'm ashamed to admit I've had my moments lately."

"That shrine to your fertility gods was a bit much," Jay joked.

"It wasn't a shrine," she played along. "Just a few talismans to our fertility gods, Metsik and Peko. Anyway, I drew up this contract."

She read it out loud to him.

I promise not to start wearing frumpy pajamas. I promise to stay up past ten, even the nights before I have to go in for bloods at five in the morning. I promise to pleasure you in the manner to which you've become accustomed.

"That's a good one," he interrupted, squeezing her nipple under the baby-doll.

I promise never to join an infertility support group. I promise not to spend any more money on Reiki or acupuncture. I promise to let go and accept our fate before we go bankrupt or if our marriage starts to suffer.

Now Jay is waving the contract at her. "Remember this?"

"But we've come this far, Jay. It's crazy to stop now with nothing to show for it."

"I'm so tired of who we've become."

"What are you saying?" she asks him. "You're tired of our marriage?"

"What marriage?" he counters. "You don't seem to feel we have one without a baby."

Kersti is silent.

"I'm going to the Four Seasons tonight," he says. "I want to be alone."

"Jay, I'm sorry I looked at donors—"

"I'm not even sure we can get back what we had," he interrupts. "We don't want the same things anymore."

"So it's done then?" she says. Even as she disbelieves it, the cold reality of his decision settles in her bones. "Just like that? We're finished trying?"

Jay glances at the pretty egg donor on her screen, makes a point of sighing, and leaves the room.

Alone in his office, Kersti tries to absorb what's just happened. He seems to mean it this time. She has no choice but to sit with that.

Now what? she wonders.

The truth is, she knows exactly what she's going to do. She's probably known since Jay first mentioned it the other day.

As a plan begins to form in her mind, she realizes she's actually a little bit relieved that Jay has put her baby crusade on hold. In spite of her inevitable disappointment, there's also the budding potential for something new in her life.

She wants to know what happened to Cressida. Maybe she's always wanted to know. She's never felt quite ready to go there, but now the timing feels fated. Here is her opportunity to start talking to people about what happened in Lausanne, including Cressida's mother; to explore all the unanswered questions she shut the door on almost twenty years ago. And if what she discovers on her journey turns into a new book, so be it.

Deirdre Strauss lives in Boston. She has a place on Beacon Hill, where she's been since Armand's fatal heart attack in 2000. Visiting her now feels like the inevitable next step.

The first time Kersti met Cressida's mother, she thought she resembled a little girl playing dress-up in her mother's closet. She was petite and ethereal, with skin like milk and haunting aqua eyes. Her tiny, childlike figure was dwarfed by an enormous blazer and swags of mothball-size pearls knotted around her slender neck. Deirdre, with her pale, veiny hands, like paper-thin insect wings. And then there was the way she gazed at and spoke about Cressida, right in front of her, as though she was a trophy she could take down from the shelf whenever she wanted, like one of her prized Tony Awards.

"She's going to accomplish great things," she once stated, with absolute confidence. "I envy the life that lies ahead for her."

Kersti has always wondered if what happened to Cressida was karmic retribution; comeuppance for her recklessness and her insatiable sense of entitlement. That's how Kersti first rationalized it anyway, even blaming herself for secretly wishing that Cressida would eventually be held accountable.

Kersti has to wonder now if the same holds true for her. What if her inability to conceive is somehow her fault, the result of her own inadequacy and passivity? Punishment for the things she did not do, the bad thoughts she had about herself and others, or simply for everything she failed to be?

Maybe if she can find out the truth about what really happened to Cressida, she might somehow be relieved of this burden of guilt and self-condemnation.

CHAPTER 6

LAUSANNE—October 1995

"Good evening, girls," Mme. Harzenmoser says, stepping inside the cramped bathroom. She towers above all six of them, her legs slightly apart, her hands on her thick hips.

"Bonjour, Madame," they mutter, not one of them daring to look into her face.

She looks at her watch. No one moves. "Do you know what time it is?" she asks them.

No one answers.

"Does Madame Hamidou allow you to be in here after curfew?"

"No, Madame."

"Does she allow smoking in here?"

"No, Madame."

"Has the Helvetia Society been resurrected?" she says, the hint of a smile coming into her eyes.

"No, Madame."

Helvetia is the national symbol of Switzerland. There's a sculpture of her down by the tennis courts—a replica of the real one that overlooks the Rhine—with braided hair, a floral wreath and draping toga, and a spear and shield in either hand. The school's famous mission is written in stone at her feet: *Preparing Young Women to Become Citizens of the World.*

"Was there really a secret society here?" Rafaella asks Mrs. Harzenmoser.

Up until now, Kersti assumed the stories about the infamous Helvetia Society were merely urban legend.

"Of course there was," Mme. Harzenmoser says, sounding almost offended by Raf's skepticism. And then she does something absolutely unexpected: she sits down cross-legged in their circle. She's surprisingly agile given how tall she is. Kersti imagines she was one of those people who used to practice yoga. Maybe she took a sabbatical from the Lycée in the sixties or seventies and went off to India on a quest for spiritual enlightenment. Looking at her now, with her silver braid resting on her shoulder like a pet snake, Kersti can picture her in her youth, a free spirit who was unwillingly tethered to this school like a balloon tied to a child's wrist. Someone who was handed a certain life—one she would not necessarily have picked for herself—but who never had the inner fortitude to leave it, or even to know she could have made a different choice.

"Was the Helvetia Society like the Skull and Bones?" Alison asks her.

"Well, interestingly, it was an American student named Mary Oxford who started it," Mme. Harzenmoser explains. "She was from the East Coast and her older brother was a member of Elihu, one of the secret societies at Yale.

"Mary chose the six most outstanding female students at the Lycée to join her in a secret society based on the tenets of Elihu. The idea was to champion the cause of their generation—suffrage—which was really gaining momentum in the States. In those early days, the Helvetians' raison d'être was social justice and philanthropy. That's why my father approved of it."

Kersti glances over at Cressida, wondering if she already knows any of this, but her expression offers no clue.

"Eventually," Mme. Harzenmoser continues, "the causes changed—war, temperance, feminism, and then, coming full circle, women's right to vote in all the cantons of Switzerland, which only happened in 1971."

"Weren't you running the school then?"

"I was."

"And the students were allowed to have secret meetings?"

"They did good philanthropic work, which, in turn, was good for the school's reputation," she explains. "So we allowed it."

"What happened?" Lille asks.

"The Helvetia Society fizzled out in the seventies. By then it had become a glorified sorority," Mme. Harzenmoser remembers. "There were no causes to rally the girls, and drugs had become prevalent on campus." She pronounces it *drogues*. "Finally, in 1974, Monsieur Bueche expelled two students for vandalism. They were both Helvetians, so we made the decision to ban the meetings once and for all. They were serving no more purpose other than to cause trouble."

"Was Madame Hamidou here then?"

"Oh yes, she started in the early sixties. She was very attached to those girls who were expelled, so it must have been hard for her. You know how she treats you, like you're her own children. She's always been very protective."

"Wasn't expelling them for vandalism kind of extreme?"

"Monsieur Bueche felt it was the only thing to do," Mme. Harzenmoser says pragmatically, and then she claps her hands together and rises to her feet. "Now to bed," she announces, her tone changing. "And I will have to let Madame Hamidou know that you've been smoking in here. You'll all have detention next Saturday."

"Madame Harzenmoser?" Lille says, as she reaches the door. "What did those girls vandalize?"

Mme. Harzenmoser turns back to them. "Our statue of Helvetia," she says.

The next night after supper, Cressida and Kersti go to the teachers' lounge to speak to Mme. Hamidou. They find her grading science papers with a trademark cigarette between her lips. The room is cloudy and reeks of Gauloises. Cressida sits down in an armchair and Kersti sits cross-legged at her feet, leaning her head against Cressida's legs. Cressida absently starts playing with Kersti's hair.

"What can I do for you?" Hamidou says, in her peculiar accent. It turns out she's half Filipino, born in Algeria and raised mostly in France.

"Why were those two girls from the Helvetia Society expelled in '74?" Cressida asks, stealing a Gauloises from her pack. She's outrageously bold with Mme. Hamidou, knowing as she does that she's untouchable. Kersti still isn't sure if it's because Hamidou adores her like a daughter or because Cressida simply doesn't give a shit if she gets expelled.

Hamidou looks surprised. "Why do you bring that up out of the blue?" she asks. "It was twenty years ago."

"Harzenmoser told us about it last night."

"Harzenmoser?" Hamidou repeats. "Since when does she talk to the students?"

"She was patrolling Huber last night."

"Hmm." Mme. Hamidou looks annoyed to hear of this intrusion on her turf, even if it is the director of the school. "She must be lonely."

"You've never mentioned the expulsions before," Cressida says. "Which is strange, considering how much you love to warn us about how Old Girls got into trouble."

"Do I?"

"Yes, you frequently use Lycée lore to make veiled threats," she teases.

Hamidou smiles. The spaces between her teeth are brown. "More like cautionary tales," she clarifies. "Vandalism has not been an issue since then."

"So it was vandalism?"

Hamidou nods.

"What did they write on the statue?" Kersti asks her.

"I never knew," she says. "Monsieur Bueche had it removed by morning. Whatever it was, he thought the punishment fit the crime."

"But you didn't, did you?"

"Bof," she says dismissively. "I've always cared more about the students than the Lycée's reputation. Of course I was against the expulsions. I tried to persuade him to be more lenient, but when Bueche make up his mind, *fini*."

"What were their names?"

Hamidou stubs out her cigarette and reaches for another. "Brooke Middlewood and Tatiana Greenberg. They were both American. The Helvetians were mostly American. The popular girls, the over-achievers, as you say."

Hamidou stands up and goes to the window. She opens it and lets in some air.

"What happened to the other Helvetians after that?"

"They graduated."

Cressida looks thoughtful. Something is on her mind. After a pause, she says, "What do you think they spray-painted on the statue that got them expelled?"

Hamidou shakes her head, looking sad. "Bueche wanted those girls out of the school," she states. "That's all I know for sure."

CHAPTER 7

TORONTO—October 2015

Kersti leans back in her seat and stares out the window, tuning out the flight attendant's safety speech. Her thoughts return to her earlier conversation with Jay and she can feel herself getting angrier and angrier. How dare he give up? He knows what's at stake, how much it means to her.

After he left the house, Kersti paced around rehashing their argument and then impulsively decided to book a flight to Boston. As the plane lifts off now, veering sharp right over Lake Ontario and leaving the island airport behind, Kersti closes her eyes. When did this happen to them? How did it happen? She thought they would always be partners, always on the same page about life's most important decisions. She sees now how childish that was, how idealistic.

She remembers the night they told her parents in a burst of optimistic solidarity that they were going to try IVF. It was the night of the festival of St. John's and her whole family was gathered around the bonfire in her parents' backyard. The sun had set and the sky was dark and smooth and speckled with stars. Jay and Kersti were sitting side by side in the red and white plastic lawn chairs her parents have been hanging on to since the seventies. They touched their bottles together. She was feeling hopeful again for the first time in a long time.

The festival of St. John, which falls on the eve of the summer solstice in June, is one of the more important Estonian holidays—not just for its religious significance but also for its rituals and traditions, which include jumping over the bonfire, drinking, dancing, singing, and, for the Kuusks, more drinking. Like all good Estonians, Kersti's father, Paavo, believes that lighting the bonfire is a way of guaranteeing prosperity and avoiding bad luck. He's a huge, hulking man. Tall, uncomfortably overweight, silver-haired and bearded, his cheeks are always dangerously flushed, his nose red and pocky. He is not a man of moderation.

That night, he rose unsteadily to his feet—much vodka had been consumed—and kindled the fire. "Who is jumping first?" he thundered in his thick accent.

Kersti's sister, Jutta, shouted her husband's name, "Rasmus!" and everyone began to clap and chant. *Ras-mus! Ras-mus! Ras-mus!*

Her six nieces were running around the fire, all with white-blond hair, round faces, and the trademark Kuusk blue eyes. Kersti was the only one in that circle without kids.

Jay was the only one with dark hair. Together, they were a pair of misfits in a clan of procreating blonds.

Ras-mus! Ras-mus! Ras-mus!

Rasmus leapt over the fire, rolling on the grass after he landed, looking like a break-dancing giraffe. "I never get tired of this," Jay whispered to Kersti.

After the rest of them jumped, Paavo boomed, "Jay's turn!"

Everyone started chanting as they passed around a bottle of vodka. *Jay! Jay! Jay!*

"I'm going to skip it this year," Jay said. "I charred my Varvatos pants last summer—"

"You have to jump," Kersti said. "Or we'll have bad luck all year." She gave him a meaningful look.

Jay downed his beer and reluctantly stood up. He removed his Sperry Topsiders and carefully set them aside. He took a breath, made the sign of a cross in front of his chest, and jumped over the fire. The Kuusks exploded in applause and Kersti ran over and lay down beside him in the grass. She was happy. It felt like a perfect night to share their news. So when the little girls were dozing in their mothers' arms and the adults were drunk and sleepy and the air smelled of high summer, Kersti said, "Jay and I are going to do IVF."

No one cheered or clapped the way they had when people were jumping over the bonfire. Anni shook her head disapprovingly. There was a long, terrible silence that made the crackling fire and buzzing crickets seem deafening.

"This goes against nature," Kersti's father thundered. Even in his late seventies, he was no less intimidating.

"Why can't you keep trying the old-fashioned way?" her mother said. "You know some women just take longer. It's in our family. You're just like me. You probably just need your tubes cleaned—"

"My tubes are closed," Kersti said. Her brothers-in-law were squirming in their plastic lawn chairs. Her sisters were quiet and typically unsupportive.

"Then it's not meant to be," Anni said pragmatically. "You have to give up now, Kersti. You don't always have to be so *jäärapäine*."

Jäär meant ram, so the literal translation was "ram-headed." Growing up, her parents always used to call her that.

"You should have married an Estonian," her father said. "We're not being racist, Kersti. Understand, it's not because you're Jewish, Jay. It's because you're not Estonian."

"Is there a difference?" Jay said, baffled.

"Of course there is a difference!" Paavo roared, his face dark red in the firelight. "This is all we have! Our community. *Each other*."

"Well," Jay said. "Happy Jaanipäev, everyone."

Kersti broke away from him and ran inside her parents' house. Jay followed her.

Her parents' kitchen was shabby, messy, outdated. The last time Anni did anything to it was in the eighties when she made the girls get on their knees and replace the original rotting linoleum with a stick-on version. She adhered to her husband's philosophy of not spending a nickel on anything that made their home feel permanent.

Kersti poured herself a chipped mug of vodka and slumped down in a chair.

"You're father's an ignorant bigot," Jay said, pouring himself a glass.

"No matter what I do," Kersti complained, "I can't fit in with them. I look like them, I talk like them, but I just don't belong."

"Look, we're going to have a kid. And even if he or she has brown hair like me—God forbid—we'll still find a way to love it."

Kersti giggled.

"And Adolf out there, with his pure, undiluted blood, can go fuck himself."

Jay took a deep gulp of the warm vodka, gagged, choked, and slammed the mug on the table. She'd never loved him more than in that moment.

The plane touches down, bounces on the tarmac, and comes to a deafening stop in the fog. Boston. A city she could have loved, if circumstances had been different.

A thick cloud of dread descends on her. She has Lille's letter in her purse and a fresh purpose for the visit. Maybe it won't be so bad this time.

CHAPTER 8

LAUSANNE—October 1995

Monday morning in English lit, Mrs. Fithern is going on about the love triangle in *Sons and Lovers*. She has a cold and keeps coughing and blowing her nose. She draws a diagram on the blackboard.

PAUL & WILLIAM—MRS. MOREL & WALTER—
MIRIAM/GYP

She circles Mrs. Morel and beside all the names, writes: *flame of life*. Turning back to face the class, she says, "Tell me about the flame of life."

Without raising her hand, Cressida responds. "The flame of life is Lawrence's metaphor for that part of a person's soul that no one else can control or possess," she says confidently. "Mrs. Morel tries to control all the men in her life, destroying them all in the process."

"Specifically, Cress, what are some concrete examples of that flame of life?"

"The coal mine for Walter," she says. "For William, I think it's probably Gyp and her superficiality. Maybe even the city, too."

"Yes, London! Absolutely," Mrs. Fithern agrees, whipping her tissue out of her shirtsleeve and blowing her nose again. "What about for Paul?"

"Nature," Cressida answers. "Mrs. Morel suppresses his life-force by making him work in the factory and separating him from nature."

"And how would you characterize their relationship? Someone other than Cress?"

"Smothering," Kersti calls out.

"Suffocating."

"Incestuous," Cressida adds.

"Incestuous," Mrs. Fithern considers aloud, followed by three short sneezes. "I would say lacks boundaries, though I wonder if their relationship doesn't fall just shy of incestuous?"

Cressida reads out loud. *"He had come back to his mother. Hers was the strongest tie in his life . . . And nobody else mattered. There was one place in the world that stood solid and did not melt into unreality: the place where his mother was . . . It was as if the pivot and pole of his life, from which he could not escape, was his mother."*

Cressida closes her book and looks up. "Sounds incestuous to me."

"Sounds like what a mother is supposed to be," Kersti chimes in, surprising herself.

"You have a pretty twisted view of motherhood," Cressida says.

Mrs. Fithern smiles, the way a mother might smile at her daughter if she was proud or impressed by her, or felt she was an extension of herself, as most mothers do. Kersti feels excluded.

The door opens then and Mr. Fithern appears in the classroom.

"Hello, luv," she exclaims, looking genuinely delighted to see him.

Charles Fithern is a bit of a legend at the Lycée. He's in his late twenties, tall and lanky, with buzzed black hair and a thick brow. He speaks with the same heavy northern accent as his wife and usually wears scuffed Doc Martens, jeans, and a button-down shirt with tie. He has a faded red, black, and yellow tattoo of the Worcester City Football Club on his forearm, and possibly, Kersti imagines, a history involving the punk subculture in England. He reminds Kersti of Sid Vicious, if Sid had been a schoolteacher. She occasionally pictures him wearing a black Sex Pistols T-shirt under his starched button-downs.

Kersti has always viewed the world from a writer's perspective, like it's an unfolding story and the people in it are characters. When she doesn't know their stories, she makes them up. When she does know them, she embellishes. At the back of her mind, she's always writing a book about everyone. The Lycée is full of characters—Mr. and Mrs. Fithern being two of the most interesting. Kersti frequently imagines their private life when they're away from the Lycée—watching *Coronation Street* together; having afternoon tea in their small English garden, which he planted for her to remind her of home; watching football at the local pub. She pictures their relationship as being quite chaste. Mrs. Fithern doesn't strike her as a sexual type. She's girlish and matronly at the same time, slightly frumpy with bouncy curls and a chipper disposition. She's clever and wry, but not sexy the way Mr. Fithern is sexy.

Everyone at the Lycée knows their story—they met at a teachers' college in Worcester, England. Her maiden name was Brains—Annie Brains—and true to her name, he thought she was the smartest, wittiest girl he'd ever met. He proposed after they'd been dating just six weeks. A year after their wedding, they left England to teach together at the Lycée.

"Sorry to interrupt," Mr. Fithern says, approaching his wife with a small white paper bag. "Sounds like you're havin' an interesting discussion about Paul Morel and his mum." He looks out into the tittering class and winks. Some of the girls giggle out loud. It's like he's Eddie Vedder or something. "Ye forgot your medicine, milady," he says, handing her the bag.

"Oh, thank you, luv. You could've given it to me at lunch."

"And miss my chance to see all these lovely ladies?"

More giggles. Mrs. Fithern looks inside the bag. "Penicillin," she says, frowning.

He blows her a kiss and the entire class goes, "*Awwwwwww!*" and he leaves.

"All right," Mrs. Fithern says, her cheeks still flushed. "Let's talk about Miriam. Someone other than Cressida tell me how she fits into our love triangle."

Next class is French 2 with M. Feuilly. Cressida has Model United Nations with Mr. Fithern and rushes off, not wanting to be late.

"Hey, Kuusk," Magnus Foley says, as Kersti takes her seat beside him.

"Hey, Foley."

She isn't very good at grammar and she speaks French with an unmelodious Estonian accent, which is why she's still in French 2. Magnus is also terrible at grammar, although he can speak it fluently. The moment she sits down, he shoves a note her way. It's a caricature of M. Feuilly wearing a mosquito headnet and a red button that says STOP SIDA, which is the French acronym for AIDS. M. Feuilly is worried he caught the disease from mosquitoes on a recent safari in Africa and he discusses his concerns at great length with the class on a regular basis.

Magnus is an excellent cartoonist and Kersti bursts out laughing as soon as she opens the note and sees M. Feuilly's large hawk nose, thin mustache, and wiry bifocals.

"Mademoiselle Kuusk?"

Kersti looks up and M. Feuilly is watching her. "Please recite the verb 'to laugh' in pluperfect," he says.

She can hear Magnus snickering.

"Je riais, tu riais—"

"That's the imperfect," he says, annoyed. "Perhaps less actual *laughing,* Mademoiselle Kuusk, and more practicing your verb conjugations. It's: *J'avais ri, tu avais ri, elle avait ri . . .*"

After he's done humiliating her, M. Feuilly tells them to open Camus' *L'Étranger*. They start reading out loud from the beginning.

Magnus stretches out his legs so that they're touching Kersti's. He's always moving around like that, unable to sit still. He stretches his legs, shifts in his seat, leans this way and that, bounces his knee, chews his pen, draws pictures. Whenever he moves, he somehow winds up brushing up against her. Her crush on him has grown exponentially since last year and she thinks he might like her, too. Although there's no concrete evidence of this other than their classroom banter, his restless legs, and their Saturday night flirtations, Kersti feels there's something burgeoning between them.

Feuilly reads the opening sentence from the book out loud and then looks up. "Is Meursault amoral?" he asks the class.

"He lives by his own truth," Magnus responds. "That's not amoral."

Abby Ho-Tai jumps up from her desk and runs out of the classroom. She takes laxatives to lose weight so she's always rushing to the bathroom. Magnus slides over another cartoon drawing, this one of Abby sitting on the toilet with a mountain of Dulcolax boxes beside her.

After class, Magnus walks out with Kersti and they stop for a cigarette in the garden, where most of the student body gathers to smoke between classes. "Let's go to the tennis courts," he suggests, lighting her Marlboro.

She looks around for Cressida, but can't find her. She's probably still at Model United Nations practice. Kersti accompanies Magnus to the tennis courts, her heart pounding. They sit down side by side on the grass, legs outstretched, faces upturned to the fall sun. The air smells faintly of Alpine jasmine. Magnus plucks a forget-me-not and hands it to Kersti.

"You going on the Gstaad trip over the holiday?" he asks her, blowing perfect smoke rings with an exaggerated motion of his jaw.

"Um, no," Kersti says, laughing. "I'll be going home to work at my dad's travel agency, so I can afford to buy my family presents."

"That's cool," he says.

"Is it though? Because I think skiing in Gstaad is a lot cooler."

"Not really. You're not like any of the spoiled weirdos who grew up here," he tells her. "I like that about you, Kuusk. You're real."

"Are you a spoiled weirdo?"

"Absolutely," he says. "But you. You're refreshing, Kuusk. You're almost normal."

It's exactly what Cressida told her in her first year. Kersti had never thought about such things before coming to the Lycée. Normal, not normal. Are the Kuusks really normal? Kersti doesn't think so, but everything is relative.

"I just got my driver's license," Magnus says. "Why don't we go for a drive this Saturday? My uncle said I could use his car. I'll take you for beer fondue."

Kersti is caught off guard by the invitation. She wants to run onto the court, jump over the net, and squeal. She can't even look at him when she answers. "Sure, Foley," she says, in the most aloof, offhanded way she can manage. "Beer fondue sounds great."

Later on in her room, still giddy about the afternoon, Kersti carefully tucks the forget-me-not he gave her inside her copy of *L'Étranger.*

CHAPTER 9

BOSTON—October 2015

Deirdre Strauss's place is on Beacon Street in the flat section of Beacon Hill known as the Flat of the Hill. She lives in a restored townhouse with a granite façade and copper roof, surrounded by birch and dogwood trees, hydrangeas and wisteria, and ivy swirling around the front door.

Kersti rings the bell. A Filipino woman wearing jeans and a stained T-shirt answers.

"Hello," Kersti says. "Is Deirdre home?"

"Not yet."

"She said it was okay if I came. I'm Kersti Kuusk."

The woman hesitates, but eventually steps aside.

"And you are?"

"Laylay," the woman says, closing the door.

The house is exactly as Kersti remembers it. High ceilings, dark parquet floors, wall-to-wall bookcases filled with old books that look more like props. Dark, gleaming antiques, fancy brocade sofas with matching armchairs, expensive knickknacks cluttering the surface of every piece of furniture in the room. The parlor has a breathtaking view of the Boston Public Garden.

"How is she?" Kersti asks.

"See for yourself," Laylay says. "She's waiting."

Kersti moves numbly down the hall, past the bedrooms. She glances inside one of them, startled. It's a room for a princess, with light pink walls and white eyelet curtains. There's a pile of stuffed animals in the center of the bed, an embroidered bolster pillow, a Barbie sitting cross-legged on a hand-painted bookcase. It's as though Deirdre reconstructed Cressida's childhood room, preserving it exactly the way it must have been. As though she's still expecting Cressida to return home from boarding school.

The den is at the end of the hall and has been converted into a hospital room. The smell hits Kersti before she even enters. Ointment layered with vanilla diffuser and perfume, an attempt to mask the scent of illness and hopelessness.

Kersti gasps when she sees Cressida for the first time in almost fifteen years. She's propped up on her orthopedic bed, staring at a flat-screen TV on the wall in front of her, looking as beautiful as she was at eighteen. Deirdre obviously goes to great lengths to maintain her daughter's appearance. Cressida's hair is clean and shiny, still curly and perfectly untamed. Her lips are glossy, her aqua eyes clear and her cheeks pink, whether naturally or from a touch of shimmery rouge, Kersti can't tell. She's wearing a white T-shirt, jeans, and a soft gray cardigan, her slender body not even hinting at paralysis or disfigurement.

Here is the beautiful, promising Cressida Strauss: a thirty-five-year-old invalid with massive brain damage. Kersti finds it easier to think of her as having died that day.

When Cressida first came out of the coma, Deirdre wrote Kersti to update her with the news. She was in a persistent vegetative state, which meant a partial state of arousal, with no sign of improvement. It sounded bleak, but by the time Kersti was finally allowed to see her three years after the accident, Cressida was able to blink, make sounds, and move her right hand enough to reach for things. And although Cressida did not seem to recognize Kersti that day, she did make eye contact with her.

"She's looking right at me," Kersti said.

"She's in a minimally conscious state," Deirdre explained. "She's a bit more aware and responsive than someone in a vegetative state. Although, frankly, it's hard to tell the difference."

"What *is* the difference?" Kersti asked.

"She can focus and sometimes she responds to people," Deirdre said. "She communicates with us, either by squeezing our hands or blinking. She can occasionally follow instructions and she's attempted the odd word or phrase over the years, but nothing significant enough to hold on to. It's all so very inconsistent, Kersti. From one day to the next, she can be alert or totally unresponsive."

"It must be hard for you."

"I was so hopeful at first," Deirdre said. "When she first began to show signs of life. It was so encouraging, but then her progress just sort of stalled."

"You mentioned she's tried to speak. What sort of things does she say?"

"Nothing enlightening," Deirdre shrugged. "'Mom.' 'Cold.' 'Thirsty.'"

Kersti turned back to look at her friend and was startled to find tears streaming down Cressida's cheeks. Kersti was baffled. Was Cressida capable of feeling things?

"She knows me," Kersti said, leaning over her friend's body. "Cress? Do you know who I am?"

"This wasn't a good idea," Deirdre said, stepping in.

She gently pulled Kersti from her daughter's bedside and curtly asked her to leave. "It's too much for her," she said.

Kersti was hurt, but frankly a bit relieved. She hated seeing Cressida like that. And yet as she was leaving, something gnawed at her. She wondered why Cressida was crying. Was it a matter of not wanting to be seen that way, or because Kersti was such an unexpected reminder of everything she'd lost and of whom she'd once been? Maybe Cressida was perfectly aware she had no more freedom or potential; maybe it wasn't beyond the scope of her reasoning at all.

The possibility of that gave Kersti a chill.

A few years later, Kersti returned to Boston on Cressida's twenty-eighth birthday, exactly one decade after her accident. She had a book signing at Trident Bookstore and decided to stop in. Deirdre told her that Cressida had edema and wasn't allowed visitors. Kersti didn't believe her, but she left flowers and hasn't been back since.

"Hi, Cress," Kersti says, stepping into the room. *The Price Is Right* is on. Cressida is staring at the television. Her head turns in Kersti's direction and Laylay—who must be her nurse—moves closer, on standby.

"How are you?" Kersti asks her, approaching the bed.

There's a flash of recognition; a spark of *something.*

"Answer her, Cressida," Laylay says brusquely.

Cressida manages to utter something—"hi" or "fine."

"Wow, you're talking," Kersti says, in a tone much like one she would use with a toddler. She reaches for Cressida's hand and is surprised when Cressida squeezes back.

"I'm sorry I haven't been in so long," Kersti says. "I would have come back much sooner, I just wasn't sure—"

Up close, Cressida is still so lovely. She barely looks older than she was when she fell, as though the accident froze her in time, stopping all growth and preserving her like a doll in a glass case. "You look amazing," Kersti whispers.

"Deirdre insists," Laylay chimes in. "She wants her to be pretty every day."

Indeed, Cressida's nails are beautifully manicured, her skin supple and moisturized, her teeth—which Kersti notices when Laylay puts a water bottle to her lips—sparkling white. She's even wearing jewelry.

Still, it's hard to see her like this. She was the smartest person Kersti ever knew. After a while, Kersti says, "Lille died."

Tears instantly spring to Cressida's eyes. *She remembers.*

Kersti is excited and wants to ask if she remembers what happened to her the night she fell. If Cressida remembers Lille, maybe enough bits and pieces have come back to her over the years. How can anyone really know what's going on in her brain?

But Laylay is hovering around them, policing the reunion, and Kersti doesn't want to upset either of them and risk being banished again.

Moments later, she hears Deirdre's crisp British accent behind her. "Kersti?"

Kersti lets go of Cressida's hand and spins around to find Deirdre standing in the doorway. "You look well," she says, looking Kersti up and down. "And you seem to be doing well, too. I read your last book."

She doesn't mention if she liked it or not. Who could blame her for her disdain? Her daughter's life was ruined at eighteen years old. The last two decades have taken their toll on Deirdre's frail beauty; though it would be more accurate to say *she's* the one who's done the damage—by way of Botox, fillers, facelifts, collagen, and chemical peels to the point of disfigurement.

"Cressida has improved," Kersti says.

"Relative to what?" Deirdre responds.

"The last time I was here."

Deirdre doesn't agree or disagree. Kersti steps away from Cressida's bedside and says, "Can I talk to you outside?"

They walk into the hallway and Deirdre fixes her frozen marionette eyes on Kersti.

"Lille Robertson died," Kersti tells her.

"How sad. She was so young."

"Breast cancer."

Deirdre lets out a muffled *oh no* and shakes her head. "Cressida was very fond of Lille."

"She wrote me a letter before she died," Kersti says. "Mostly about Cressida."

"What about her?"

"Lille didn't think she fell by accident."

"What did she think?"

"I'm not sure. She didn't finish the letter."

"The school confirmed what happened to Cressida," Deirdre says, her mouth tightening. "Why wouldn't Lille believe the official party line?"

"Do *you* think it was a party line?"

Deirdre sighs, wringing her hands nervously as though she's trying to pump the circulation back into them.

"Lille was dying when she wrote me," Kersti perseveres. "I think she knew something. I get the feeling she needed to unburden herself—"

"Or maybe she was just speculating. The mind goes at the end—"

"I don't think so," Kersti says, challenging her. "And I don't think you really do, either."

Deirdre doesn't respond at first. She just stands there contemplating something, her paper-thin skin pulled back so tautly over her cheekbones there's no way to guess at what she's feeling. Finally, she turns and walks down the hallway to the living room, her heels click-clicking on the swirling black and white marble. Kersti follows her.

"There's something I never told you," she says.

Kersti's heart accelerates.

"There was a note," Deirdre confides, her voice a whisper. "A suicide note."

CHAPTER 10

LAUSANNE—November 1995

On Saturday morning, Kersti spends the entire two-hour study hall choosing something to wear. Cressida can't help her with an outfit because she's at Model United Nations practice again; they're going to The Hague at the end of November, so she's never around. Kersti will be happy when it's over.

Lunch is the usual roast chicken and french fries, but Kersti saves her appetite for beer fondue. When the bell rings and they're released from school, all the boarders spill out the front door, wild with their freedom. Kersti hangs back for a few minutes, not wanting Magnus to think she's overly anxious, and then saunters out to find him leaning against his uncle's Mercedes, wearing a leather jacket over a Nirvana T-shirt. Kersti tries not to look at him as she slides into the passenger seat. She doesn't want him to see how red her face feels or how hard it is for her not to smile.

They drive through the countryside outside Lausanne, neither of them saying much. Kersti is looking out her open window, still awed by the scenery. In the autumn sunlight, the grass shines like emeralds against a backdrop of flaming red and orange trees. Beyond the hills, which are patched with cobblestone villages and red-roofed farmhouses, the jagged Alps rise up to meet the white sky, taking her breath away.

"Does it still impress you?" she asks Magnus, turning to face him for the first time since they left the Lycée.

"What?"

"This countryside, the Alps, Lake Geneva . . ."

He shrugs.

"How can it *not*?" she asks, incredulous.

"This is why I like hanging out with you, Kuusk," he says, smiling at her.

She doesn't respond, choosing instead to savor the moment and not bungle it with one of her awkward, overthought retorts.

They drive until they reach a red-shuttered farmhouse in the middle of a meadow, where cows are mingling languidly and the air smells of Edelweiss. There's something charming about the way the place has been preserved in time, nestled in the shadows of the Jorat forest. The name of the restaurant, Auberge de Chalet-des-Enfants, is painted on a wooden sign out front. In spite of the November chill, people are eating outside under a canopied patio.

Magnus orders for her—beer fondue for two and a bottle of Chasselas—which is thrilling. She doesn't drink wine when she's out with friends, only beer, and it feels wonderfully grown-up, something her parents would do.

"My mom loves Chasselas," he says, lighting a cigarette. She notices his knee bouncing under the table. Every so often, it hits the table and their glasses shake.

"Are your parents together?" she asks him.

"No. My mom's remarried. She lives in Stockholm with her new family. I spend the summers with my dad in California."

"When do you see her?"

"I don't," he says matter-of-factly. "I used to go home for Christmas, but I can't stand my stepfather and their kids are assholes. I go to Gstaad now with the school."

"That's kind of sad."

"Is it?"

She can't tell if his response is bravado or genuine indifference. "It must bother you," she says. "Never seeing your mother?"

He shrugs. The fondue shows up and he looks relieved. It's sublime and they're both happy to eat for a while in silence. "Don't pretend your life is *The Cosby Show*," he says, looking up at her.

"I never did—"

"Most of us don't wind up at the Lycée because we're wanted," he says.

She looks down at her plate, stung. He's right. The chasm between Kersti and her family has become even more palpable since she's been in Lausanne. Her three sisters are inseparable. They look the same, dress the same, finish each other's sentences. They even speak their own language, which their mother calls "Estonglish." They're twenty-three, twenty-four, and twenty-six. They all still live at home, although Jutta is engaged to her boyfriend, Rasmus, and will probably move out after her wedding. Kersti has nothing in common with them. When Kersti goes home for the holidays, they call her Swiss Miss and exclude her from everything. Even though they're so much older than her, she finds them immature, silly, and unworldly. She feels much closer to her friends at the Lycée. In some ways, she even feels closer to Mme. Hamidou than to her own mother, whose silent recriminations have always shone through her judgmental blue eyes.

"Don't sulk, Kuusk," Magnus says.

She has an urge to smack his smug face, but he returns her anger with an irresistible smile and she softens.

"How do you like the fondue?" he asks her.

"It's delicious," she mutters, pulling a rope of cheesy bread out of the pot.

"Wait till you taste the flan."

He orders dessert and more wine, which alarms her. He has to drive back to Lausanne.

By the time they leave the restaurant, the sky is dark and they can see their breath in the air. Magnus can barely walk in a straight line and Kersti is afraid to get in the car. She's drunk, but not completely incoherent. "What are we going to do?" she asks him. "You can't drive."

"Hmm," he says. "What can we do?"

She's not sure what his agenda is, but she's starting to feel nervous. He takes her by the hand. "Follow me, Kuusk."

He leads her to the woods and she's so caught up in the thrill of holding hands with him, she forgets to worry about what's going to happen next. Leaves crunch beneath their shoes as they trip over branches and rocks, leaning on one another for support. "Are you going to murder me?" she asks, half-joking but really beginning to wonder.

He laughs.

"You know, like that preppy murder in Central Park a few years ago?"

"Murder's not what I had in mind."

She stops walking and makes him stop and face her. "What *do* you have in mind?" she asks him.

"Well. We need to kill at least an hour, right?"

"Don't tell me a hike through the woods in the dark?"

"You don't know me at all," he says. "I smoke too much to hike. You're not really afraid, are you?"

The moon, just shy of being full, is throwing a fair bit of light across the night sky. "Should I be?"

"Of course not," he says, laughing and pulling her toward him. Her heart is thrashing inside her chest. She hears some little creature scurrying nearby, but doesn't care. She's standing in the forest with Magnus Foley and his face is coming toward her. She closes her eyes and it's exactly like in her fantasies: his lips on hers, soft and wet; the taste of cigarette, which somehow is a turn-on; his big hands on either side of her face, holding it in place while he kisses her. Everything happens quickly after that.

Magnus manages to find a big rock and, breathing heavily, gently eases her down onto it. He opens her coat. She squeals when she feels his cold hands on her bare skin, but when his fingers find her nipples, the squeals turned to moans. No one has ever touched her like this before, or anywhere for that matter. She's never even been kissed.

He's her first. Her first real kiss, her first breast touching, and finally, her first lover. He has a condom in his jeans pocket. "SIDA," he mumbles in her ear. "We have to be safe."

She's too confused, elated, and drunk to protest. She's outside of herself, experiencing it almost as a bystander. He whips off his coat and, gentleman that he is, lays it on the rock underneath her. He has his pants down at his knees almost as quickly as he has hers down. She's grateful for the fur lining of his leather jacket. She feels warm. And there's also the heat from his body and their heavy breathing, and from all the moving and grinding up against each other.

"Are there wolves here?" she asks him. He just laughs some more and resumes what he's doing, which is making her feel damn good.

"I don't know what to do," she murmurs, not really embarrassed but wanting to warn him in advance.

"Don't worry," he pants, kissing her on the mouth and then her neck and in her ear. His tongue feels so good. He knows exactly where to put it to make her spine arch. Her fear begins to vanish, her anxiety quiets down.

And then the pain comes. An excruciating stab between her legs, like something tearing. It's worse than when she had her ears pierced and she screamed in the middle of the department store. She cries out now, her voice echoing throughout the woods.

"You okay?" he manages, but doesn't stop. The deeper he pushes himself inside her, the better it feels—for *him*. His pleasure seems to increase proportionally with her pain. She's in agony. Each thrust makes her cry out again. She's gripping his shoulders, digging her nails into his shirt, which has the effect of riling him up even more. He starts pounding harder, faster, making weird noises. *Fuck, fuck, fuck. Oh. Fuck. Uh. Uh. Uh. Uh. Fuck. Uh. Uh.*

Kersti's eyes are wide open, staring up at the dense black canopy of trees where two raccoons are fighting noisily on a branch. She remembers her Natural Biology teacher mentioning something about how the North American raccoon is becoming a problem in some Swiss forests. It's almost funny, the way they're scrapping up in the tree while she and Magnus go at it down here. Magnus is still pumping away on top of her like he's doing push-ups on a gym mat, but she never takes her eyes off those raccoons. It's a good distraction and makes her think of home—bonfires in the backyard, camping trips in Gravenhurst. She pretends she's enjoying the sex, moaning where it seem appropriate, calling out his name here and there, like she's seen in movies.

And then he lets out a loud noise, like a goat bleating, and he collapses on top of her. She's sopping wet between her legs and hopes it isn't blood. She strokes the back of his head, something else she's seen in movies.

"Oh my God," he says, panting in her ear. "Oh my God. You sweet little virgin. That was . . . wow."

Now that it's over, she feels so close to him. She holds him tight while he tries to catch his breath. She's never felt so wanted, so revered. It's absolutely empowering, lying beneath the full weight of him, his heart beating against her breast. She tickles his neck with her fingers and he rests his face in the slope of her neck. She forgets they're on a rock outside in the cold. She's warm and content, the pain completely forgotten.

"I think I'm in love with you," she whispers. She knows it's impulsive, but after the things he's just said to her, it feels right. "I'm so happy right now."

"You're so real," he says hoarsely. "So down-to-earth and authentic. It's beautiful. Really." He leans up on one elbow and kisses her nose. "You sweet little virgin," he repeats. "What a nice surprise."

"I told you I didn't know what to do."

"I meant when I invited you out for a drive," he clarifies.

"So your plan all along was to have sex with me?"

"Of course," he admits, sitting up and pulling on his pants. "There's just something about you."

She looks down at herself and even in the dark, she can see blood all over her thighs and the fur lining of his jacket. "Oh God, I'm sorry," she mumbles, embarrassed.

"That's what dry cleaners are for," he says, tousling her hair. "Don't worry."

She pulls up her pants and they each light a cigarette. The moment is utterly perfect. The moon, the rustling trees, Magnus.

She's no longer a virgin. Magnus Foley is her first, will always be her first. Nothing and no one can ever change that fact and the realization fills her with indescribable joy. She can't wait to tell Cressida. Cressida lost her virginity at thirteen to an actor in one of her father's plays; Kersti is relieved to have caught up to her and have it over with now.

When she gets back to Huber House, still dazed and euphoric, Mme. Hamidou is about to lock the doors. She looks at her watch and frowns.

"Sorry," Kersti says, rushing upstairs. She's surprised to find her room dark and Cressida already asleep. It's barely after ten. "Cress?" she whispers.

Cressida rolls over. "Kerst?"

"Are you asleep? Didn't you go out tonight?"

"Too tired," Cressida says. "I was at MUN till after dinner. We got Malawi. How was your date?"

Kersti turns on the bedside lamp and snuggles in next to Cressida. "We *did it*," she blurts.

"You slept with him?" Cressida says, sitting up, fully awake now.

"I'm not a virgin anymore," Kersti confides, beaming. "Can you believe it? But oh my God it *killed*. Why didn't you warn me?"

"Where were you? Where did you do it?"

"He took me for lunch at this place called the Auberge de—"

"Chalet des Enfants."

"How do you know?"

"It's his favorite place."

Kersti doesn't like the sound of that. It implies Cressida knows things about him.

"Then what?" Cressida says, not sounding nearly as happy for Kersti as Kersti thought she'd be.

"We had a lot of wine," Kersti tells her. "He couldn't drive, so we went for a walk in the woods—"

Cressida interrupts with a snicker.

"And then it just, like, happened."

"On the ground?"

"On a rock," Kersti says, beginning to get annoyed. "What's your problem? You've never liked him—"

Cressida shrugs.

"*Do* you like him?" Kersti asks, panic flooding her chest.

"Of course not," Cressida says, her expression inscrutable. She leans over and turns off the light. "I'm happy for you," she mutters, lying back down.

But she doesn't sound happy at all.

CHAPTER 11

BOSTON—October 2015

Deirdre opens the locked drawer of her desk, an elegant Louis something with cabriole legs and gilt edges, and retrieves a note. It's handwritten on a piece of lined paper that's been torn from a school notebook.

"Cressida left a suicide note?" Kersti's question is a breath, a gasp.

"Yes."

"You've had this all along?"

"Yes."

"I thought they never found a note," Kersti says, glaring at Deirdre in frustration. "You *told* me there was no note."

"They sent it to me with her things after she was safely back in the States and far enough away not to damage their reputation," Deirdre says. "It was Armand who found the note when he went there to pack up her things. Bueche said they missed it when they searched her room the first time. Covered it up is more like it. That school wouldn't have wanted to be linked to an attempted suicide. All they ever cared about was their reputation."

The creases from where the note is folded are worn from having been opened and closed so many times. It looks hastily scribbled, practically illegible.

I will miB you. Im sorry

"I will 'mib' you," Kersti reads.

"She was very drunk," Deirdre says. "That's what they told me."

"It's uncharacteristically brief," Kersti remarks, not knowing what to make of it.

"The truth is," Deirdre admits, "I've never been one hundred percent convinced she wrote it." She covers her mouth with a pale hand. "I suppose it's hard for any mother to accept that her own child wants to die so badly she's capable of taking her own life, but I never thought of Cressida as being suicidal—"

"I didn't think she was, either, but then I guess some people hide it well."

"Cressida never did hide anything, though, did she?" Deirdre reflects. "Whatever she was feeling or going through, the world had to know about it."

"So you don't think she jumped?"

"I've never known what to think, Kersti. But in my heart of hearts? No, I don't think she did. But let's face it," Deirdre sniffles. "I wasn't around. What did I really know about her? I like to think there's no way she would have tried to kill herself and the note was just teen melodrama—a coincidence, a bid for attention. Then I think maybe I'm just deluding myself. It certainly hurts less if it was an accident. She had so much promise—"

"Does she remember anything?" Kersti asks. "She seemed to remember Lille just now. Is that possible?"

"It's possible," Deirdre says.

"Have you ever asked her what happened, Deirdre?"

"Of course," Deirdre says. "Many times. She just stares back at me, empty. Maybe it's for the best that she doesn't remember—"

She shakes her head then, her face a mask of anguish and confusion, tears collecting in the corners of her eyes and spilling slowly down her cheeks. Amazing her ducts still function, Kersti observes.

"Why did you make me leave the first time I came to visit her?" Kersti asks.

"I told you then. It was too painful. I knew she wouldn't want you to see her like that."

"*She* wouldn't, or *you* didn't?"

"Both, I suppose," Deirdre admits.

"What if she just missed me?"

"Maybe she did. She's had such a disappointing life, Kersti—"

"I'm sorry." Kersti reaches out and places her hand on the sharp bone of Deirdre's shoulder. "Do you remember when I visited last time, I asked you about a ledger?"

"Vaguely."

"Lille also mentioned the ledger in her letter to me. She thought there might be something incriminating in it."

"Incriminating for who?"

"She didn't say."

"I never came across a ledger. The school never sent it to me."

"Are you sure?"

"Of course I'm sure."

"You said there wasn't a suicide note, either," Kersti reminds her.

"I swear, Kersti. There was no ledger with her things. There's no reason for me to lie about that, but I'm sure you can imagine why I never wanted anyone to know about the suicide note. Cressida was above suicide."

Kersti hands back the note, not sure she trusts Deirdre.

"Whom did the ledger belong to?" Deirdre asks, refolding the note, something she's probably done hundreds of times before.

"I don't know," Kersti lies, deciding not to say anything. Cressida fell the very same night she got her hands on that ledger. Whether she jumped, fell by accident, or was pushed, Kersti—like Lille—has probably always known the ledger contains the answers. Why they both chose to ignore their instincts for so long can only be attributed to post-traumatic stress and adolescent self-preservation. It was just simpler to accept a drunken fall.

"Do you think someone could have pushed her?" Deirdre asks.

Kersti recalls the web of people Cressida had hurt by the end of her final year at the Lycée—the relationships destroyed, the friends betrayed, the hearts broken—and yes, Kersti considers it's very possible. She can think of two people in particular.

"What about Magnus Foley?" Deirdre says, reading her mind. "He's the one she snuck out to meet that night—"

What Deirdre doesn't know is that Cressida snuck out to tell Magnus she was in love with someone else, and that later on, according to Lille, Magnus came looking for Cressida at Huber House. Who knows how he took being dumped? He was crazy in love with her, spoiled, entitled. What if he pushed her and wrote a suicide note? Which would mean Kersti lost her virginity to a murderer, the possibility of which she doesn't want to think about right now.

And if Magnus didn't push her, does he know something? "I have to find that ledger," Kersti says, more to herself. Knowing where she has to go next.

"Please keep me abreast," Deirdre says, touching Kersti's wrist with her translucent blue hands. "If you find anything out, I'd like you to let me know."

There's an ambivalence in her request that Kersti recognizes, which comes from wanting to know the truth and being afraid of it at the same time.

They return to Cressida's bedside and Kersti sits down beside her. Cressida turns to face her, her aqua eyes focused and lucid. "*Statch*—" she says, startling them.

Kersti looks at Deirdre and Laylay for a translation.

"What are you trying to say?" Laylay asks her.

"*Statch*," Cressida repeats. "*You*."

"Say again—"

"*Statch. You*."

"She's saying statue," Kersti cries. "Do you remember the statue, Cress?"

Cressida blinks.

"What statue?" Deirdre says.

"There was a statue of Helvetia at the Lycée," Kersti explains.

"My God," Deirdre says hopefully. "Cress? Darling? Is that what you meant to say? Statue?"

Cressida's beautiful face reveals nothing. It's a porcelain mask, blank and impenetrable, magnificently concealing a damaged mind full of God only knows what.

CHAPTER 12

LAUSANNE—November 1995

Kersti knows something is different in French class on Monday. Magnus barely acknowledges her when she sits down next to him, other than to grunt, "Hey." He doesn't even call her Kuusk, the way he normally does, doesn't scribble any notes to her or stretch his legs out so they touch hers. When she tries to catch his attention or make eye contact, he deliberately looks away, pretending to concentrate on whatever M. Feuilly is saying.

It goes on like that for the entire two-hour class and when it's finally over, Magnus gets up quickly and runs off, muttering, "See you later." Not even looking back at her.

She wants to scream after him, "You devirginized me, asshole!" Instead she rushes to the bathroom, ashamed and bewildered. She figured they were a couple. She spent the entire weekend imagining them holding hands after class, kissing each other good-bye as they parted ways. Everyone in the school knowing they were together.

She locks herself in the stall and sobs very quietly because she can hear Abby Ho-Tai in the stall beside her. Maybe Magnus is embarrassed about what happened on Saturday, she rationalizes. Maybe he regrets taking her virginity on a rock when they were both so drunk. She spins it all kinds of ways before concluding it's probably a good idea to talk to him.

She splashes water on her face and goes off in search of him. It's lunch and he usually hangs around the school grounds socializing and smoking before walking home. She looks for him in the garden, but he isn't there. She asks around. Someone saw him heading around back, so that's where she goes.

She follows the dirt path behind Huber House and stops immediately when she spots them standing together by the tennis courts. Her first reaction is paralyzing jealousy. Cressida's back is to Kersti, but when Kersti recognizes her wild hair, she's hit with such intense despair it knocks the wind out of her. She watches them for a long time, feeling betrayed, and more inadequate than ever. She contemplates fleeing, hiding in her room and never speaking to either of them again, but then it occurs to her, what if Magnus is asking Cressida for advice? Who else would he turn to if not Kersti's best friend?

Feeling slightly buoyed, Kersti continues along the path that winds around the statue of Helvetia and decides to play it cool. *Hey guys. What's up?* But as she approaches, she notices they're standing very close together and that Magnus's fingers are hooked inside the front pocket of Cressida's jeans. There's a perceptible intimacy between them that makes Kersti feel instantly sick. Where did this relationship come from? "Hey, guys," she says, and it comes out sounding like an accusation.

They both spin around and Magnus guiltily steps away from Cressida, pulling his fingers out of her pockets. Before Kersti can think of anything clever to say, she starts to cry.

"Kerst—"

She instantly regrets confronting them. Now she feels like an idiot, a loser. He used her. They're probably laughing at her behind her back. Before she can humiliate herself further, she runs off toward Huber House.

Cressida runs after her. "Kerst!" she cries out. "Wait!"

Kersti swings open the front door and goes inside, with Cressida right behind her. "Stop being a baby," Cressida says. "Just talk to me."

"Fuck you! You know how much I like him! You know he was my first!"

"It's not that simple."

"Excuse me?"

They're alone in the narrow corridor outside the TV lounge. Everyone else is in the dining hall for lunch.

"Magnus and I have been here a lot longer than you," Cressida says, as though that explains something.

"And?"

"We have a history."

"You're only telling me this *now*?" Kersti fires. "I've been confiding to you how much I like him for over a year and all you've ever said is he's not your type. Now all of a sudden he shows some interest in me and *you* want him?"

"It's not like that."

"Isn't it?" Kersti says. "You have to win. You have to get everything you want. You can't let anyone else have anything—"

"It's complicated."

"You're a bitch," Kersti tells her. "You are a real bitch."

"He was my first, too!" Cressida blurts.

Kersti steps back. It takes her a few seconds to recover before she's able to speak again. "You said it was that actor—"

"It was Magnus," Cressida states. "We were thirteen. It was the year before you came to the Lycée."

"Thirteen?"

"I got pregnant," she explains. "Hamidou took me to Zurich for the abortion."

"Hamidou took you?" Kersti cries, incredulous.

"I couldn't have anything to do with Magnus after that," Cressida says. "But I never stopped . . . I've always had feelings for him. We've liked each other since fifth grade."

"Does Magnus know you were pregnant?" Kersti asks, forgetting her own stake in their triangle.

"Yes, but we were kids. Literally. Like, little kids."

"And now?"

"I don't know. I'm sorry—"

"So because he liked me and he slept with me, *now* you've decided you want him back?"

Cressida looks down at her feet. "Maybe," she murmurs. "Do you know how hard it's been for me to listen to you go on and on about him? And when he asked you out and then you guys . . ." As she wipes away tears, Kersti has to wonder if she's acting. It's in her blood, after all.

"Does he still like you?" Kersti asks her.

Cressida gives her a look, as though to say, "What do you think?" but doesn't respond.

"Because he sure seemed to like *me* on Saturday," Kersti says.

"I'm sorry you're hurt, but don't you get it? He used you to get to me."

"I find it hard to believe that he made everything up," Kersti says, remembering his tenderness when he thought he was hurting her, the things he said to her. *You're so real. So down-to-earth and authentic. You sweet little virgin.*

How could he not have meant those words? He sounded so sincere. "He can decide for himself," Kersti says. "You don't have any more right to him than I do. Let's see who he wants to be with."

CHAPTER 13

TORONTO—October 2015

The Estonian House is on Broadview, near Chester Hill Road. It used to be a school, an ugly, brown brick building that the Estonian community took over in 1960. It's nothing fancy, but it's serviceable and satisfies just about every need of the community, including its own credit union, the Estonian Family Services office, the Estonian consulate, the Estonian language school, Girl Scouts, and the Estonian travel agency owned by Kersti's father. Kersti practically grew up here and knows it as well as her own home: the front and back stairwells, the musty basement, the dingy offices and pale green classrooms, the cafeteria and banquet halls. Between the Estonian classes every weekend, Girl Scouts, the art center, and all the holiday parties over the course of her life, she's probably spent more time in this building than anywhere else.

Kersti climbs the stairs to the third floor and pokes her head inside her family's travel agency—really just a small office—which moved into the Estonian House in 1998, two years after Expedia came on the scene and turned the travel-booking industry on its ass. The rent is much cheaper here than its former location on Broadview, and her father has a loyal clientele of elderly Estonians who don't book online and keep him in business.

Jutta and Tuule both look up from their computers. "Tere," they say, at the same time. They both have the same haircuts—short bobs—and wide round faces, which make them both look about a decade younger than their forty-something years.

"Hi," Kersti says, opting for English.

Her sisters still speak Estonian as much as they speak English. As with many second- and third-generation Estonians, their children's first language was also Estonian. When Paavo Kuusk arrived in Canada with that first wave of refugees after the war, he—like the rest of his fellow countrymen—never stopped believing they would all eventually return to the homeland as soon as Estonia regained its independence from Russia. While they lived in Canada, which Paavo always believed would be temporary, he and Anni were diligent about raising their kids fully immersed in the Estonian culture, so that their generation could be wholly, seamlessly reintegrated.

It wasn't enough that Kersti and her sisters spoke or understood Estonian as a second language, either; they had to be, first and foremost, Estonian. They were put into Estonian-immersion kindergarten, followed by Estonian elementary class every weekend until high school. After high school, it was Tartu College for Kersti's sisters, which is affiliated with Tartu University in Estonia; her sisters were also members of the Estonian sorority in Toronto, where they met their future Estonian husbands, who of course belonged to the Estonian fraternity. Kersti escaped all that when she was sent to Lausanne, and later, when she married a Jew, her one and only act of rebellion against the family.

"What're you doing here?" Tuule asks her.

"I've got an appointment at Family Services," Kersti says, plunking down in one of the swivel chairs.

The office, like the rest of the building, is dreary and utilitarian:

dim lighting, industrial carpet, fake chestnut-stained MDF furniture from Office Depot, and beige IBM computers from the year Paavo moved the agency here. He's never believed in wasting money on prettying up a place or making it warmer or more hospitable, lest he should find himself feeling too comfortable. He's lived his entire life in Toronto as though everything is temporary. *Why spend money on a new couch when we could be moving back to Estonia anytime? Why get new computers? Why invest in a new kitchen floor? A bigger house?*

And yet, even when Estonia reestablished its independence from the Soviet Union in 1991, Paavo did not return. Though he still claims he will go back there one day to die, the thought of gathering up the whole clan—daughters, sons-in-law, families of his in-laws, grandchildren, close friends—has proved too daunting. At eighty-four, he's planted his roots too deep. The Estonian-Canadian community that grew up around him over the years has become his true homeland, more than Estonia ever could be again. He's just too stubborn to admit it. And so he stays, secretly content in Toronto, not willing to invest in or commit to anything too binding that might anchor him here.

"What appointment?" Tuule wants to know.

"Counseling."

Jutta and Tuule are quiet. Jutta pops the end of a croissant in her mouth. They don't ask questions.

She leaves their office, feeling a little depressed. The whole building has that effect on her. She's always found it to be gloomy and shabby, a statement in itself about its culture of impermanence.

She runs down to the second floor, where Jay is standing outside the Estonian Family Services office waiting for her. It's been tense between them since she got back from Boston. He wasn't very happy that she'd left without discussing it with him. She reminded him that he was the one who'd gone to a hotel. Other than that, they haven't spoken much at all, other than to agree—reluctantly—on counseling.

Eva Sepp opens the door. She's tall and broad, about Kersti's age, with dirty blond hair and florid cheeks. The blue eyes are a given. She's wearing a red acrylic sweater with black leggings that reveal thick, cross-country skier's legs. Or so Kersti imagines.

"*Tere*," she says, inviting them both inside.

Jay and Kersti sit down side by side on a green leather couch, separated by a box of Kleenex.

"What brings you here?" Eva asks, putting on a pair of bifocals and tucking her hair behind her ears.

"We're having problems," Kersti starts. "Due to my infertility."

"Our infertility," Jay corrects. "It's *our* problem."

"Okay, well, that's very supportive, Jay," Eva commends him.

"Well, it's funny though," Kersti says. "Because if it's *our* problem, why is it *your* decision that we stop trying? I don't get a say?"

"Are you kidding me?" Jay says, his voice rising. "We've been at this for years, Kersti. I would've thrown in the towel ages ago. When do I get to say stop? Or don't I?"

Kersti snatches a Kleenex and blows her nose.

"I can already see this is a very emotionally charged issue for both of you," Eva says.

Jay lets out an exasperated sigh. "Listen," he says. "I agreed to come here for Kersti because I know this is a rough time for her. But—and I don't mean to disparage what you do—nothing you say can convince me to use an egg donor."

"My role is not to convince you of anything," Eva says neutrally.

Jay turns to face Kersti, his expression softer, desperate. "I'm here to say this one more time. I'm not using an egg donor. I want us to go back to how we were, no more trying to have a kid, or else—"

"Or else what?"

"Kersti," Eva says softly. "What would it take for you to accept that you may not be able to have a baby?"

"Nothing," she says unequivocally. "Do you have children, Eva?"

"Yes," Eva admits. "But that's not—"

"Would you have been able to accept not having children?"

"I can't speak to that."

"Not being a mother makes you no less a woman," Jay intervenes, trying—and failing—to console her.

Kersti turns on him, wanting to choke the pedantic tone right out of his voice. "How would you know?" she snaps.

"*I* don't think any less of you," he says.

"What about what *I* think of me?"

He looks confused. Eva is leaning back in her chair, watching the scene unravel. Watching them unravel.

"There are certain expectations I have to live up to," Kersti says, looking back and forth between them, shredding the Kleenex in her hand. "As a woman, as an Estonian. And if I don't, then I feel bad about myself."

"That's fucking ridiculous," Jay mutters.

"No, it's not," Eva says sharply. "I completely understand that, Kersti. I do."

"Whose expectations are they?" Jay wants to know.

"Everyone's!" Kersti says. "My mother, my father, my sisters, women. Estonians."

"Estonians," Jay repeats, with a disgusted eye roll.

"You know I've never fit in with them," she reminds him. "I've always felt like an outsider in my family and with the other Estos.

All I have to do is have a baby and carry on the great Estonian legacy to set things right, and you want me to accept that I *can't*? You want me to just move on and give up on the one thing every woman on the planet should be able to do?"

"You've had three novels published, for Christ's sake! That's not enough of an achievement for you?"

"It sounds to me like this is about belonging," Eva gently interjects.

"That's part of it," Kersti acknowledges.

"So it's not really about maternal longing," Jay accuses. "It's about conforming?"

"That's cruel," Kersti says, brushing warm tears from her cheeks, knowing, at last, that she's not going to get her way. How can she possibly explain to him that her inability to conceive is just more proof of her inadequacy? The way it makes her feel is a perfect mirror of that overriding sense of inadequacy she always felt next to Cressida, especially after Magnus, and continues to feel to this day.

"Having a baby won't change how Kersti feels about herself," Jay tells Eva, as though reading Kersti's mind. "Or how anyone feels about her."

Kersti tunes him out and drifts off. *I have to get out of here,* she thinks.

"Because they've never accepted her, she refuses to accept herself," he says. "Infertility is just the tip of the iceberg. We could have a happy life together without children if only she would just—"

"We're going around in circles," Kersti interrupts, reaching for her purse. "Maybe we do need some time apart to regroup."

"Why can't you let go of what they think?" he asks her.

She doesn't bother answering him. She's already working out a plan. Where she's going next, who she needs to talk to.

"Kersti?" Eva says, drawing her back to the conversation with a tone one might use on a five-year-old. "Are you hearing what Jay is saying?"

"Yes," Kersti says, standing up. "I'm hearing him."

"Where are you going?" Jay asks her. "This was your idea—"

"You were right. It was a waste of time."

"So now what? You're going to take off again without telling me where you're going?"

"I'm going to New York," she says, leaving him there with a very bewildered-looking Eva Sepp.

As the front doors close behind her, she rushes away from the Estonian House, feeling more purposeful than she has in a long time.

CHAPTER 14

LAUSANNE—December 1995

When the students return from the Christmas concert at the church, they all gather in the dining hall for the traditional hot chocolate and *spitzbuebli*. It's a magical night, with snowflakes like eiderdown dusting the pine trees and copper rooftops as they land. Kersti is standing by the buffet with Alison and Lille, all of them giddy and flushed from the cold, gorging on the jam cookies. Tomorrow they go home for the holidays.

In spite of the lovely night, Kersti still feels like she's lost everything that mattered to her this semester—her best friend, her virginity, the guy she thought she was in love with. *Gone*. Cressida and Magnus are back together and Kersti has been unceremoniously relegated to the sideline. Every morning she wakes up with what feels like a vise tightening inside her chest. The weight of her hurt bears down on her, a burden that feels physical as well as emotional.

Magnus has gone back to calling her Kuusk and scribbling notes to her in French, but the flirtatiousness is gone. There's a new dynamic between them—she's his pal, his French buddy. His girlfriend's best friend. Kersti has taken on the role of sidekick. He never acknowledged the night they spent together, the virginity he stole from her. If he does talk to her outside French class, it's to ask where Cressida is, what does she want for her birthday, is something bothering Cressida that he should know about? Like that.

When Kersti sees them together, kissing between classes, holding hands and walking to his apartment on Saturday afternoons, the sting of their betrayal feels as fresh as if it's just happened. It makes her feel worthless, deficient. She finds herself frequently asking the question, "What's wrong with me?" And in the absence of any specific, concrete answer, Kersti concludes it must be everything. Before long, the question turns into a statement, uttered silently almost every day. *Something is wrong with me.*

She's not even sure what hurts more—losing Cressida to Magnus, or the other way around. At times she feels more jealous of Magnus. He's the one monopolizing Cressida's time, her affection, her attention. Either way, Kersti feels abandoned, the fall semester marred by their rejection.

She's almost relieved to be going home for the holidays.

"I think I'm going to *spitzbuebli*," Alison jokes, reaching for another cookie.

"Me, too," Kersti says. "I feel really *spitzbuebli*."

"You look a bit *spitzbuebli*," Lille says, just as Cressida arrives at the buffet.

"Are you guys *spitzbuebl*ing?" she says, without missing a beat. "I don't want to interrupt."

Everyone laughs, even Kersti.

"Can I talk to you, Kerst?" Cressida asks her. She's wearing tall leather boots with a tweed miniskirt and a creamy turtleneck through which the lace of her bra can just barely be seen. Her hair is pulled back in a ponytail that looks like a giant pompom, and her skin is glowing pink and luminous. She is dishearteningly beautiful, Kersti thinks, feeling crappier than ever.

"I know it's been kind of tense between us," Cressida says. "But I really miss you."

"We share a room."

"You know what I mean."

"You're always with Magnus."

"Kerst, I'm sorry. I know I hurt you and I wish it hadn't happened that way. I wish it had been anyone but you who got hurt. But I miss us."

"Doesn't seem like it."

"Spend Christmas with me in Telluride," Cressida says, clasping Kersti's hands. "We can ski and hang out and rekindle our love—"

"You know I can't," Kersti says. "I have to go home."

"Why? You had the worst holiday ever last year."

It's true. Kersti felt like an alien at the Estonian House Christmas party, and even more so with her family. She bought her sisters handmade Swiss chocolate snowmen and in return they gave her a package of airmail envelopes, a role of stamps, and bubble bath from the pharmacy.

"We'll have so much fun," Cressida says, still holding her hands. "I miss my best friend. I want to spend time with you."

"What about Magnus?"

"He's going to Gstaad."

"Don't you want to go to Gstaad with him?"

"No. I want to go to Telluride with *you*."

Kersti has to admit she's touched, even a bit flattered that Cressida is choosing her over Magnus. She dismisses the fleeting thought that Cressida has a way of making her feel special and shitty about herself at the same time. "My parents can't afford to send me to Telluride," Kersti says. "Why don't we just talk after the holidays. Maybe we both need some space—"

"I don't want space," Cressida sulks. "We've already had too much space between us."

Kersti can feel herself softening, her resentments and jealousy melting. In spite of everything that's happened, she knows Cressida loves her. She can't forget the way Cressida took her under her wing right from the start, stood up for her and made sure she was welcomed into the group. *You're the most normal, grounded one here,* she once said to Kersti.

Cressida needs her. Deep down, Kersti knows that.

"Come to Telluride with me," Cressida pleads. "I'll buy your ticket. You can go home first and then come to Colorado on the twenty-sixth. We'll spend New Year's together and then fly back to Lausanne."

She has it all worked out; she always does. And she is utterly seductive.

CHAPTER 15

NEW YORK—October 2015

Kersti glances out the little egg-shaped window at the glistening tarmac where a steady drizzle has been falling since late afternoon. The sky is already dark as the plane begins to roll out. She's always enjoyed flying at night, something about being cocooned in blackness, like soaring into space. She was able to book a last-minute flight and was out of the house before Jay got home from work. They haven't spoken since their disastrous counseling session.

When the plane smooths out at its flying altitude, Kersti reaches into her purse for the stack of mail she grabbed from home and quickly shuffles through the magazines—*Vanity Fair, British House & Gardens*—finding the one letter in the pile. She recognizes the embossed emblem of Helvetia on the envelope and opens it.

Dear Kersti,

Our 100th birthday celebration is fast approaching on Saturday June 11th, 2016. This is a friendly reminder that we are still waiting for your RSVP both as a "One Hundred Women of the Lycée" speaker, and as an attendee of the festivities. If you are unable to make it, please inform us at your earliest convenience so that we may arrange our speaker schedule accordingly. We hope to see you in the spring!

Best,
M. Bueche

Kersti folds the letter and puts it back in her purse. She's been mulling over whether or not to go for months; she can't blame Bueche for wanting an answer. She's still waiting to hear from Noa and Rafaella. Maybe she'll ask Magnus if he's planning to go. It will be a good opener since they haven't spoken since the day of Cressida's accident. They reconnected on Facebook about two years ago, but only to add each other as "friends." They've never had an actual conversation. Once in a while she trolls through his pictures, but he rarely posts anything. He's never commented on or "liked" any of hers. She messaged him as soon as she left the Estonian House this afternoon, asking him to meet with her. His response came quick: *Kuusk! Quelle surprise. Text me when you arrive.* With his number.

She couldn't help smiling. She was relieved he remembered her, even called her Kuusk. She still thinks about him. The ego has a way of hanging on to unrequited love as though it's some kind of personal failure, an irrevocable blight on past achievements. That's how it's been for Kersti, no matter how much time passes or how much she loves Jay.

Outside her hotel on Seventh and Fifty-Fourth the street buzzes and hums until the sun comes up. She lies awake most of the night, listening to the noises below, thinking about her marriage, babies, Cressida, Lille, the Lycée, what she would say if she spoke at the birthday celebration in Lausanne. *It's an honor to stand before you on the Lycée's hundredth anniversary. I'm truly humbled.*

She wonders if Harzenmoser is alive. What became of their beloved Mme. Hamidou? Mostly she wonders how Magnus Foley will look tomorrow. Will they reminisce about the night she lost her virginity? The beer fondue, the fighting raccoons? Cressida's momentous fall?

By the time she arrives at his office on Thirty-Fourth, breathless from having walked too fast, she's conjured him in her mind a dozen different ways—overweight and bald; silver-haired and debonair; openly gay with two earrings and a flamboyant lisp. She's still got this dogged need to prove herself to him, so it would be a relief if he's let himself go.

He's got his own graphic design firm on the thirty-fourth floor, overlooking Gramercy Park. Kersti announces herself to the receptionist and is instructed to sit and wait on an uncomfortable orange couch—one of those pretentious, contemporary pieces that look more like a sculpture than furniture—and given a bottle of water with the orange and gray MAFD logo on it.

She waits about ten minutes before Magnus shows up, striding toward her with that cocky smile she'd almost forgotten. He's wearing ripped jeans and a snug black T-shirt that looks like it would have to be peeled off. She realizes instantly that everything she imagined he would look like was wrong. He's still gorgeous and youthful, a reminder that they're still only in their thirties, even though most days she feels so much older. Or maybe *weary* is the better word. The truth is, there may still be plenty of time before thinning hair and paunchy middle sections, sagging body parts and reluctant surrender. Magnus's skin is smooth and vibrant, he's in good shape, and he has the same thick blond brush cut of two decades ago, which is somehow both a relief and demoralizing.

"Kuusk," he says, still grinning, giving her an approving once-over.

"It's Wax now."

"How are you? Shit, it's been, what? Like seventeen, eighteen years?" He hugs her and she smells soap in his skin, probably from a recent hand wash. "What the hell brings you here after all this time?"

"A couple of things, actually."

"I get so many notes on Facebook from people from my past . . . I never expect anyone to actually show up."

People from my past. Strange to realize that's what she is, that they are this. He once fucked her on a rock in the woods and told her she was authentic and real. *You sweet virgin.*

"Anyway, you look great, Kuusk."

She's wearing skinny jeans with knee-high boots and a fitted leather jacket. Her hair is pulled back in a high ponytail, which also acts as a de facto facelift. She hopes she looks good. "You, too," she says, trying not to stare at him for too long.

She's fourteen again, seeing him for the first time. Her pulse is thumping, her palms are clammy. What is it about him? What was it back then about both of them—Magnus and Cressida—that so powerfully attracted her, beyond their obvious good looks? Some intangible magnetism or special charisma that she wanted to attach herself to and absorb by association? Or, more disturbing, was it closer to a sadomasochistic instinct, knowing on some unconscious level that they were both dangerous for her and she would get hurt over and over again and still not be able to walk away? She suddenly feels compelled to resolve that for herself.

"You still haven't said why you're here," he says, and she wonders if he even remembers having sex with her. *Devirginizing* her. If he does, he isn't acting the least bit sheepish or embarrassed about how he handled things afterward.

"Can we go somewhere and talk?" she asks him, glancing over at the receptionist. "I can come back—"

"Not necessary," he says, leading her out of the office and back to the elevators. "Let's grab coffee."

He calls for the elevator and they wait for it in awkward silence. When it finally arrives, they look at each other with relief. "So how have you been?" he asks her, as soon as the doors close, trapping them inside together. "You're still living in . . . ?"

"Toronto."

"Right. What do you do there?"

"I'm a writer."

"What do you write?" Most people assume when she says she's a writer that she's a copywriter, a dabbler in poetry, or someone who sits in Starbucks all day working on a screenplay that will never be finished.

"Novels," she tells him. "Historical women's fiction. Nothing you'd know."

"Published?"

"Three so far."

"Wow. Very cool."

"You seem to be doing pretty well," she returns, thinking of his view of Gramercy Park.

"I'm good at design," he says, not elaborating.

Between uncomfortable stabs at small talk, they both stare up at the floor numbers as they descend to the lobby. She notices he's not wearing a ring on his wedding finger. His status isn't posted on Facebook, so she isn't sure if there's a Mrs. Foley.

"Kids?" he asks her.

"Not yet," she says, avoiding the longer version of that answer. "You?"

"Divorced. No kids."

Her eyes are still fixed on those numbers. Nine, eight, seven. Why is she so happy to hear he's divorced? When they reach the lobby, he extends his arm to let her out first. "Madame," he says.

The coffee shop is one of those standard New York institutions you always find in the lobby of these art deco buildings—a long counter with stools, straight-up coffee percolating in glass pots—no lattes and cappuccinos here—and a queue of suits out the door.

"The usual, Jahmir," Magnus says. Kersti orders a black coffee. Magnus treats.

They settle side by side on a lone bench by the elevators. "Did you get your invitation to the Lycée's hundredth anniversary celebration?" she asks him, as per the speech she rehearsed all night.

"They don't know where to find me," he says, fiddling with the sleeve of his cup.

"*I* found you."

"The Lycée probably hasn't figured out Facebook yet. You going?"

Kersti shrugs. "I don't know." She doesn't mention that she's been chosen one of their Hundred Women. "I'm still debating."

"It's too hard to go back there," he says, and she figures he means it both literally and figuratively.

"Remember Lille Robertson?" she says, lifting the lid off her cup to let the coffee cool.

"The little weirdo with the white hair and the black nose?"

"She died."

"How?"

"Breast cancer."

"Shit. That's too bad."

"Have you kept in touch with anyone?" she asks him.

"Me? No. No one." He's staring into his tea, distant. "You?"

"Noa and Rafaella. Mostly on Facebook. Noa and I Skype sometimes."

"What are they up to?"

"Raf lives in Paris. She's divorced. As far as I know, she doesn't work. Noa's still in Rotterdam. She's got a lot of kids. She's an environmentalist. She posts a lot of anti–Royal Dutch Shell messages. That's about it. Well, and Cressida."

"Cressida?"

"Yes. I was just in Boston visiting her. She's living with her mother."

He nods, his expression clouded. She wonders what he's thinking. He doesn't ask how she is.

"Anyway, Lille wrote me a letter before she died," Kersti continues. "And it . . . I brought it, actually. If you want to read it."

He looks at her as though to say: "What the hell has this got to do with me?"

She hands him the letter. "Her mother sent it to me. She found it unfinished on Lille's computer."

"You never spoke to Lille after graduation?" he says. "Weren't the three of you best friends?"

"I didn't even graduate. I left right after . . ." She leaves it unspoken. The accident. The fall. "Lille sort of vanished. I was never able to find her on any of the usual social media."

Magnus unfolds the letter and reads it. When he's done, he hands it back to Kersti without saying a word.

"Lille didn't think Cressida fell by accident," Kersti says.

"I see that."

"I didn't know you were there that night."

"Why would you?" he says. "I snuck in."

"Why?"

"Does it really matter anymore?"

"I think so."

"Why?"

"You were the last person to see Cressida that night."

"No, I wasn't."

"Weren't you?" A thick man in an overcoat bumps Kersti as he brushes past. "I just want to find out what really happened to her," she says. "What she was like before she fell—"

"Why? Why now?"

"Timing, I guess," she tells him. "First I got the invitation from the Lycée, then the letter from Lille. I figured the universe was trying to tell me something, like maybe I need some closure on this. Or maybe I didn't do enough when it first happened."

"We were kids," he says. "What could any of us have done?"

"I know, but now I feel like I can at least ask some questions," she says, thinking about her conversation with Deirdre the other day. "And frankly, the more I do the more my curiosity is snowballing. I may even write about it for my next book."

"Cressida was an alcoholic, Kersti. We both know that. You want to know what she was like the last time I saw her? She was wasted."

"I know she dumped you."

Magnus looks at her for a moment and breaks into a smile. "This isn't the place for a real conversation," he says, checking his watch. "Do you want to have dinner tonight?"

"Sure," she says, trying to sound nonchalant but secretly feeling like he's just invited her to the school dance. *Do you remember fucking me?* She has to bite her tongue in order not to ask him.

"To be continued," he says, getting up and disappearing inside the elevator.

CHAPTER 16

LAUSANNE—February 1996

Cressida's father, Armand, rips a piece of his crusty bread in half and stuffs a hunk in his mouth. It's Parents Weekend and Cressida invited Kersti to join her and her parents for dinner at the Maison de Raclette. Kersti's parents didn't come for Parents Weekend. They couldn't afford the trip. Kersti was disappointed when she received the apologetic letter from her mother. She realized after reading it that she missed her parents. Her visit with them over the holiday was short. She spent Christmas eve and morning with them—most of it at the Estonian House, surrounded by all her parents' friends, which was essentially the entire Estonian community—and then she boarded a plane to Telluride to spend the rest of the holiday with Cressida at her family's log cabin.

They had a wonderful time, just as Cressida planned. The cabin was more of a log mansion, with picture windows overlooking the Rockies and a back door that opened onto the mountain. They skied, made chocolate chip pancakes in the middle of the night, dyed each other's hair, and watched a lot of movies in their pajamas, sprawled on an L-shaped couch the size of Kersti's entire main floor. Mostly, they reconnected. It was a lot like the first year of their friendship. Just the two of them, rediscovering one another. Kersti didn't have to fight for Cressida's attention, or feel threatened by anyone else encroaching on their time together. As the week went on, Kersti remembered with a softly swelling heart what she loved so much about Cressida—her irreverence, her wit, that feeling she gave Kersti of being completely adored and special.

On New Year's Eve, they sat in front of the TV and watched the ball drop in Times Square, drinking Baileys in chocolate milk. Cressida's parents had gone out and they had the house to themselves. At midnight they opened a bottle of champagne that Armand had left for them. They drank from the bottle and danced to ABBA and *Grease*—the anthems of their childhoods—and got so drunk, Cressida fell in the bathroom and split the porcelain toilet lid in half. They rolled on the floor laughing about that for a while, and then Cressida got in a cold shower so she wouldn't pass out.

When she was done, she gazed at her perfect, naked self in the medicine cabinet mirror and then covered up in a white terry robe with the initials *DSP* monogrammed on the pocket. Kersti still could not imagine Cressida ever being pregnant. Her body was obviously never meant to be disfigured or desecrated in any way. The thought of her smooth, flat stomach distended over elastic band maternity pants, or her milky skin vandalized by blue stretch marks, was utterly incongruous.

"What was it like being pregnant?" Kersti asked her.

Cressida sat down on the ledge of the tub and lit a cigarette from the pack she'd left on the soap dish. "Horrid," she answered. "I was so nauseous I couldn't stand up. I couldn't eat, I couldn't read. All I could do was sleep and puke into a garbage can next to my bed. It was a nightmare."

"Weren't you afraid to tell Hamidou? Couldn't she have expelled you?"

"She would never," Cressida said, giving her a funny look.

"Did it hurt? The abortion?"

"No."

"Do you and Magnus ever talk about it?"

"Never," she said, standing up. "You're the only person I've ever talked to about it, Kuusky. You're my soul mate."

That week in Telluride, Kersti was reminded why being Cressida's best friend was a privilege. So she resigned herself, once they were back in Lausanne, to be diplomatic and share her with Magnus as best she could. She was still bruised over the way he'd used her, but what choice did she have other than to accept what they were offering?

Armand looks at his watch and frowns. Magnus is meeting Cressida's parents for the first time and he's late. "*I* wouldn't have showed up late to meet your mother's father when we were dating," he states, crumbs flying like sawdust from his mouth. "It's disrespectful."

"Let's just order the raclette," Deirdre suggests, trying to placate her husband. "I'm famished."

"He's not earning any points with us," Armand says, ignoring his wife.

Armand Strauss is an intimidating man. Broad-shouldered, immaculately dressed, with a neatly trimmed silver mustache and gelled silver hair that shimmers like diamonds beneath the light of the chandeliers. Being a world-famous composer and musical theater producer—he created the decade-long running play *And Then There Was One*—he demands respect from everyone who crosses his path, or as Cressida likes to put it, he sucks the blood out of them.

Cressida gives Kersti an amused, conspiratorial look. She's working her way through a bottle of red wine and her cheeks are gorgeously flushed. "So he's late, " she says. "Big deal. He's not one of your stagehands, Armand."

"Cressida," Deirdre says sharply, her British accent more pronounced. "It's a matter of courtesy. It's got nothing to do with who your father is."

"Everything has to do with who my father is."

"He should want to impress me if he cares about you," Armand adds, holding up his hand, gold rings glinting. A waiter appears and Armand orders in French. Raclette for five and another bottle of Pinot Noir.

The waiter nods and scurries off, almost colliding with Magnus. "Sorry I'm late," he says. "The bus from Verbier broke down."

He unzips his ski jacket, the lift tickets jangling like keys. His cheeks are red from the cold, his usual spiky hair somewhat flat from his hat. He's wearing a white shirt and a tie, dark dress pants.

Cressida looks over at her father with a satisfied expression. Armand says contritely, "Glad you could make it, Magnus."

Magnus sits in the chair between Cressida and Kersti. He looks at Cressida adoringly, kisses her cheek, and completely ignores Kersti.

"How was the skiing today?" Armand asks him, stabbing a tomato slice on his salad plate.

"A little icy," Magnus says, lighting up a Philip Morris. "I'm going to try Chamonix next weekend."

"I wish we had more time for skiing this trip," Armand says, turning to Deirdre. It's the first thing he's said to her all night.

"You look gorgeous," Magnus whispers to Cressida, as though they're the only two people at the table. She's wearing a lavender cashmere sweater and has her hair straightened. It looks like mink.

"She doesn't know how beautiful she is," Deirdre comments, and it's unclear whether she's proud or jealous.

"I think she does," Armand says, observing his daughter. "I suspect she knows exactly how beautiful she is."

"Maybe she'll follow in my footsteps and be an actress," Deirdre says.

"She's way too smart to be an actress," Armand counters.

Deirdre flinches and looks down at her plate. Cressida hardly seems interested in what everyone is saying about her. She's used to it. She's effortlessly dazzling, always the centerpiece. Kersti is starting to feel invisible again.

"I'm thinking of producing a play about the Gulf War," Armand announces. "Enough time has passed since it ended. I think we have some perspective now."

"Will it be, like, a ten-minute play?" Cressida jokes.

"It's a parody," Armand explains. "It captures our American grandiloquence."

"I used to love watching Desert Storm on TV," Magnus remarks, refreshing his wine.

"That's rather cavalier," Armand tells him. "Which is exactly what this play is about. It *was* a war, not just a TV show to garner good ratings."

"I think it *was* for ratings."

"You say that because, like most Americans, you think it was a victory for us," Armand lectures. "But we've yet to see how many of our returning soldiers will die from the chemical and biological warfare you never heard much about. CNN didn't feature *that* aspect in its nightly war broadcasts."

"But I'm not American," Magnus says.

The waiter shows up with their raclette and expertly shaves

globs of melted cheese onto their plates. They eat in silence for a few minutes, stretching melted Gruyère from their plates to their lips.

"What's with all those SIDA stickers everywhere?" Armand says, changing the subject.

"Stop AIDS," Cressida answers.

"It's an epidemic here," Deirdre murmurs, nibbling her potato and avoiding the cheese. "It's because of all the heroin addicts in Zurich."

"They just closed one of those needle parks in Zurich to try to stop the spread of HIV."

"Our French teacher is worried he's got it," Magnus says. "He thinks he contracted it from a mosquito when he was in Africa last year."

"Is that possible?" Deirdre asks, turning white.

"Anything is possible," Armand says. "We still know so little about it."

"People are still so ignorant," Cressida mutters.

"Maybe you could make a musical parody about AIDS," Magnus says.

Later, after her parents go back to their hotel, Cressida, Magnus, and Kersti head down to Ouchy with a bottle of vodka. They climb the Molecular Structure—their name for what's supposed to be some sort of art sculpture, but is really just a massive 3-D metal star—and settle in for a few more hours of drinking in the bitter cold, looking out over the black lake.

"Is it just me or are my parents assholes?" Cressida asks them.

"They're assholes," Magnus agrees.

"They're so pretentious. I can't stand them."

"I love that the word *grandiloquence* was dropped into the

conversation," Magnus says. "Well done, Armand. You obnoxious fuck."

"What's the point of Parents Weekend anyway?" Kersti says.

"Maybe spending two days a year with us alleviates their guilt?"

"The alternative is they don't come at all," Magnus says. "Which is just as bad. Isn't it, Kuusk?"

"Are you sad your parents didn't come?" Cressida asks him.

"My father's doing an album," he says, sounding a little defensive.

He takes a swig from his bottle and crawls over to Cressida. "It's with the Edge," he brags. "He can get you an autograph if you like."

Cressida snorts in response. Then they start kissing and Kersti stares up at the starless sky, feeling unwanted. She peels off a STOP SIDA sticker and wonders why she keeps subjecting herself to this new arrangement, a threesome in which she is the extraneous third. "I'm going," she announces. "I'm freezing."

"Don't go, Kerst!"

"Let us at least drive you," Magnus says, slurring his words so it sounds like *less least drivoo*. Vodka is dripping out of the Rikaloff bottle, which is tipped sideways in his hands.

"I'll get a taxi," Kersti says.

"He's fine to drive," Cressida assures her, climbing down from the top of the Molecular Structure.

"He's not fine," Kersti argues. "He's wasted. You can kill yourself if you want."

"It's just straight up the hill," Magnus says. "I'll drive slow."

They jump down, all three of them stumbling as they land. Magnus throws the vodka bottle out toward the lake but it doesn't reach and instead smashes on the concrete.

"Gotta work on my throw," he says, draping his arm around Cressida's shoulder and leaning on her for support. They stagger over to his uncle's Mercedes, and against Kersti's better judgment—which is now highly impaired—she slides into the backseat.

He starts the car. One hill, straight up to the school. All he has to do is not kill them.

Cressida turns back to look at Kersti. She's typically a happy drunk. Or she's happy drunk, if there's any difference. Kersti thinks there probably is. Magnus pulls onto the street with an abrupt jerk and a loud screech of the tires. Kersti reaches for her seat belt and buckles up, instantly regretting her decision not to get a taxi. She looks back wistfully at the lineup of them at the taxi stand. As Magnus swerves around the corner, Cressida flops sideways and slams against the door. Both girls cry out, half-exhilarated, half-terrified.

"Put your seat belt on!" Kersti shouts. Cressida doesn't listen.

Magnus cranks up the radio. It's an angry Alanis Morissette song that throbs in sync with Kersti's pounding heart. She's got her eye on the speedometer and it's climbing fast. Sixty, seventy, eighty, ninety kilometers per hour on the curvy cobblestone streets. "Slow down!" she cries. "Are you fucking crazy?"

Magnus ignores her, taking the corners like a Formula 1 driver, recklessly pressing down on the gas, relishing the girls' terror. "Stop the car!" Kersti yells, gripping the seat in front of her. "Stop the fucking car! I want to get out!"

Without any warning, Magnus abruptly stops. Kersti flies forward but the seat belt jerks her back, probably saving her life. Cressida, unbuckled in the front, instinctively throws up her leg to protect herself. There's a terrible smashing sound, a loud scream—possibly Kersti—and then silence.

Kersti opens her eyes, looks around to assess the damage. See who's still alive. They haven't crashed into anything.

"Holy fuck," Magnus mutters. "Look what you did, Cress."

That's when Kersti notices the windshield. The glass is cracked in a spiderweb pattern. It looks like a bullet hole, but it's Cressida's boot heel that did it.

"Look what *I've* done?" Cressida says, incredulous. "That would have been my head if I hadn't put up my leg!"

"Fuck," he moans. "Fuck. My uncle's car."

"Serves you right," Cressida admonishes.

"Are you okay?" Kersti asks her. Her voice is a tremor, her whole body shaking.

"Yes, thank you for asking. What about you?"

"I'm okay," Kersti responds, too shaken to move.

"You should go, Kerst," Cressida says. "Or you'll get in trouble. It's almost curfew."

Kersti leaves them sitting in Magnus's car, battered and fighting, with their shared death wish and extraordinary sense of entitlement. When she gets back to school, Mme. Hamidou knocks on her door.

"Where's Cressida?" she asks. "It's past curfew." She has her usual nighttime smell of toothpaste and cigarettes. She's wearing a green velour robe with running shoes.

"She was in a car accident," Kersti says.

"A car accident? With her parents? Why hasn't anyone called the school?"

"Not with her parents."

"With who? Is she all right?" The panic on Hamidou's face is as genuine as if Cressida were her own daughter. She more or less is.

"She's with Magnus Foley. Her foot went through the windshield—"

"*Mon Dieu* . . ."

"I walked back alone."

Mme. Hamidou sits down on Kersti's bed. She's very pale. "Are they waiting for the police? Does she have to go to the hospital?"

"I doubt it."

"Was he drinking?"

Kersti doesn't answer.

"Les idiots," she mutters, shaking her head. "Are you okay?"

"I guess."

Hamidou shuts the door and Kersti lies down, her head sinking slowly into the feather pillow. She's mad at herself, not just for getting into Magnus's car, but also for allowing herself to be their third wheel. Did they have to make out in front of her at Ouchy? Were they punishing her for having tagged along, even though they begged her to come?

She tosses and turns late into the night, ruminating over what happened, her chest burning with self-righteousness. And yet no matter how angry she is, her feelings inevitably wind up circling back to jealousy. She deplores this about herself. It makes her feel weak and petty. What kind of person is she? After almost getting killed tonight, her biggest grievance is that she wasn't the one chosen by Magnus, and her most significant lingering emotion is envy.

But there it is. She still occasionally lulls herself to sleep at night replaying her first and only date with Magnus, picking apart their conversations, analyzing his every gesture, reliving how she'd felt when he was inside her. She sometimes argues the case in her head as though she's a lawyer. *Your honor, when you look objectively at all the evidence leading up to and including the night in question, there is no way Magnus Foley could have been faking it! Therefore, we must conclude that he had real feelings for the plaintiff. . . .*

Kersti feels something warm under the duvet.

"Kerst?" It's Cressida, cuddling up to her, folding herself into a spoon position against her back. Kersti can smell cigarette and alcohol on her breath. It's sour and uncharacteristically repellent.

Cressida flings an arm over Kersti's waist and presses her face into the space between her shoulder blades. "I'm sorry," she murmurs, her words muffled by Kersti's T-shirt.

Kersti says nothing. She pretends to sleep.

"I know I get out of control when I drink," Cressida goes on. "My parents put me in a bad mood tonight and I drank too much and I was reckless. I wanted to punish them—"

"Well, you punished me instead," Kersti says, sitting up. "You almost got us both killed."

"I'm sorry, Kuusky. I'm going to stop drinking for a while."

"And I hate it when you and Magnus make out in front of me," Kersti adds, unable to hold back. "It's so rude. What do you think? I'm fucking invisible?"

"I'm sorry. I know I'm a terrible friend. But I love you, I really do. I love you so much."

Kersti sighs and lies back down. Cressida slips right back into the spoon position and within seconds, she's snoring softly in Kersti's ear.

CHAPTER 17

NEW YORK—October 2015

In a dark booth at Le Singe Vert in Chelsea, Magnus orders a bottle of Sancerre, hands the wine menu back to the waiter, and turns his full attention to Kersti. "I looked up your books on Amazon," he tells her. "I'm impressed."

"The first one is kind of embarrassing—"

"Don't do that," he stops her. "I know all about the awards—"

"Nominations."

The waiter sets down two wineglasses and returns a moment later with their bottle. He opens it, pours a splash into Magnus's glass, and waits. Magnus sniffs it and has a sip. "Fine," he says, dismissing the waiter. "So, are you working on a new novel?"

"I'm always working on a novel," she says. "This one isn't really going anywhere, though."

Magnus is suddenly full of questions. How long has she been married, where did they meet, does she dedicate her books to him. He doesn't mention anything about his own marriage. She doesn't ask.

Finally, he puts his glass down, fixes that clear blue gaze on her, and says, "So why are you here, Kuusk?"

"I told you," she says, her tone slightly defensive. "I want to ask you some questions about the night Cressida fell."

"Now?"

"I know it was a long time ago," she says. "But I've always wondered. I guess Lille reaching out to me kind of propelled me out of my inertia."

"What do you want to know?"

"People don't just fall off balconies, Magnus. No matter how drunk they are. The railing was too high, for one thing."

"She might have been sitting on it," Magnus says. "And toppled backwards."

"I guess," Kersti concedes, deciding not to mention the suicide note just yet. "You said you weren't the last person to see her that night. Who was?"

He's swishing the wine around his glass, fidgeting with his hands. Tapping his fork like a drumstick, buttering bread and not eating it. Same old nervous Magnus. "You know who it was," he says. "After she 'dumped' me, she went to his place."

"So you knew?"

"She told me she was in love with someone else and that we were over. I knew who it was." Kersti can feel the vibration of his knee bouncing under the table, like a subway passing below them. "I'd heard the rumors."

"Then what?"

"She left my apartment to go meet him."

"She told you that's where she was going?"

"Not in so many words. But I knew."

"How did you take it?" she asks him. "What did you do?"

"What *could* I do?" he says, and the way his face collapses as he remembers makes him alluringly vulnerable, reminding Kersti that the memory of Cressida—the perfect enduring mythology of her—cannot be diminished by time, neither for him nor for her, as she'd hoped it would be.

"So you just let her go?"

"*Let* her?" He laughs. "When did Cressida ever not do what she wanted? I had no choice but to let her go."

She watches him carefully—the bouncing knee, the chewed nails, the way he's staring morosely into his wine rather than squarely at her—and she doesn't believe him.

"Did you follow her?" she asks him quietly. "After she left your place?"

He lets out a noise—something between a sigh and a grunt, possibly even a laugh.

"You mean did I chase after her?"

"You must have been pissed off—"

"No. I mean, yes. I was pissed off. No I didn't chase after her."

"You went to the Lycée to wait for her."

Magnus reaches for the bottle of wine in the ice bucket and refills his glass, not even noticing that Kersti's is also empty. "I did go to Huber House," he says.

"Why?"

He places his hand lightly on top of hers, startling her. She shivers, withdraws it quickly.

"You don't think I pushed her, do you, Kuusk?"

"No, of course not," she answers quickly. The truth is, she isn't sure what to think. She's not even sure what she was expecting from this reunion; she really just wanted to see him.

The food arrives precisely at that moment, silencing both of them. The waiter sets down the plates, wishes them "bon appétit," and vanishes.

"Smells good," Kersti says, attempting to lighten the mood.

"To Cressida," he says, raising his glass.

"I went to see her before I came here," she says.

"You mentioned that."

When he doesn't say anything else, she continues. "I really went to see Deirdre."

"Looking for that ledger?"

"I asked her about it," Kersti says, pressing her fork down on a small mound of mushroom risotto.

"And?"

"She says she doesn't have it, which I'm still not sure I believe. But she did tell me something interesting."

"What's that?"

"Cressida left a note."

"A suicide note?"

Kersti nods and his mouth falls opens slightly, as though to ask a question that never comes. "Shit," he manages. "I thought they never found one—"

"Deirdre says Bueche sent it to her later with the rest of Cressida's stuff. Supposedly Armand found it when he went to pack up her things, after the dust had settled, coincidentally."

"No doubt," he says. "They wouldn't have wanted a suicide on school grounds getting out. That's all they cared about. Their reputation."

"That's what Deirdre said."

He's shaking his head, looking pale and discombobulated. "Shit," he says again.

"You're surprised."

"Hell, yeah."

"Why?" Kersti asks him, leaning forward. "I know you said she was wasted, but how did she seem to you that night?"

"You mean was she suicidal?"

"Depressed? Acting weird? Anything . . ."

"She was the same Cressida as usual. Infuriating, aloof. She didn't seem depressed at all. In fact—"

"What?"

"She was . . . I think she was really happy. She was kind of . . . I don't know. I guess she was in love." His tone is conciliatory, defeated. They both know she was never really in love with *him*.

He reaches for the wine and this time he refills Kersti's as well. "So this whole time we've been talking, you knew she jumped?" he asks her.

"That's the thing," Kersti says. "I don't necessarily think she did."

"A suicide note is pretty cut-and-dried, isn't it?"

"I read her note and something about it isn't right."

He rests his elbows on the table, his face drawing nearer to hers. For a second she imagines them as a couple, him leaning close to tell her she looks beautiful tonight, that he's in love with her. . . .

"Doesn't feel right how?" he wants to know.

"It just wasn't her."

"What does it say?"

"I'm sorry I'll miss you."

"That's it?"

"Pretty much. Not her style at all. She would have quoted Anne Sexton or Sylvia Plath. There would have been more drama and flair. Nothing about this fits."

They stare at each other for a few moments, both of their plates untouched. Finally, Magnus says, "Does it matter anymore, though?"

"We both loved her," Kersti responds. "No matter what she did, we loved her. Don't you want to know how she fell? And why?"

"To what end?"

"Curiosity. Closure. Justice?"

"Justice," he repeats, scoffing.

"I'm not doing this to be noble—"

"Maybe it was Colonel Mustard in the library."

"Maybe it was you," Kersti teases, emboldened by the wine. She says it almost flirtatiously. "A crime of passion?"

"Or maybe it was *you*, Kuusk."

At this, Kersti draws back.

"Weren't you always jealous of her?" he goes on. "Weren't you in love with me? Maybe you guys fought about it. She didn't really want me, but she wouldn't let you have me, either, would she?"

Kersti's face heats up. "Do you even remember having sex with me?" she blurts, finally getting it off her chest. "That day in the woods?"

Magnus's face turns deep red. "Of course," he says. "You were a virgin."

"You remember."

"Of course I remember."

She waits for him to say something else, but nothing comes.

"It hurt," she tells him.

"Well, it's supposed to the first time—"

"I don't mean that. I mean afterwards. How you never really spoke to me again once Cressida decided she wanted you back. You never acknowledged what happened between us. It was like it never happened. I was crushed."

Magnus sighs and Kersti can't tell if it's remorse over his behavior, or dread at having to have this conversation twenty years after the fact. "I'm sorry, Kuusk. I liked you. You were a cool chick. But me and Cressida . . ."

"I get it," she says. "It's just how you did it."

"I was an asshole," he says. "I only knew how to be an asshole."

They resume eating in silence. Kersti figured that telling him how she felt after all these years would be freeing. She imagined that having him acknowledge what he did and apologizing for it would be cathartic, healing. But she feels no different, no better about herself. Turns out it changes nothing.

"What about this ledger Lille mentioned?" he says, trying to change the subject. "Why would she think there's something incriminating in it?"

"Because Cressida got it in the mail the day she fell," Kersti tells him. "She took it with her when she went to meet you."

"The plot thickens," he mutters. And then, at length, "What's she like now?"

"You've never been to see her?"

"No," he says, disappearing for a moment. His eyes go dim, his expression vacant. She wonders where he's gone. "I know we were just kids, but I really . . . she meant a lot to me. Obviously much more than I meant to her."

"Same," Kersti says, feeling a beam of compassion for him, remembering how Cressida had once described their relationship as a "trivial high school thing." "She's still beautiful."

He nods, probably grateful he's never seen her in her current incarnation. "What now?" he asks Kersti.

"I don't know," she says. "I don't exactly have a plan."

She thinks of Jay with a shudder of sadness, imagining him home alone, worrying about what she's doing in New York, when she's coming home, where she's going next. She feels guilty for having fled Toronto. She misses him, but she doesn't miss their fertility stalemate. Besides, it can't hurt to let him suffer a bit, to let him miss her and rethink his position on using an egg donor.

"You know, Kuusk, maybe Cressida was sitting on her balcony railing drunk off her ass and she just fell backwards," Magnus says pragmatically.

"And then someone wrote a fake suicide note for no apparent reason? Or wait, maybe *she* wrote it and then accidentally fell. What a coincidence!"

"Okay, so maybe she jumped. Maybe she was fooling us all and she did want to die. She hated her parents; she grew up in a boarding school. Wouldn't be the first time someone who seemed to have it all was really miserable inside. My point is, Kuusk, I don't think you're ever going to know the truth. Too much time has passed."

"Mrs. Fithern was there," she says, ignoring him. "She was the one on duty. She must know something. Do you think they even questioned her? Or anyone?"

"No. I'm pretty sure they just cleaned up the whole mess and swept it under the rug."

"I'd like to speak to her."

"So now you're going to Europe?" he says, teasing her. "She'll never speak to you."

"I'm good at research. I can find things out."

"Is that what this is about? Research for your next novel?"

"Maybe," she says, already feeling excited about the possibility.

The bill comes and this time Kersti insists on paying half. "It was good to see you," she tells him, not quite sure she means it. She can't say anything has been resolved for her as far as Magnus is concerned, or that there's been any diminishment of that baked-on, twenty-year-old hurt. What does closure feel like, anyway?

"Do you want to come back to my place?" he asks her, smiling that cocky grin that used to make her melt inside. Nothing's changed. She despises his arrogance and is fiercely attracted to him at the same time.

"You never told me why you went to Huber House that night," she says. "Why did you want to see her after she broke up with you?"

"Cressida wasn't at Huber when I got there," he says. "She hadn't come back."

"Why did you go to her dorm then, if you knew she wasn't there?"

"This is starting to feel like an interrogation."

"I'm sorry. I'm just . . . I'm curious. I've wanted to ask you these questions since the night it happened."

"I went to talk to the house mother on duty," he says.

"To tell her what?"

"Where Cressida was."

CHAPTER 18

LAUSANNE—February 1997

It's Saturday morning study hall. Kersti is still lying in bed, rereading the letter from her mother.

> Dad wasn't able to find cheap flights. He tried right up till the last possible minute. We won't make it for Parents Weekend. Sorry to disappoint you.

Kersti crumples the letter and tosses it at the garbage can. It misses, but she leaves there, not caring.

"What's wrong?" Cressida asks, looking up from her book. She's reading *Gatsby* again.

"My family's not coming again this year."

"They're telling you the week before?" Cressida says. "I thought it was all booked. You told me it was for sure this year."

"It was supposed to be," Kersti says, embarrassed.

That's what they promised her over the holidays. It was supposed to be her Christmas present from them. She opened up her card and inside it said: *Four plane tickets from Toronto to Geneva in February! Love, Mom, Dad, Tuule & Maaja.*

Her parents and two of her sisters were going to fly over for five days and let Kersti show them around. Kersti was thrilled. She even brought the card back to school with her, hung it on her wall, and was secretly counting down to Parents Weekend.

"Why aren't they coming?" Cressida asks her.

"They can't afford it."

"I'm sorry, Kerst."

"Whatever," she mutters, but hot tears are already sliding down her face. "They just don't want to come."

"I'm sure that's not true."

"They don't give a shit about me," Kersti says. "Let's go down for lunch. I'm hungry."

"Let's skip it and go to McDonald's."

"It's Saturday."

"So?"

"We can't just not show up for lunch."

"Of course we can," Cressida says. "Hamidou's in Bern and Ms. Bowell is on duty."

Ms. Bowell is basically senile. Aside from having a name that demands ridicule, she's also really old—at least in her eighties—both of which render her utterly ineffectual as a teacher.

"We're free," Cressida says, throwing on a pair of Uggs with her sweatpants. "Let's go."

Kersti grabs her ski jacket and tuque and they set off, deciding to brave the cold and walk all the way down to the Gare. They link arms and sing most of the way down.

"*What if God was one of us?*" Cressida bellows, deliberately singing off key.

"*If God had a face,*" Kersti chimes in, already feeling better, "*what would it look like?*"

"Monsieur Bueche," Cressida returns.

The following Saturday morning, Cressida charges into Kersti's room, flushed and breathless. "You're still in pajamas?" she says.

"I told you I'm not going with you and your parents."

"Get dressed and come down," Cressida says. "You at least have to say hello to Armand and Deirdre."

"No I don't. I'm staying here all weekend."

"Stop sulking and come and say hi to my parents," Cressida says, starting to sound annoyed.

"It's humiliating."

"Stop thinking about yourself," she scolds, which Kersti finds both hilarious and ironic coming from Cressida. "They'll be insulted if you don't make an appearance."

Kersti reluctantly rolls out of bed and puts a cardigan over her pajamas. She slides her feet into her fur-lined moccasins and follows Cressida out into the hall. "I know they're going to try to convince me to spend the day with you guys," Kersti says. "And I'm telling you now, I'm *not*."

"Fine."

They head downstairs, Kersti shuffling her feet to annoy Cressida.

"You could have brushed your teeth," Cressida mutters.

When they reach the main floor, Kersti looks around. Other parents are showing up to collect their daughters—it's the usual flurry of hugging and crying—but no Deirdre or Armand.

"They're in the smoking lounge," Cressida says.

Kersti rolls her eyes and follows her there but when she steps inside the first person she sees is her father, filling most of the small room with his substantial height and girth. He pulls her into his arms and squeezes her tight against his belly before releasing her. Anni pops out from behind him and then her sisters, Maaja and Tuule, rush over to her with outstretched arms. Kersti is flabbergasted.

"Was that letter your idea of a joke?" she says to her mother. "Were you planning on coming the whole time?"

"Not exactly," Anni says, looking over at Cressida.

"I don't understand. Why did you tell me you weren't coming?"

"We weren't," Paavo says, his deep voice reverberating off the walls.

"We couldn't afford anything," Anni tells her. "We tried, but even one flight with our best rate through the agency was too much for us right now."

"It hasn't been a good year," Paavo mutters.

"Cressida called us and told us how upset you were," Tuule explains.

"You did?" Kersti says, turning to Cressida.

"She paid for our flights," Anni says.

"We're going to pay her back," Paavo adds.

"Please," Cressida says dismissively. "I just arranged it through Armand's secretary. It's no big deal."

"When did you arrive?" Kersti wants to know.

"Late last night," Anni says. "We're staying at the Ibis hotel."

"Aren't you happy we're here?" Maaja asks her.

"Yes!" Kersti cries, hugging her.

"You guys are clones," Cressida says, looking at Kersti beside her sisters. Maaja and Tuule still have the same hair—white-blond bobs held to the side with those old metal clips from when they were little. They're wearing knee-length skirts with crisp white shirts and cardigans. Kersti is happy to see them.

"I have to shower before Deirdre and Armand get here," Cressida says.

"Show us your room, Kerst," Tuule says.

Kersti takes them upstairs. She's floating, proud. She glances into the staff room on the second floor and notices Angela Zumpt sitting there, staring at nothing. Hamidou is reading in the armchair beside her. Angela's parents aren't here. The rumor is she has no parents and lives with an uncle during the summers. For the first time ever, Kersti feels sorry for her. She looks so lonely sitting beside Hamidou, like a pet dog. Waiting to be petted or acknowledged, any shred of attention she can get.

Kersti continues up the stairs, not wanting to think about Angela or pity her.

When Cressida heads off to her room, Kersti catches up to her and hugs her. "Thank you so much," she says. "I can't believe you did this."

"Life is short."

"No it's not," Kersti responds. "It's long and slow as hell."

Cressida smiles, like she knows something Kersti doesn't.

CHAPTER 19

TORONTO—October 2015

Kersti comes home in the late afternoon to an empty house. She timed her return flight so Jay would be at work. She texted him while she was away—short, terse messages to let him know her hotel, her flight information—but he never responded.

She settles at her writing desk with a cup of tea and a pile of Social Tea cookies. She hasn't written in way too long. There have been too many distractions, none of them pleasant. These dry spells make her very anxious. She always feels tremendous pressure to get a new book out before she vanishes into obscurity. Her last one was published two years ago, a long gap, given that this one won't go to print for at least another year after she writes it.

She dunks a cookie in her tea and stares grimly at her computer. *Chapter One.*

She thought Magnus might text her today. Thought he might follow up, see if she was able to track down one or both of the Fitherns, which she did. It was as simple as typing Mrs. Fithern's maiden name and up she popped on LinkedIn. *Annie Brains-Chowne. Teacher at Abberley Middle School, Abberley, Worcestershire.* Among her credentials was the Lycée Internationale Suisse, 1985–1993, and if that wasn't enough, her professional email address was also listed. All that was missing was a recent photograph.

Kersti debated whether to reach out to her by email. She concluded she was less likely to get a response, whereas if she calls her—perhaps at home one evening, without any warning—she will have a much better chance of connecting with her. So, thanks to the whitepages.co.uk, Mrs. Brains-Chowne's phone number is now safely stored on Kersti's phone.

Surprisingly, Kersti also found Mr. Fithern as effortlessly as she found his former wife. She thought he might be in hiding, still running from the scandal at the Lycée and its lingering cloud of shame, but there he was on LinkedIn, his fifty-year-old face smiling back at her as though he had nothing to hide. His once-black hair was gray and significantly thinned out, which made his ears look disproportionately huge, and his chin looked weaker than she remembered. His teeth were crooked and slightly buck, much less forgiving to his overall appearance than when they'd been brighter and whiter in his youth, but his eyes still had that twinkle of mischievousness and rebellion, or whatever it was that had once made him so enthralling.

He's still teaching, though now at an all-boys school, where he's been since the late nineties. Prior to that, he taught at the international school in Lilongwe, Malawi, no doubt a period of soul-searching and regrouping in the aftermath of Cressida and the evident dissolution of his marriage. Staring at his picture, Kersti can't believe that the legendary Mr. Fithern—the love of Cressida's short, young life—is now a middle-aged schoolteacher with bad teeth and big ears, and a secret past that probably no one gives a shit about anymore.

She wonders if he ever really loved Cressida. In retrospect, it's doubtful. He was probably just seizing his opportunity to screw a young girl of her stature while he had the chance. By virtue of being one of the only male teachers at a small girls' boarding school—his only competition was old M. Mahler—he was lucky enough to be able to choose from the crème de la crème of teenage heiresses. In the real world a girl like Cressida would have been way out of his league.

Chapter One

Imbi stepped out from the twisting cobblestone lane into Raekoja plats, the town square where she had last seen Gunnar twenty years ago. Built out of the thirteenth-century town of Reval, Tallinn's Old Town was a bustling enclave of Hanseatic architecture, colorful gabled houses, Gothic-spired churches, hidden courtyards, and markets. But on that morning, Imbi was preoccupied, her thoughts consumed with her memories of Gunnar

She hears the front door slam downstairs and stops writing. Jay's home early.

She realizes, as she waits for his footsteps on the stairs, that she's nervous. She has no idea where his head is at, if he's angry with her or if he's had time to reflect and calm down. Her heart is racing and she's bracing for a fight, even though it's possible he won't speak to her at all. He's been known to give her the silent treatment for days. It doesn't happen often, but when he makes up his mind to punish her by shutting down, he can be frighteningly unyielding.

The Sonos goes on and for a long time she hears nothing but the sound of Drake's moody rapping. She returns to her work and tries to sink back into the lives of Imbi and Gunnar, but it's pointless.

"Hi."

She looks up, startled, and he's there in the doorway. Instinctively, she jumps up from her desk and rushes over to him, throwing her arms around his neck and holding on to him. Soon she's sobbing out loud, her whole body making jerky little spasms in his arms. He rubs her back and she can feel his heart beating against her cheek. "I missed you," she tells him. "I'm sorry."

"I'm sorry, too."

"Why do we keep doing this?" she asks, looking into his face, not caring that her nose is running and her eyes must be red and puffy.

"I guess because we're both hurting." He sits down on her swivel chair and gently pulls her onto his lap. "This hasn't been easy for me, either. I've always wanted to be a father."

"But you're ready to give up now—"

"Isn't it time? When will you be ready?"

She shrugs, not knowing the answer.

"When our marriage is over?" he continues. "When we're bankrupt?"

She snuggles up against him and presses her face into his warm neck. She's always loved the smell of his skin. She doesn't want to lose him. But. *But.* How can she be expected to release her dream of motherhood? Not just the dream, but also the sense of purpose inherent in raising a child? "I guess the journey would end for me if we couldn't get pregnant with an egg donor."

"Would it, though?"

"Yes, of course. I mean, I would consider adoption, but the fertility part of the journey would end—"

"After how many egg donor cycles?" he flares. "Because I know you. You wouldn't stop at one."

She doesn't bother to argue, because he's right. She would never stop at one. She will never stop. It's not in her DNA. "Let's be friends," she says, suddenly feeling exhausted. "I miss you."

"Me, too." He kisses her and touches her hair. "What did you do in New York?"

"I met with Cressida's old boyfriend," she says, leaving out the part about him being her first love, her first lover and the Guy Who Broke Her Heart. "Magnus Foley."

"And?"

"We had dinner."

Jay gives her a strange look.

"I went there specifically to talk to him," she explains. "About the night Cressida fell. It was *your* idea, remember? You said it would be a good distraction for me. A good idea for a new novel."

"And?" he asks calmly. "Was it?"

"Yes, actually. I found out that he was at Huber House that night. But he wasn't there to see Cressida. He was there to see Mrs. Fithern."

"Why?"

"She was the housemother on duty that night," Kersti says, getting excited as she recounts her conversation with Magnus. "He told her that Cressida was having an affair with her husband."

"What did she do when she found out?"

"That's the thing. Magnus said she didn't even react. She didn't seem surprised or angry, which is strange."

"She could have been trying to save face."

"What if she went up to confront Cressida in her room? She'd just found out her husband was screwing her favorite student—"

"You think she pushed Cressida?"

"They could have fought. I'm not saying it was premeditated, but it's just as plausible as any other theory—"

"Sounds like the makings of a great mystery."

"I'm still not entirely convinced Magnus was telling me the truth."

"How did he look?" Jay asks her.

"Who, Magnus? That's a weird question."

"Is it?"

"He looked the same," she says. "Pretty good, I guess."

"Where did you have dinner?"

"A French place in Chelsea."

"What time did you get home?"

"I don't know. Ten?" She kisses his face and rubs his sideburns, omitting Magnus's invitation to go back to his place. "What's this about, babe?"

"This is how affairs happen," he says. "We're going through a rough patch, you're feeling vulnerable and sad. You reach out to an old guy friend on the pretext of finding out what happened to your friend, and next thing you know . . ."

"First of all, it wasn't a pretext."

"What exactly are you hoping to accomplish hopping from city to city, interrogating all these people?"

"You're the one who suggested it," she repeats, frustrated. "I guess it was convenient for you at the time to get me off your back?"

"Yes! It was before you took off to New York and had dinner with an old boyfriend at a French restaurant in Chelsea while *we* were fighting!"

"Not *my* old boyfriend—"

"It doesn't fucking matter, Kersti."

She gets up off his lap and moves away from him. "It so happens I *do* want to find out what happened to Cressida," she tells him. "Nothing I've found out so far makes sense and frankly I want to dig a little deeper. No one else ever investigated or asked questions and I'm doing it now. Better late than never, don't you think?"

"Do what you need to do," he says.

"Meaning?"

"We just can't seem to get back to where we were."

He shakes his head and leaves the room, defeated.

Alone again, Kersti returns to her swivel chair, faces her computer, and stares at it for a long time. Tears come again, blurring the words on her screen, and she doesn't move. Eventually, the tears dry up on her cheeks, leaving salty streaks and a faint headache. She reaches for her phone, feeling like a naughty child who's been told not to do something and wants to do it all the more. She scrolls through her contacts, her finger stopping at the name Brains-Chowne.

It's nine o'clock at night in England, a good time to catch someone at home, either putting the kids to sleep, reading in bed, or watching TV with her husband. She impulsively dials the number. While it's ringing, she pictures the two of them snuggled on the couch watching *Downton Abbey* with a hand-knit blanket thrown over their legs, a tea tray spread out in front of them, and a fire blazing in the stone fireplace. She imagines Mr. Chowne to be tall and lanky with bad teeth, wearing a serviceable brown robe over his pajamas and slippers on his large feet; and then she realizes she's unfairly superimposed middle-aged Mr. Fithern onto her picture of Mr. Chowne.

"Hullo?" A chipper woman's voice on the line.

Kersti freezes.

"Hullo?"

"Mrs. Fithern?" Kersti blunders, forgetting to call her by her new name, Mrs. Brains-Chowne.

After a beat of silence, Mrs. Fithern says, "Who is this?"

"It's Kersti Kuusk. I was in your English Lit class at the Lycée in Lausanne—"

More silence.

"Ninety-four to ninety-eight?"

Kersti is sure she can hear her sighing on the other end. Neither of them says it out loud, but it's there, unspoken and intractable: *Cressida's year. Cressida's best friend.*

"I'm speechless," she says. "How did you get my home number?" Her voice sounds exactly the same, warm and youthful, familiar. Twenty years collapse like a ribbon of dominos, and she might just as well be talking about Paul Morel in *Sons and Lovers.*

"I'm sorry to intrude," Kersti says. "I remembered your maiden name and I looked you up in the white pages. I . . . it's not for myself. It's for Lille."

"L'il Lille Robertson?"

"Yes," Kersti says, encouraged. "She died recently. She had breast cancer."

"Oh, good God, not 'er, too?"

"She wrote me a letter before she died," Kersti continues. "Her mother found it on her computer and sent it to me."

"Oh, dear—"

"Lille wanted me to let you know how much you meant to her," Kersti lies. "And to make sure you're okay."

"*Me?* After all these years? Why?"

"She cared about you. You were her favorite teacher. And . . . well, she really wanted me to get in touch with you and find out how you are. She always wondered after—"

"She was such a sweet girl. A really good human being. Marked for tragedy though, I suppose."

"I'm sorry to call you out of the blue like this," Kersti says. "I just felt I owed it to Lille. And the truth is, I've thought about you a lot, too. We all cared about you."

"That's very nice to hear," she says, her voice sounding choked up. "You hope as a teacher to have some impact on your students. I'm touched, really."

"I'm relieved I didn't upset you. I just wanted to tell you about Lille." *And ask you if you went up to Cressida's room the night she fell and possibly scuffled with her and pushed her off her balcony in a fit of jealous rage?*

"I'm remarried," she volunteers, quite matter-of-factly. "Simon and I have four girls. He tells people we live in Abberley-Upon-Hormones, in Hormoneshire." She chuckles at their inside joke and right on cue, Kersti can hear a chorus of girls' voices in the background, squealing or arguing. It's hard to tell with girls.

"I still teach here in Abberley," she goes on. "I have a good life. Simple and quiet. Lille can rest assured, wherever she is. It's all turned out rather well."

"It sounds nice," Kersti says, elaborating on her earlier picture of their life and placing them in a charming stone cottage nestled in the Cotswolds. Kersti visited there once, in her second year at the Lycée. It was the Ascension holiday in May and they went to watch the annual cheese rolling in Gloucester. She remembers standing on the side of a hill, surrounded by turreted stone churches and medieval cottages and Union Jacks flapping alongside her under a steady drizzle, and a horde of people chasing a ten-pound cheese wheel down a steep hill with all the fervor and passion of the running of the bulls in Pamplona. Afterward, they drove through the rolling, rain-soaked Cotswolds, stopping at a place called the Crown & Crumpet for scones and clotted cream.

"And how are you doing, Kersti? Are you still in Canada?"

"Yes, in Toronto," Kersti responds. "I'm a writer."

"A writer? Really."

"I write fiction. Historical novels."

"Can I take any credit?"

"Absolutely."

"I knew you had a talent for it," she says, probably fibbing. "You just needed to polish your diamond."

"You should be able to find my books in the UK," Kersti tells her, and then rattles off the titles, rationalizing that if you're going to brag about your literary success to anyone, it should be your English Lit teacher. "I was chosen one of the Hundred Women of the Lycée as part of their centennial anniversary celebration."

"Congratulations, Kersti. My time there wasn't all for nothing then."

Kersti doesn't know what to say. She remains quiet. Both of them do, for what feels to Kersti like an excruciatingly long time. The only thing crackling on the line between them is the tension from what they dare not speak out loud—the very public humiliation that ended Mrs. Fithern's tenure and her marriage.

"Is she still alive?" Mrs. Fithern finally asks.

It takes Kersti a moment to figure out she's talking about Cressida. "Yes," she says. "She has permanent brain damage, but she's alive."

"I've often wondered. I think about her often."

"You do?"

"Of course. She was only a child and I was very fond of her." Her voice is tender, extraordinarily generous, given what Cressida did to her. And yet Kersti wonders, does some part of her believe that Cressida got what she deserved? If so, she doesn't say it. What she says is, "Charles was the predator."

Kersti can't imagine what it must be like to find that out about your husband. She thinks of the early days of her own marriage, how life had once brimmed with promise, and how it's turned out now. Disappointment is a thing you don't see coming. It's something you crash into, like the back of a bus.

"Did you know about the affair before Magnus told you?"

"I suspected, but I didn't know for sure," she admits. "Charles admitted everything to me after Cressida's accident."

"If it was an accident."

"You know what I think?" Mrs. Fithern volunteers. "I think Cressida jumped from her balcony. She was an unhappy girl who got in over her head and tried to kill herself. Charles didn't want that baby any more than she did. Suicide was her way out. That's what I've always believed."

"What baby?"

"She never told you?"

"No—"

"He got her pregnant."

"Mr. Fithern did?"

"Indeed," she says, as though Kersti should have known. Like it was common knowledge. "Charles always thought she jumped to punish him."

CHAPTER 20

LAUSANNE—May 1997

Mrs. Fithern has a new haircut. It's very short on the sides and puffy on top, like a poodle with a Mohawk. She's also put on some weight in recent months and there's speculation she might be pregnant. "What's the book about?" she asks the class.

They're studying Fitzgerald's *Tender Is the Night* in AP English. Cressida is obsessed with it, has read it three times. Kersti finds it dull and depressing.

"It's about rich people doing nothing in the Riviera," Rafaella answers. "It's about my parents."

The class erupts in laughter. Naturally, they can all relate. Except Kersti.

"It's about the dissolution of a marriage," Cressida says. "About two people who bring out the worst in each other—mental illness and alcoholism."

Mrs. Fithern sits down on the front of her desk. "What about themes? I want you thinking thematically."

"Youth," Cressida calls out.

"Yes," Mrs. Fithern cries. "And specifically, the sheen of youth. The *promise* of youth."

She slides off the desk and scribbles on the blackboard: "YOUTH." "Dick was obsessed with his own mortality and lost youth," she tells them, as though she's speaking about mutual friends.

"And Zelda's," Cressida adds.

"You mean Nicole's," Mrs. Fithern corrects.

"Aren't they one and the same?" Cressida responds. "Isn't this book Fitzgerald's attempt to rationalize his own decline and unrealized potential by blaming it on Zelda's schizophrenia?"

Kersti and Rafaella look at each other and roll their eyes. Cressida is a brilliant student, but she can be cloyingly pretentious.

"Be careful in your essay, luv," Mrs. Fithern cautions. "The protagonists are Dick and Nicole Driver. Not Scott and Zelda. It's fiction."

And then, as though suddenly remembering the other dozen students in her class, she randomly calls on Kersti. "What other character symbolized the promise of youth in the book, or of something new and better?"

"Um. Their children?" Kersti guesses.

Mrs. Fithern sighs. "You're being way too literal," she says, sounding annoyed. "I mean thematically."

Her obvious disappointment gives Kersti the impression she would much rather continue this discussion of *Tender Is the Night* with Cressida, one-on-one, over coffee.

Around midnight that night, after they know Hamidou has gone to sleep, Kersti and Cressida creep down the flight of stairs to the third-floor bathroom, cigarettes in hand. The other girls are already there, consoling Noa, who's crying.

"What's going on?"

"Noa's ex-boyfriend tried to kill himself," Raf says.

"Andries?"

Noa nods, sniffling. She unravels a strip of toilet paper and daubs at her eyes. "It's not the first time," she tells them. "He did the same thing last summer."

"And you never told us?"

"I was embarrassed."

Kersti can't imagine anyone being so in love with her that he'd want to die if she broke up with him. She's dated a couple of guys since the debacle with Magnus. One was from a finishing school in Villars, a jet-haired Colombian named Miguel. He didn't speak much English and although he was good looking, they fizzled out pretty quickly. The other one she met at the local hangout, Captain Cook's. His name was Roger. They went out for a few months in the fall, but didn't survive the holidays. Neither guy held a candle to Magnus.

"How did he do it?" Lille asks.

"Razor blade. The wrong way, of course."

"And this time?"

"Same. I got an emergency call. Madame Hamidou came and got me during study hall. It was Andries from the hospital."

"Pathetic," Cressida mutters. "Anyone who doesn't die didn't really mean to."

Noa stands up and splashes water on her splotchy face. "I'm going to bed," she says, and leaves the bathroom.

Lille starts to braid Kersti's hair, tickling her scalp with her fingers. "Poor Andries," she says. "Talk about a cry for attention."

"You don't even know him," Cressida says.

"Lille feels everyone's pain," Alison says. "That's why we love her."

Kersti closes her eyes, enjoying the moment. Lille's fingers in her hair, the draft of sharp cold air in her nostrils, the comforting banter of her best friends. She's content. She feels more at home than home here; she always has. She tries not to think about the end of the year too much.

She dozes off for a bit and the next thing she knows, Cressida is up on her feet.

"Where you going?" Kersti asks her, turning her head slightly in Lille's lap.

"Out."

"You're sneaking out again?"

There's a certain combination of fearlessness and gall required to make a nightly escape from school. Plenty of rebellious students have tried and gotten caught over the years—suffering a suspension or a loss of weekend privileges—and maybe the odd one actually got away with it and didn't need to prove it could be done again. Cressida isn't like that. She doesn't care about proving anything to anyone. She's immune to that teenage albatross—approval. She only serves herself, with no fear of consequence.

"One of these days you're going to get caught," Kersti warns, hurt that Cressida would rather sneak out to meet Magnus than hang out with them.

"What'll they do? Expel me?"

"Maybe."

"You are adorably naïve, Kuusky. Don't wait up for me."

The door closes behind her and Kersti lies there, pissed off.

"She's fearless," Lille says admiringly, tugging on Kersti's hair.

"She doesn't care about anything," Kersti mutters. "Is that fearlessness?"

"Rules don't apply to her."

"Why not?" Kersti wants to know. "Why does she get to do whatever she wants? Hamidou must know."

"You sound jealous."

"Maybe I am."

"There's no point punishing her," Lille says. "A person has to care in order for a punishment to be effective. Hamidou knows that."

"So she just goes through life doing whatever she wants?"

"Life is much bigger than the Lycée," Lille says. "The real world will be different."

"Will it?"

"Why does it bother you?" Raf asks her. "It's her life."

Kersti has no answer for that.

She's still up when she hears the door creak open and then close. It's four thirty in the morning. She sits up and turns the light on, startling Cressida.

"What the fuck!" Cressida cries, stumbling backward. "You scared the shit out of me!"

"What the hell happened to your face?" Kersti asks her. Her lips are swollen and bloody.

Cressida peers at herself in the mirror. Kersti gets out of bed and stands behind her. Up close, there are bite marks on her top lip. The skin around her mouth, all the way down to her chin, is bright red, chewed and raw.

Cressida studies her wounds, inspecting the damage. And then she laughs. "It's pretty bad this time," she says.

"This time?"

"Look at this," she says, peeling off her jeans. She stands before Kersti in her panties, exposing violently bruised inner thighs, a kaleidoscope of blue and purple.

"Holy shit. Magnus did that to you?"

Cressida doesn't answer. Instead, she goes over to the sink and brushes her teeth.

"Did Magnus do that to you?" Kersti repeats.

"Why are you still up?" Cressida asks her, her ravaged mouth full of toothpaste suds.

Kersti sits on the bed and waits for her to finish.

"It was just sex," she says, gently patting her face with a towel.

"That was just sex?" Kersti cries. "You've been battered."

"He likes it rough."

"I've never seen you look like this before," Kersti says, horrified. "Those bruises . . ."

Cressida gets into bed and pulls the duvet up to her chin. She groans from the pain. She must be sore everywhere.

"Has he always been like this with you?" Kersti asks.

Cressida looks away.

"Did you let him do this to you, Cress? Or were you trying to stop him?"

"Oh, Kerst," Cressida says, as though Kersti could never be expected to understand.

"Because if you wanted him to stop and he did it anyway—"

"Yes, I know what rape is, Kersti. This wasn't rape."

"But if Magnus forced you—"

"It *wasn't* Magnus."

Kersti falls silent. Cressida turns off her lamp and rolls over on her side, giving Kersti her back.

"Who was it?"

Silence.

"Cress. Who was it? Did someone rape you?"

"It wasn't rape!" Cressida responds impatiently. "I love him. It was consensual. It's just getting way more intense, but it's amazing."

The room begins to swirl around Kersti. She feels dizzy, winded. "Who the hell is it?"

After a long moment, Cressida's voice cuts through the dark. "Mr. Fithern," she says, her tone defiant, unapologetic.

A million things run through Kersti's mind—Mrs. Fithern and

Cressida discussing *Tender Is the Night* together; Nicole and Dick Driver's disintegrating marriage; Mr. Fithern biting Cressida's lips until they bled. Magnus.

Magnus.

"What about Magnus?" Kersti manages.

"He's the one you're most concerned about?"

"And Mrs. Fithern—"

"It hasn't been good between them for years," she says with authority.

Kersti can't even speak.

"I've always had a thing for him," Cressida informs her, as though this is ample justification for what she's done. "I love him. For the first time in my life, I'm really *in love* with a man."

"I thought you were 'in love' with Magnus," Kersti snaps, using air quotes to make her point. "Isn't that what you told me?"

"I do love him," she says. "But he's not a man. With Charlie it's on a whole other level."

Kersti wants to slap her. "What if Mrs. Fithern finds out? The whole school would know. You'd be expelled for sure, right before graduation—"

"We've been seeing each other since The Hague," Cressida says.

The Hague? *Almost two years ago?* Around the time Kersti slept with Magnus and then Cressida *had* to have him back because she couldn't live without him?

Kersti stands up and backs out of the room, feeling like she might throw up.

"Where are you going?"

"Away from you," she says, closing the door behind her and retreating to Lille's room.

CHAPTER 21

BOSTON—November 2015

Kersti and Jay hop in a cab at Logan Airport, the mood between them still tense. She convinced him to come to Boston with her and make a mini-vacation out of it, but their interactions have been strained. They're being civil to one another, making an effort to avoid all potentially perilous topics, but their usual jokey camaraderie is noticeably absent.

They ride in silence to the XV Beacon hotel, with plans to spend Saturday afternoon at the spa and have dinner at Moo, in the hope of resuscitating their marriage. But first, Kersti is going to pay Deirdre another visit.

As they veer onto Route 1A, Kersti pulls out her Moleskin and tries to recap everything she's discovered since she embarked on this journey, trying to fit it all into some cohesive timeline. She knows Cressida snuck out to see Magnus, broke up with him, and then went to Mr. Fithern's. As soon as she left his place, Magnus went to Huber House and told Mrs. Fithern about the affair. He left Huber without seeing Cressida and claims never to have seen her again.

"What are you working on?" Jay asks her, putting his hand on her knee.

"Just some notes."

"For which book?"

"Possibly the story of a beautiful but troubled girl who mysteriously falls from her balcony at a Swiss boarding school." Even as she says it out loud, her whole body tingles.

"I'm happy to see you excited about a new book," he says. "I feel like maybe you've been a bit bored with the other one."

"We'll see how this all plays out," she says, returning to her notebook and writing, "Mrs. Fithern?"

Mrs. Fithern claims not to have gone to Cressida's room after Magnus told her about the affair, which Kersti finds hard to believe. Wouldn't it be the very first thing any woman in her shoes would do? The fact that the Fitherns both think Cressida jumped—when either one of them had much to gain from silencing her—seems a little too convenient.

And then of course there's the missing ledger, this being the most frustrating dead end of them all.

"Kerst? We're here."

Kersti looks up and realizes the taxi has come to a stop in front of a regal-looking building with a black iron façade and intricate copper cornices. The doorman opens the car door and helps her out. Inside, the lobby is sleek, done in tones of espresso and cream with mahogany built-ins, taupe couches on a zebra-hide rug, bold modern art on the walls, and two original cage elevators. After they check in, it's decided Kersti will go straight to Deirdre's while Jay explores Beacon Hill.

"I'm glad I came," he says, pulling her into his arms. "We needed this. It was a good call."

As she kisses him, she feels a surge of relief. "I'll be quick," she promises. "And then I'm all yours. There's a restaurant on Newbury we can try for lunch—"

"I love you."

"Love you, too."

Laylay opens the door. "Mrs. Deirdre is waiting for you," she says, stepping aside. "In the parlor."

The parlor. Who still uses words like that?

Laylay takes her coat and Kersti finds Deirdre reading on one of the brocade couches, her feet neatly tucked beneath her, her face tilted slightly into the sunlight, as though she's posing for a portrait.

"Hi, Deirdre."

"Kersti," she says, looking up and setting her book down. "What's going on? You sounded so cryptic on the phone."

Kersti sits down on the other sofa.

"Do you want a drink? Or some tea?"

"I'm fine, thanks."

"Tell me then," she says. "What did you find out that was so pressing?"

"Cressida was pregnant."

The color disappears from Deirdre's cheeks, leaving two circles of bright coral blush on the stark white canvas of her skin.

"Why didn't you tell me, Deirdre?" Kersti asks her.

"Why would I?" Deirdre snaps. "You didn't need to know. No one did."

"Deirdre, didn't you think it warranted some investigation at the time?"

Tears spring to Deirdre's eyes and she looks away.

"I know it couldn't have been easy," Kersti says.

"That's right!" she cries. "It wasn't easy. I was trying to protect her reputation!"

"Hers or yours?"

"That's unfair, Kersti."

"I'm sorry. I didn't mean that."

Deirdre reaches for a fur throw that's draped on the arm of the couch and pulls it over her bird legs. "You don't have children," she says. "You don't know how hard it is to protect them from what the world thinks of them. People can be so cruel, Kersti. I didn't want anyone to know she was pregnant. Or that she tried to kill herself. She was special. That's how I wanted her to be remembered."

"What about getting justice for her?"

"Justice?" Deirdre sneers. "You think she cares about justice? She'd rather be able to feed herself and go to the bathroom. There can never be justice."

"What if someone pushed her?" Kersti perseveres. "The fact that she was pregnant . . . I mean, if you think *you* didn't want anyone to know about it, what about the people who had even more to lose?"

"I don't understand," Deirdre says. "Why would Magnus—"

"Magnus wasn't the father."

Deirdre sighs.

"She was having an affair with her history teacher."

"Mr. Fithern?" she cries, sitting upright. "From the Model United Nations?"

"Yes."

"She worshipped him," Deirdre remembers. "She talked about him all the time—"

"She was in love with him. And he was supposedly in love with her."

"Wasn't he married?" Deirdre says. "To one of the teachers at the school?"

Kersti nods, giving Deirdre time to absorb it all.

"Still," Deirdre says, her voice smaller, barely audible. "It was so long ago."

"For what it's worth, I think someone might have pushed her," Kersti says, the sentiment crystallizing even as she says it out loud. "I spoke to Mrs. Fithern the other day. She's the one who told me Cressida was pregnant."

"She knew?"

"Fithern told her. She thinks Cressida tried to kill herself. Apparently they both do."

"Well, we do have the suicide note," Deirdre acknowledges. "Maybe they're right."

"Yes, it's very neat and tidy. But we both know that note is bullshit."

Deirdre is pulling nervously at the strand of pearls around her neck. "Oh, Kersti. Honestly, what can we do now?"

"You can open an investigation in Lausanne."

"What for?" Deirdre cries. "It won't give Cressida her life back. It will just humiliate her and ruin her—"

"Her what? Her life? Her reputation? Does *that* really matter anymore?"

Deirdre buries her face in her hands and cries silently, her narrow shoulders shaking. She flings out an arm in search of a tissue. Kersti jumps up and hands her the box.

"You really think someone pushed my baby?" she says, blowing her nose.

"I think it's worth looking into it, Deirdre. At least worth talking to Bueche and Harzenmoser."

"I can't go back there—"

"I'll go with you," Kersti says. "I've been invited back for the Lycée's hundredth birthday. We can go together."

"There must be some sort of statute of limitations," she says. "Besides, what would I ask them? What could they possibly tell me after all this time? I would just embarrass myself."

"Bueche and Harzenmoser covered up the note and they covered up the affair. They must have known about it. Everyone knew at the end. They shut it down before the police even had a chance—"

"I don't know."

"Madame Hamidou could help you," Kersti says. "She might still be there. She loved Cress like a daughter."

Deirdre frowns.

"Is there anything else you haven't told me?" Kersti asks carefully. "Do you have the ledger, Deirdre? Is there something in there . . . Are you still protecting her?"

Deirdre shakes her head and opens her mouth to say something, but before she can respond, a young girl about eight years old gusts into the room, breathless and red-cheeked. "Mama?" she says, flopping down next to Deirdre and eyeing Kersti with curiosity. *Mama?* Kersti thinks, shocked.

The girl is exquisite, with pale green eyes and curly auburn hair tied up in two high pigtails. She's nearly as tall as Deirdre and just as slender, wearing sparkly leggings and a sweatshirt with a bejeweled peace sign.

"Darling," Deirdre says, daubing the corners of her eyes and trying to regain her composure. "I didn't hear you come in."

"Why are you crying?" the girl asks, staring at Kersti.

"We're talking about Cressida," she says. "You know that makes Mama sad. Sloaney, this is Kersti, Cressida's friend from school. Kersti, this is Sloane."

"Hi, Sloane."

"Hi."

"How old are you?"

"Seven and three-quarters."

"Sloaney," Deirdre says, "the heels of your socks are filthy. Please go and change them and start your homework."

"Can I have a snack?"

"Laylay will cut you a mango."

Sloane slides off the couch with a reluctant groan and shuffles out of the parlor. When she's gone, Kersti turns to Deirdre. "She's beautiful," Kersti says. "She called you Mama."

"Yes."

"She can't be yours," Kersti says, guessing by the child's crazy mane of curls, her pale green eyes, and the perfect curve of her mouth who she belongs to.

"When Cressida was twenty-seven," Deirdre explains, "I flew her to a fertility clinic in Colorado for in vitro."

"My God. She's Cressida's daughter?"

"Right after Cressida got back to the States, I had them do a D-and-C to make sure nothing from the first pregnancy would interfere with a future pregnancy. Just in case. At the time, I still hoped Cressida would recover and lead a normal life. Eventually, it became apparent that she wasn't going to get better. So in 2007, I found a sperm donor and a surrogate, and now I have my Sloane."

Kersti remembers the little girl's room she saw the last time she was here. She should have guessed. Deirdre has created a replica of Cressida.

"She's the light of my life," Deirdre says. "My second chance."

"Does she know Cressida is her mother?"

"*I'm* her mother," Deirdre states.

"You're her grandmother."

"I've raised her as my own."

"Who does she think Cressida is?"

"Her sister. My first child."

Kersti is speechless. She has to concede that the frozen eggs were an ingenious idea if the goal was to preserve Cressida's legacy, rather than to re-create her.

"I have no regrets," Deirdre tells her. "We've still got fifteen frozen eggs in storage—"

Fifteen eggs.

The words land like a bomb. What occurs to Kersti in that moment is so utterly insane, it astonishes her with its perfect irony.

"Anyway," Deirdre says. "I'm going to think about it."

"About what?" Kersti asks, completely lost in her own thoughts.

"About going to Lausanne and speaking to Bueche and Harzenmoser—"

"Deirdre," Kersti blurts out, knowing this is her only chance; that if she's going to have a baby she has to make it happen any way she can. "I have a proposition for you."

CHAPTER 22

LAUSANNE—November 1997

At midnight, Kersti bursts out of her room to get Cressida. She still isn't used to them not sharing a room. They both have single rooms on the fourth floor now, which is supposed to be a privilege for the top senior students. Kersti's lonely, though. Her small room with the single bed and the sloped ceilings sometimes feel like a cell. She misses Cressida's company.

Their feud at the end of last year is mostly forgotten. The night Cressida confided about her affair with Mr. Fithern, Kersti decided she wouldn't speak to Cressida for the entire summer. It was already May, which meant only a few weeks of silent treatment to get through until the end of the school year.

She lasted about two weeks, which made things very awkward in their room. Cressida kept trying to explain, tell her side of it. But Kersti was too hurt. At first, she couldn't get past the fact that Cressida had claimed to still be in love with Magnus while she was already seeing Mr. Fithern, but morbid curiosity ultimately trumped Kersti's self-righteousness. She couldn't stand being excluded from Cressida's unfolding drama. It was killing her not to be able to ask Cressida all the questions that kept popping into her head. She wanted to know everything about the affair. She wanted details. Where did they rendezvous? Was he going to leave his wife? Who else knew? And naturally, Kersti wanted to know if Magnus would be available again.

She finally caved the night of the Ascension holiday. She was in bed unable to sleep and Cressida was at her desk, working on an essay. She always did her homework in the middle of the night—an afterthought. "You told me you loved Magnus and that's why you wanted him back," Kersti blurted into the dark. "You knew I liked him, but you had to take him anyway—"

"I didn't take him *from you*," Cressida said, turning around to face her.

"And the whole time, you were also screwing Mr. Fithern. *Why*?" Kersti demanded. "Why couldn't you just let me have Magnus?"

"It wasn't my decision to make," Cressida said. "Magnus is his own person. He made his own choices. I had no control over that. Besides, I did have feelings for him."

"Did?"

"Do."

"But you have stronger feelings for Mr. Fithern," Kersti said, turning on her bedside lamp. "You said so. I don't get why you had to have both!"

"Haven't you ever loved two people at the same time?"

Kersti thought about Cressida and Magnus and the answer was yes, but she said nothing.

"I didn't think Charlie and I had a future," Cressida said.

"So you used Magnus as your backup, which also kept him away from me. Just because you could."

"No, Kersti. I had a fling with Charlie. I never planned to fall in love with him. I planned to be with Magnus. Magnus and I made sense. Charlie and I . . ."

She shook her head, bewildered. Like she was the victim in all this. "I may be impulsive," she said. "I follow my heart and sometimes it's reckless and people get hurt, but I'm not a bad person, Kersti. I don't make calculated decisions to deliberately hurt people. Especially not you or Magnus."

"You think that makes it okay?"

"I don't know if it makes it okay," Cressida said. "I don't worry about what's okay or not."

Kersti knew that to be true. She just wasn't sure if it was an admirable quality, or reprehensible. She thought about *L'Étranger* and wondered if Cressida was amoral or just living by her own truth.

For most of the summer, their friendship was like a fragile artifact. Still in one piece, but full of filament-like cracks that weakened its integrity. They emailed each other regularly—Cressida from London or Belize or wherever she happened to be—but their exchanges were terse, formal. Kersti was still aggrieved and didn't want Cressida to think she was forgiven.

And then on Kersti's birthday in August, she received a FedEx package with a plane ticket to Greece. *Seventeen years on earth deserves seventeen days on the Greek Islands. Happy B-day, Kuusky. I'll meet you at the Athens airport. Cress*

Her parents agreed to the trip, deciding it would be an early graduation present. They gave her a cell phone and two hundred dollars and off she went. Armand and Deirdre were supposed to be there the whole time, but Deirdre got a role in the West End and it was decided the girls would have a chaperone instead, Armand's twenty-five-year-old personal assistant. Armand flew in on his private plane to meet them for a few days in Corfu and Samos, but for all the other islands they were basically alone.

The Greek Islands in August were teeming with tourists. Everywhere they went it was hot, crowded, and exciting. They quickly fell into a rhythm—sleeping until noon every day, Greek coffee, a few hours at the beach, siesta in the afternoon. Dinner at 10 p.m. Partying until four, five, six o'clock in the morning, dancing and downing tequila slammers and then capping off the night with a gyros at sunrise. Kersti had a fling with Boyd from Brisbane. That's what they called him. He ended up following them to Santorini and Ios, but eventually Kersti decided to lose him. She actually really liked him, but she started to think Cressida was the one he wanted. How could it not be? Maybe she was being paranoid—maybe she simply couldn't believe that anyone would like her and not Cressida—but she couldn't face the possibility of another rejection.

For seventeen days they celebrated her seventeenth birthday, hopping from island to island. The best part was having Cressida all to herself for such a long time. On their last night, when they were on the ferry back to Athens, Kersti reached for her hand and held it. "Thank you," she whispered.

They were lying side by side on the deck, surrounded by dozens of other stargazing backpackers. "I had the best time."

"I'm the one who's thankful," Cressida returned. "I don't deserve you."

Kersti knew their friendship was restored. The cracks were gone; the surface was smooth again. Her heart was full.

She knocks on Cressida's door and Cressida pops out, grinning mischievously. "I have a surprise for you," she says.

"What?"

She pulls her into the room, closes the door, and whips a joint out of her kangaroo sweatshirt.

"Where'd you get that?" Kersti asks. She knows Cressida smokes up a lot—with Magnus and with Mr. Fithern—but she usually doesn't do it at school.

"We have to do it here," she says. "One time before the end of the year." She means in Huber House. Whenever they've smoked before, it's been at Ouchy or outside one of the bars.

They bundle up in sweaters and coats and go outside on the balcony. Cressida lights the joint, has a toke, and hands it to Kersti. They pass it back and forth, their smoke mixing with their frozen breath. "It's freezing," Kersti says, her teeth chattering.

"Does it seem weird to you that Celine Dion is married to that old guy?" Cressida says, sounding quite vexed by it.

"What made you think of that?"

"She's Canadian and you're Canadian. I just kind of put that together. Plus I have that stupid song in my head from *Titanic*."

"He was her manager," Kersti tells her.

"I know, but he's old enough to be her dad. She was like twelve when she married him."

Kersti laughs. "She was twelve when he discovered her, not when he married her."

"Still," Cressida says. "She was a kid and he was like forty."

"*You*'re in love with an older man," Kersti reminds her.

"Charlie is thirty and I'm almost eighteen. And he's not fatherly. He's sexy."

Cressida suddenly leans forward against the railing and raises her arms in the air. "I'm the queen of the world!" she cries, and starts singing the *Titanic* theme song.

Kersti stands behind her and places her hands on Cressida's hips, pretending to be Leonardo DiCaprio from the movie. "I've got you, Rose!"

Cressida turns around, playing along. "Where are you going, Rose?" she says dramatically. "To be with *him*? To be a whore to a gutter rat?"

"I'd rather be his whore than your wife, Cal!" Kersti responds, and they both burst out laughing, Kersti not letting on that she secretly loved the movie.

They go inside and strip off their coats. "Let's go bake something," Cressida says.

They head down to the kitchen on the first floor, where the students in the Econome program take cooking classes and learn how to fold napkins. The door has an old lock, which everyone in Huber House can easily pick open with a hair clip. The fridge is always stocked with baking basics—flour, sugar, butter, eggs—and occasionally something special, like jam or chocolate chips.

"Anything good?" Kersti asks, as Cressida starts opening all the pantries.

When she finds what she's looking for, she holds it up like a trophy. "Cocoa powder!" she cries. "We can make brownies!"

They both start cheering and hugging each other, dancing around the room. They open the fridge and discover a jar of Hero jam and a bottle of whipping cream. "We can make scones, too," Cressida says.

Kersti turns on the oven while Cressida takes more stuff out of the fridge. "Maybe Celine thinks her husband is sexy," Kersti says, going back to their earlier conversation. "Maybe you're in love with Mr. Fithern because he reminds you of Armand."

At this, Cressida erupts laughing. "Armand is an ass," she says, mixing cocoa, coffee grounds, and cream in a mug. "And frankly I think he's gay."

"Your dad's gay?"

"I'm pretty sure."

"What about Deirdre?"

"I don't think she cares," Cressida says. "She probably has her own lovers."

"How long have you known?" Kersti asks her. "Why didn't you tell me?"

"Well, it's not like they sat me down and made an announcement. And I don't know for sure. I just started to suspect the last time I was home. I mean, they're never together."

"That doesn't mean he's gay."

"He leers at guys," Cressida says. "Flirts with them. He always has."

"Your poor mom," Kersti says, thinking about young Deirdre on her wedding day, not having a clue she was about to marry a homosexual.

Cressida adds boiling water to her coffee-cocoa concoction and has a sip.

"Armand reminds me of Thurston Howell from *Gilligan's Island,*" Kersti says, creaming butter and sugar in a bowl. "You know how he wears that ascot and talks with the locked jaw and clenched teeth?"

Cressida stretches her mouth as wide as it will go and says through clenched teeth, "*Gilligan.*"

"*Lovey,*" Kersti says, in the same clenched-teeth voice. "*Skipper.*"

"Shit," Cressida says. "I never thought about it before. For sure Mr. Howell is gay."

"Do you think Mrs. Howell knew?"

"They slept in separate beds—"

Kersti adds cocoa and eggs to her brownie batter while Cressida gets started on the scones. She could do it blindfolded if she had to. They must have made a million scones over the last few years; it's the one thing for which they can always find the ingredients.

"It must be weird to grow up super-poor and then one day be a kajillionaire," Cressida says, kneading her dough.

"Thurston Howell grew up poor?" Kersti says, shoving the brownies in the oven.

"No. Celine Dion."

They look at each other in a moment of mutual confusion and then collapse on the linoleum floor laughing.

"Do you think it's wrong for me to expect that I should always get what I want?" Cressida asks, turning serious.

"Um. Yes, probably."

"Does it make me a bad person?" she asks, her tone more curious than concerned.

"Of course not," Kersti says, leaning on her elbow. "It's normal to you. You've always gotten everything you want so you don't really know another way."

They lie there for a while, the smell of their baking wafting around them.

"What am I going to do without you, Kuusky?"

"It's only November."

"Have you decided what you're going to do next year?" Cressida asks.

"Maybe U of T, or Ryerson. Or I might just work at my dad's travel agency."

"Why would you ever do that?" Cressida says.

"They'd like it if I went into the family business."

"What about you? What do you want?"

"I don't know. To write. But that's lame . . . I need a real job."

"I hate when you say shit like that," Cressida says, reaching up for the mixing bowl and scooping out a glob of brownie batter with her fingers.

"Hate when I talk like what?"

"Like: 'I need a real job,' 'I can't be writer,' 'I'll do what my parents want me to do.'" She turns to face Kersti with brownie batter all over her face. "It depresses the hell out of me."

"Sorry I'm not like you," Kersti says. "I don't expect to get everything I want in life."

"Maybe you should."

"I prefer to please people rather than to hurt them or disappoint them."

"That's your problem," Cressida says. "You need a little more Cressida in you."

On their way back upstairs, with their bellies full of brownies, scones, and coffee, they clutch the mahogany banister for support. How many times have they made this climb over the last four years, Kersti wonders? Everything she does now, that's what she thinks about. *How many times have we done this and taken it for granted?* Climbing the Huber stairs; baking scones in the middle of the night; gossiping in the bathroom; roast chicken and french fries on Saturday; Sunday morning treks to McDonald's by the Gare; chasing each other through the *passerelle* that connects Huber and Lashwood.

Cressida places her hands on Kersti's lower back and starts pushing her up, one step at a time. They're both suppressing giggles. When they come to the second-floor landing, Kersti stops abruptly.

"Look," she whispers, and points down the hall to where someone is creeping stealthily toward them—a tall figure with short hair, mannish, ungraceful. As the person approaches, her face is momentarily lit by a slice of moonlight coming through one of the dormer windows. It's Angela Zumpt.

Angela gasps when she spots them both standing at the top of the stairs, waiting for her. "What are you doing?" she asks them.

"We were hungry," Kersti says. "What are you doing on the second floor?"

"Using the washroom," Angela answers, trying to get past them.

"What's wrong with our bathroom?" Kersti wants to know. Angela's room is also on the fourth floor, where there's a perfectly good bathroom.

"I prefer this one," she says, flustered. "Iss none of your business anyway."

Kersti laughs and looks over at Cressida, expecting her to jump in, but her expression is strangely solemn. She's dead quiet. "Cress?"

"I ate too much," Cressida says. "I have to puke."

Angela hurries up the stairs on her way back to the fourth floor, with Cressida not far behind.

"What was that all about?" Kersti asks Cressida, trying to keep up with her. "What do you think she was doing? Policing someone on the second floor? Spying?"

"Probably," Cressida responds absently, rushing to the bathroom.

CHAPTER 23

TORONTO—February 2016

A light snow is falling outside. The lobby of the clinic is decorated for Valentine's Day, with a banner hanging in the window. Kersti and Jay are sitting side by side in the waiting room. She looks up from the "Everything You Need to Know about Your Sperm" pamphlet and notices Jay clutching his laptop bag so tightly his knuckles are white. He's staring miserably out at nothing. "You're not nervous, are you, babe?" she says gently. "You've done this before."

She holds up the pamphlet. "Did you know that motile sperm are called spermatozoon?"

"Sadly, I do. I've read that one before."

"It's been at least forty-eight hours, right?"

"You've asked me that fifty times already. Yes. It's been forty-eight hours."

"I just want to make sure they're fresh—"

"They're fresh, Kerst. Believe it or not, I'm capable of going forty-eight hours without jerking off. I also ate your oyster and pumpkin seed casserole, took my zinc, my folic acid, and my vitamin D. My sperm is fucking FRESH."

She touches his hand and rests her head on his shoulder. "This is it, babe. I know it. I had a beautiful thick uterine lining this morning and the nurse said my cervical mucus was gorgeous."

"That's why I married you," he mutters. "Gorgeous cervical mucus."

"And my inner labia isn't swollen anymore—"

"Babe?" he says. "I don't ever want to hear the words *labia* and *swollen* come out of your mouth again."

"Jay Wax?" The nurse is standing in the corridor with a clipboard. "We're ready for you."

Jay stands up and salutes her. "Spermatozoon reporting for duty," he says.

Kersti hands him his laptop bag. "Here's your porn. Now go make us a baby."

She still can't believe they're at the Colorado Center for Reproductive Medicine making a baby with Cressida's eggs. The journey to this point has been surreal and yet divinely fated—starting with Lille's letter, which ultimately led to this moment. If not for that first visit to Deirdre, Kersti would still be in Toronto, reluctantly giving up her dream of motherhood.

It turns out Deirdre was thrilled to donate as many of Cressida's eggs as Kersti needed. The only catch is if Kersti gets pregnant, Deirdre wants to be in the children's lives. "I would never impose myself," she said. "Never expect them to think of me as their grandmother, but I would need to see them once in a while, to be kept abreast of their development. Technically, even if they never know, I *would be* their biological grandmother."

It seemed fair, a small price to pay. Deirdre agreed to have her lawyer draw up a contract, and Kersti left that day with only one more obstacle to overcome: *Jay*.

She managed with great restraint not to say a word about it until dinner that Saturday night in Boston, after their day at the spa and a couple of rounds of make-up sex. And then, when Jay was relaxed and flushed from wine, with a belly full of filet mignon and creamed spinach, she said, "I want you to know, you're a hundred percent right."

"I am? About what?"

"About me, not ever being willing to give up on having a baby."

He looked at her nervously. "And is that a good thing or a bad thing?"

"I would have kept going until it bankrupted us."

"You're scaring me, Kerst—"

Kersti shifted in her chair and sipped her wine, carefully choosing her words. "What if the cycles were free?" she asked him.

"It would help," he admitted. "But they're not. Especially with a donor—"

"I've found a private donor," she said. "Hear me out. She's already got fifteen superb-quality eggs frozen at one of the best fertility clinics in the United States. She would donate them to us for free. There's a lot of legal stuff involved—it's like adopting a baby—but I know her very well. She's not a stranger. I know her family history. We would only pay for my drugs, which would be minimal, and the transfer—"

"Who is it?"

"Listen to me," she said, reaching for his hands. "Look at me, Jay, and just answer this question. Do you want to have a child? Forget everything else—"

"I *can't* forget everything else—"

"Do you want to have a child?" she repeated.

"Yes," he answered, and she was moved to see he had tears in his eyes. "Of course I do. You know how much I want to be a father."

"Then think about this. As many high-quality eggs as we need *for free*, from someone I know. It's meant to be, Jay. We can't walk away from this."

"Who is it?"

"Cressida."

Jay's mouth fell open. "How the hell?"

"Her mother had her eggs frozen."

"Holy shit. This is fucked up."

"She's already had one child with those eggs," Kersti continued. "I met her. She's beautiful. Perfect. Deirdre used a sperm donor, but of course we would use your sperm and you would be the father—"

She pulled out her phone and showed him the pictures she'd taken of Sloane, as well as a few she'd added of Cressida as a baby and in her teens. "That's her daughter, Sloane. And this is Cressida. That's her at two, and then here at five. . . ."

Jay scrolled through the pictures. "She was gorgeous," he said, lingering on one of Cressida from the Lycée.

"I spoke to Deirdre about their family history," Kersti said. "There's nothing alarming or unusual—"

"Except suicidal tendencies," Jay said, handing back her phone. "She tried to kill herself, Kersti."

"No, I don't think she did," Kersti said. "I haven't had a chance to really talk to you about it, but I don't think she did. And at some point, when all this is behind us, I'm going to prove it—"

"Wasn't she fucked up, though? Didn't she do some messed-up shit? These can't be the genes you want for our child."

"I knew her, Jay. She had a good heart. She was her own worst enemy, that's all. She was raised in a boarding school from the time she was seven. How could she not have been fucked up? But that's got nothing to do with genes."

"Still—"

"You want to talk about genes?" Kersti went on, getting more fired up. "She had a brilliant mind. She was scary smart. And obviously gorgeous and perfect in every way—"

"This is madness, Kersti. You know that, don't you?"

Kersti fell silent when he said that. "Yes," she confessed, welling up. "I know it."

And for the first time since she'd left Deirdre's that afternoon, all her rationalizations and justifications fell silent too. It *was* madness, even she couldn't refute that. But it was also exquisitely, poetically ordained.

"I want a baby," she said plainly. "I know you think I'm losing my mind—and maybe I am—but this opportunity has presented itself and I can't turn it down. I feel like it's meant to be, that it's our last chance."

"And you're going to do it with or without me, aren't you?"

"Of course not," Kersti said, not sure she was telling the truth. "We're partners, remember?"

He was quiet for a long time. She had a few bites of her molten cake while his crème brûlée sat untouched. The irony of their situation was not lost on her; in using Cressida's eggs to make a baby, Kersti was showing herself to be a lot more like Cressida than she ever realized. As poor Jay contemplated her outrageous request, she knew she would get her way one way or another, no matter how scandalous or controversial.

Was she really all that different from Cressida then? In their relentless pursuit of a passionate, personal desire, in their stubborn willfulness and refusal to accept no or back down, did they not possess at the core the very same self-centeredness and single-mindedness? Maybe it wasn't even a bad thing. Maybe it spoke more to inner strength and perseverance than to poor character. That's how Kersti decided to frame it, anyway. And with that realization, she came to have a new respect for Cressida and for her younger self.

After a while, Jay said, "Give me a few days to think about it, okay?"

She knew then he would do it. She could tell he was almost on board. She sensed that something about his demeanor had shifted. Perhaps it was the money, as well as the fact that their donor wouldn't be a stranger, but she was convinced he wanted a child as badly as she did.

It's a good thing, too, because once the seed was planted there was no turning back for Kersti. The idea of breeding her own little Cressidas was too compelling. Beautiful, intelligent, magnificent creatures just like their biological mother, only with all the love and nurturing that Kersti and Jay would provide. In Kersti's more stable hands, Cressida's genes would surely flourish and thrive in a little girl or boy.

She watches Jay now as he follows the nurse down the corridor and her heart swells. He turns back to her and gives her the thumbs-up, a big smile on his face. Desperation can make a person do unimaginable things, she thinks. Or become someone they never thought they'd be.

Two weeks later, Kersti finds herself lying on the couch, waiting for that portentous, dreaded phone call. The pregnancy test results. They went to Mount Sinai this morning for the test; drove downtown in absolute silence, their moods solemn. For most couples, it's the moment of joy and celebration. For them, it's sheer anxiety.

Two weeks ago today, on Valentine's Day, two perfect ABB blastocyst-stage embryos were painstakingly transferred inside Kersti's uterus with all the promise of a sunrise. They stayed in Denver for a week after the procedure, with Kersti overcautiously lying flat on her back in the hotel room the whole time. Since returning to Toronto, she's been obsessing over potentially real or imagined pregnancy symptoms. She knows from experience and from having read too many fertility blogs that swollen breasts and fatigue can be symptoms, but her doctor warned her these could also be the effects of the progesterone she's injecting and not to get too excited.

The call usually comes close to noon, after the hospital gets the blood results back from the lab. Kersti's had several of these calls before and they usually begin with, "I'm sorry, Kersti." Twice the results were positive—she was technically pregnant—but in the follow-up blood tests, her hCG levels did not increase the way they should have, and by the time she had her eight-week ultrasound, no heartbeat was detected. Dr. Gliberman called them miscarriages, but later told her that neither of her brief pregnancies had ever been viable. She wasn't sure what that meant, if it was supposed to console her or be less traumatic since they weren't "real" pregnancies in the first place, but it felt like a cruel joke after everything they'd already been through.

After an unsuccessful attempt to nap, Kersti goes into the kitchen, boils water for chamomile tea—she's been forbidden caffeine—and butters toast, just about the only thing she can eat due to her nerves. She settles at the counter with the mail, wishing Jay hadn't gone to work. She knows it's how he copes, but it would be easier if he was here and they could talk and pass the time together. Her mother offered to come over, but Kersti isn't up to facing Anni or any of her sisters. Not if it's bad news.

There's a thick envelope from Deirdre in the mail, probably more copies of the legal documents. She had her lawyer draw up a series of ironclad contracts. Kersti opens the envelope and pulls the rubber band off what appears to be a pile of letters. There's a note from Deirdre attached to the top.

Kersti,

I should have given these to you a long time ago, when you were in Boston. I intended to, and then we were sidetracked by more "pressing" matters. You know me by now and you will soon see why I kept these to myself for as long as I did: shame/embarrassment/prudishness. My daughter never ceased to shock me. I was nothing like her as a teenager, I assure you! I know it's not the mysterious ledger, which I promise I do not have, but these notes may give you insight into what was going on before she fell. I never knew whom they were from before you told me, though I confess when you were here, I did know she'd been seeing someone other than Magnus. These "love notes" (if you can call them that) were sent to me with her things, hidden between the pages of a book. I have to get rid of them now—Sloane is at a snooping age—and it's either to you or the incinerator. Perhaps they can help you, should we decide to investigate further after you have the baby.

That said, I'm waiting by the phone for your good news. I have every faith that our Cressida's eggs will bless you with one if not two (three or four?) beautiful children. Take good care of yourself and our precious cargo. Best, D.

Kersti opens one of the notes.

C,

No one else makes me cum like you. It's all I can think about all day long. I'll be waiting for you tonight. Wear that thing you wore the last time.

C-

Kersti has never thought of herself as a prude, but even she's a little shocked by it. Cressida would have been sixteen or seventeen at the time.

Kersti doesn't recognize the handwriting, but assumes it's Mr. Fithern. Charlie, as Cressida used to call him.

C,

Why after all this time would you worry about me getting caught? It's not for you to worry about. It's my problem. I love you. Now get over here soon so I can fuck you.

C-

C,

When you came last night and your beautiful body was convulsing in my arms, I knew I could give everything up to have you forever. And yes, to answer your question again, no one makes me cum like you.

C-

C,

Dreaming of your perfect body and what I'm going to do to it when I see you tonight. And no more talk like the other night. You know you are the only one for me, the only one I love. You mustn't forget that, no matter what the situation seems on the outside.

C-

C,

Why do you say we can't be together? Your age and all the other irrelevant points you make are utterly meaningless to me, this at least you should know! I don't like all these doubts you're having. I can't live without the taste of you, the feel of you, the smell of you. Our relationship transcends societal norms. You've never adhered to any rules before. Don't start now. We do as we please. We always have.

C-

Kersti feels flushed and embarrassed even though she's alone. She imagines Mr. Fithern slipping these notes into Cressida's history textbook during class, or handing them to her as they passed each other on their way to class. Did he give them to her when he was returning a test or homework he'd graded? Did he fuck her in the school bathroom, with Abby Ho-Tai in the stall beside them, sick from her laxatives? Did they get off on crossing lines, shattering boundaries, disregarding everyone at the Lycée but themselves?

He must have had his own pile of dirty notes from her, tied up in rubber bands and stashed all over his house; the house he'd shared with his wife. Does he have them still? Did he keep them as a souvenir, a reminder of his youthful virility, his underage conquest?

Kersti can't help wondering what Cressida would have written to him. How was she able to do it? One minute, giggling and gossiping and being silly with her girlfriends up in the third-floor bathroom like any normal teenage girl, and the next, writing those things to her married lover, things Kersti had never even heard of, or wouldn't have dared *think* about, let alone say to another person.

Maybe Mrs. Fithern found Cressida's letters and read them. She must have been shocked and horrified—more than Kersti is now. And not just by the betrayal, but by their vulgarity and the sheer recklessness of their behavior. She must have despised Cressida.

And yet, when Kersti spoke to her, she'd sounded positively sympathetic. *Charles was the predator.* Something about that comment never rang true for Kersti. Their whole conversation had left her feeling unsettled.

I think she was an unhappy girl who got in over her head and tried to kill herself.

As Kersti broods over their conversation, she realizes she's already made the decision. She's going to go to Lausanne for the centennial celebration and speak to Bueche and Harzenmoser herself. If by some miracle she's pregnant, she'll be past the first trimester by then; if not, it will be her consolation trip. Maybe they can go to Estonia, do that Baltic cruise Jay had talked about, travel around for a few weeks to regroup. Either way, she can't stop here. There are too many loose ends and unanswered questions.

When the phone rings, Kersti nearly jumps off her stool, having completely lost track of the time. She takes a deep breath and tries to steady her galloping heart before she reaches for it.

Please God Please God Please God

"Kersti?"

"Yes," she manages, on the brink of vomiting.

"Congratulations, Kersti!" the nurse says, her voice the most beautiful sound Kersti's ever heard. "Your test was positive. Your levels are great."

Her levels are great. Kersti exhales and realizes she hasn't breathed in at least a minute. The phone is shaking in her hand. "I have to call Jay—"

"We want you to come back Wednesday for your follow-up blood test."

Not out of the woods yet, but it's different this time. She can feel it. This is Cressida's baby and it's meant to be.

CHAPTER 24

LAUSANNE—January 1998

Kersti keeps a careful eye on Cressida, curious to see how she'll handle herself surrounded by the entire faculty. She's standing over by the lavish pastry table with Mrs. Fithern, wearing a floor-length jersey skirt slit up to her thigh. They're talking animatedly. A waiter approaches them and hands them each a glass of champagne. They clink flutes, laughing.

It's the grand unveiling of the new library, a project M. Bueche undertook as part of the Lycée's eightieth anniversary back in '96. After two years of fund-raising and construction, the new library is complete with new IBM computers, an elegant mahogany study hall, and an expanded historical archives department. Kersti watches as Cressida's eyes find Mr. Fithern's at the opposite side of the library, both obviously aware of the other's every movement. Something lustful and secretive passes between them, and Kersti is disturbed by how effortlessly Cressida is able to simultaneously enjoy herself with Mrs. Fithern—no doubt trading their usual quips, debating literature, and glibly mocking the stuffy alumni together.

Alison follows Kersti's gaze and frowns. "It's sickening," she mutters, and walks away in a huff. Kersti regrets telling Alison and Lille, but she couldn't keep it to herself. Cressida's secret was like a grenade; she would have exploded with it if she hadn't gotten rid of it. As far as boarding school gossip goes, it's the gold standard. Deliciously irresistible.

Kersti continues to watch Cressida until she finally looks up and notices her. She excuses herself to Mrs. Fithern and comes over to Kersti, champagne flute in hand. "Isn't the library absolutely breathtaking?" she jokes, mimicking M. Bueche's earlier speech.

"Formidable, formidable," Kersti plays along in French

They drift over to the new archives, where framed photographs from the last century are hanging on the walls and a collection of Lycée artifacts is displayed in a museum-style glass case. There are athletic ribbons from the twenties and thirties; an original school uniform—a high-collared Edwardian blouse and navy ankle-length skirt—as well as a later version, a navy blue tunic with the motto sewn onto the crest. *Bene qui latuit, bene vixit.* One who lives well, lives unnoticed.

Among the other paraphernalia is an old menu from 1918, featuring Zürcher Geschnetzeltes and Rösti for supper; a poster for the first Festival de la Cité, June 28–29, 1968; the very first school yearbook from 1916–17. Beneath the glass display, there's a gleaming mahogany bookcase lined with all the other yearbooks from 1918 to 1997.

Cressida kneels down, the slit of her skirt opening and revealing the full expanse of her lovely white leg. She runs her finger over the identical yellow spines of the yearbooks, tracing the gold writing as though she's reading braille.

Her finger stops at 1973–74 and she pulls it out of its tight slot. She stands up and flips through the yearbook. Kersti knows exactly what she's looking for. "Why are you so interested in those girls who got expelled?"

"I'm curious."

"About what?"

"What they did."

"Why?"

"No one gets expelled here," she says, slipping the yearbook under her sweater.

"What the hell are you doing?"

"Let's go," Cressida whispers, hugging the yearbook against her body.

Kersti follows Cressida out of the library and they run all the way back to Huber House, exploding into a peal of laughter as they reach her room. When the door closes behind them, Cressida lifts her sweater and the yearbook falls out. They sit on the floor, breathless and giddy from having stolen it. Cressida starts to look through it page by page, as though she's looking for the clue to a mystery. Maybe she is.

The mildew smell makes Kersti queasy. She's never liked the smell of old books. It reminds her too much of her parents' house—damp and neglected. Cressida studies the grad portraits, where the seniors are posed with their best friends. The students of that era all looks the same—long straight hippie hair parted down the middle and hanging in their faces like nuns' head coverings.

"Here they are," she says, pointing to a photograph of three attractive girls sitting side by side, arms linked. Their curtains of hair conceal most of their features, revealing just a sliver of skin and lips, tips of noses, corners of eyes. None of them are smiling.

"These are the two girls who got expelled," Cressida says. "Brooke Middlewood and Tatiana Greenberg."

"Who's the third girl?"

"Amoryn Lashwood."

"As in Lashwood House?"

"Maybe," Cressida says, staring at the photograph, which must have been taken before two of the three of them were expelled. The quote next to the picture reads:

> I saw the best minds of my generation destroyed by madness . . .
>
> *—Allen Ginsberg*

Cressida continues going through the yearbook, pausing every so often to read a caption or examine a photograph. "Look at this," she says, turning it so Kersti can see. "Amoryn Lashwood's Bequeaths."

The Bequeaths are where the grads list inside jokes and special memories or leave personal messages to their friends. Kersti is already planning to bequeath a certain history teacher to Cressida, nipples to Lille, a smoke-filled bathroom to Alison, rolling paper to Noa, et cetera, et cetera.

Amoryn Lashwood's Bequeaths are comparatively short: "I bequeath the HS & the Ledger."

"Here's another one just like it," Cressida says. "I bequeath the HS & the Ledger."

"And this one," Kersti cries, finding herself swept up in Cressida's excitement. "I bequeath the HS & the secrets in the Ledger—"

They find a total of five similar Bequeaths.

"HS has to be the Helvetia Society," Cressida says, pleased with herself. "The girls who left these Bequeaths must have been Helvetians. The ledger was probably like a meeting log or something."

"I wonder what secrets were in there."

"Probably the same thing that got them expelled."

"You mean whatever they spray-painted on the statue?"

"Their Bequeaths were obviously a message."

"To who?"

"Bueche," Cressida answers, with such certainty Kersti considers she might know something. "What the fuck happened to that ledger?" Cressida wonders aloud, getting up and going over to her mirror. She gazes at herself for a moment before putting on some lip gloss and a dusting of blush.

"Going somewhere?"

"To meet Magnus."

"Magnus?"

"He's still my boyfriend," Cressida says, turning away from her beautiful reflection in the mirror. "I still have feelings for him."

Kersti bites her lip.

"Besides," she rationalizes, "if Charlie doesn't leave Mrs. F., why should I leave Magnus?"

Kersti wants to shout: "I actually loved him! I'm the one who deserved him!" But Cressida has long since forgotten that Kersti was the collateral damage in their love story. And although part of her can't help rejoicing that Magnus is finally getting his comeuppance, it still makes her bristle that Cressida would so easily dump him for someone better. It feels almost personal, slyly vindictive.

Cressida shoves the yearbook in one of her drawers and runs a hand through her curls. "I love you, Kuusky," she says sweetly, wrapping her arms around Kersti. "You're always here for me."

Kersti's muscles tense. "Are you going to bring the yearbook back to the library?" she asks her.

Cressida looks at her strangely. "Does it matter?" she says. And for some reason, it does.

CHAPTER 25

TORONTO—April 2016

Kersti lifts her head out of the toilet bowl and lies down on the cold tiles. You asked for this, she reminds herself, loving and hating her morning sickness equally. Loving it because it's a privilege and a constant physical reminder that she's carrying two babies inside her, and hating it for obvious reasons. She's ten weeks pregnant. There were two heartbeats at her eight-week ultrasound; two healthy, normal heartbeats, the sound of which was met with a floodgate of relief and tears. It was the sound of life and hope and possibility itself.

"We did it," Jay whispered, his hand on her stomach, tears streaming down his face, the music of those racing heartbeats in the background.

At the clinic in Colorado, they gave Kersti and Jay a thick binder of instructions on how to tell their children they come from donor eggs, but Kersti is going to tell them in her own way. She's going to write it. She's been working on a letter to them since the day she heard those heartbeats. Maybe since the day she knew she would use Cressida's eggs. She wants them to understand that everything she did was for love; the kind of pure, inflexible maternal love that knows no limitations.

She reaches for the pack of saltines on the floor beside her and stuffs one in her mouth, her only relief from nausea.

"You okay in there?" her mother calls out, opening the door and finding her on the floor.

"When does this end?" Kersti asks.

"Twelfth week with every one of my pregnancies," she says. "Do you need help back to bed?"

"I'm going to stay in here awhile," Kersti tells her. "I'll be fine."

When the nausea begins to subside in the late morning, Kersti manages to scrape herself off the floor and go downstairs to the kitchen. "At last," her mother says, looking up from a pot on the stove, with a strand of white hair falling over her face. She's been here almost every morning for the last two months, feeding Kersti toast and soup and preparing meals for Jay. "Try this," she says, placing a bowl of soup in front of her, with two pieces of toasted black rye on the side. "Tell me if it's too sweet."

Kersti dunks the toast in the soup and realizes she's starving. "It's good," she says, and finishes everything.

"Let's hope it stays down," her mother says, scooping sour cream into a pot.

Feeling better, Kersti heads up to her office to write.

Hello again, Gunnar and Imbi. She types *Chapter Three,* and stares at her screen, uninspired. It doesn't take long before an email pops up on her screen.

Congratulations on twins! How are you feeling? Will you know the sex by June?? My hotel is booked. I arrive the 12th. I'm staying at the Angleterre. I think Raf is staying there too. Where are you staying? It will be like old times . . . without the smoking! (You'd better not be smoking!!) Have you heard from Alison? I can't wait to see you. Bisous. Noa

Kersti types back a short note. We're booked at the Chateau. Can't wait to catch up in person. I guess I'd better start working on my speech! No word from Alison yet. I'll keep you posted. KK

She smiles to herself as she hits send. Now that it's decided, she can't wait for the reunion in Lausanne. It will be eighteen years since she last saw Noa and Rafaella in person, or set foot in Switzerland. She's still waiting to hear back from Alison, whom she found living in Whistler and working as a buyer for a ski apparel company, but she's not very optimistic about making contact. Deirdre is also going to meet her there, so they can speak to Bueche together.

"Kersti?" her mother calls out.

"In here!"

Anni sticks her head in the room and says, "I'm going now. I left the *leivasupp* on the stove and there's supper in the fridge for Jay. Don't eat it. It's *pirukad*. The herring will make you sick. I'll see you tomorrow morning."

"Love you."

"Yup."

Anni disappears, leaving behind a trail of Opium perfume, the same one she's been wearing for as long as Kersti can remember. For the first time ever, Kersti can actually appreciate how set in their ways her parents are without being offended or taking it personally. Maybe it's hormones.

Kersti stares at her notes for the novel and realizes *The Jewel of Reval* is just not happening. The other book is calling to her—loudly. No matter how many times she sits down in this chair and turns on the computer with the very best of intentions of finishing this one, she just can't bring herself to write it. She keeps telling herself, Maybe tomorrow. But the truth is she has no inclination.

She leaves it aside for the moment and settles cross-legged on the floor with her box of mementos from the Lycée. She had Jay bring it upstairs so she could sort through it. She's going to bring some photographs with her to Lausanne, to share with Raf and Noa. She imagines them in the bathroom of Huber House, exactly as it was back then, their adult selves reminiscing about old times. They'll surely feel the void of Lille and Cressida—they were very much the nucleus of the group—but they'll celebrate stoically in their honor anyway.

She pulls out her yearbook with its faded yellow cover and looks through it with an overwhelming sentiment of nostalgia. There's a picture of Kersti and Cressida, part of a collage of random snapshots, where they're arm in arm in the Lycée's garden. Cressida's hair is pulled back in dozens of tight, intricate cornrow braids—she must have just gotten back from a trip—and her skin is golden brown, luminescent. She's wearing a white sundress with the strap slipping off her shoulder, smiling at the camera, statuesque and resplendent.

And there's Kersti beside her, eclipsed as usual by that astounding beauty. Paler, shorter, unremarkable in a generic, adolescent way. A bad eighties haircut, the ends crimped and overlightened, a loose gray sweatshirt to hide whatever is beneath it, an apologetic half smile, itself an acknowledgment of her inadequacy. In essence, an average teenager who is achingly unsure of herself, with blackheads and social awkwardness and a painful self-consciousness that leaps off the page.

Kersti touches her stomach where Cressida's eggs are transforming themselves into what she's come to think of as her chance for redemption. She never could compete with Cressida, but now she's got a part of Cressida inside her.

Hopefully Kersti's children will be exceptional, inherently right. Something Kersti never was, or at least never felt.

There's nothing like a pregnancy to mark the plodding passage of time. Kersti tracks the babies' development week to week. *Your baby at thirteen weeks is the size of a pea pod. Your baby at sixteen weeks is the size of an avocado. He even has toenails!*

As her mother predicted, the morning sickness disappeared in her twelfth week, just as she entered her second trimester. Her tummy still hasn't popped, so it just looks like she's gained about twenty pounds, evenly spread. She can already tell she does not have the sort of body that will stay thin everywhere except for a hard basketball at the front. In another month, she'll find out the sex. She's secretly hoping for at least one girl. No names have been decided; Jay wants to wait until they know what they're having. Kersti's parents are pushing for Estonian names, but Jay isn't sold. "I'm not having my kids named Jaagup or Ivar or Nuut," he said, all names of her uncles.

Kersti snips the stems off a handful of cherry blossoms and drops them into one of the crystal vases she got for her wedding. She sets it on the Venetian mirrored table in the foyer and admires her first flowers of the season. It's the nesting instinct, her mother says.

Her phone vibrates with an incoming text while she's crouched in the dirt. She wipes her hands on her jeans and sees it's a Vancouver number. She knows immediately that it's Alison Rumsky.

Sorry for the late reply. I'm in T.O on biz. I can meet you for coffee/lunch?

Kersti texts back: Yes!! Where & when?

They meet at La Carnita, a dark, hipster place on College that Alison suggested. *Craving Mexican,* she wrote. All the arrangements were made via text.

When Kersti arrives, she spots Alison at a back booth, looking identical to her teenage self. Astonishingly, she hasn't changed at all. Her red hair is cut in a practical bob that she's probably chosen for its convenience and ease, not for its style, and her skin is freckled and unfairly youthful, smooth in the places where Kersti is starting to detect lines. She's still lanky and fit, wearing a chambray blue button-down shirt and Capri jeans.

"You haven't aged!" Kersti cries, staring at her in disbelief. "You look sixteen! How is that possible?"

"Fresh mountain air?" she says, standing up and hugging Kersti. "You look great, too."

"No, I don't. I'm almost four months pregnant and wearing elastic waistband maternity jeans."

"Congratulations," Alison says, sitting back down. "What number is this?"

"My first. And second."

"Twins?"

Kersti nods, tenderly rubbing her tummy the way pregnant women do, something that used to annoy the hell out of her. "How about you? Kids?"

"No," she says, not seeming the least bit bothered or embarrassed about it. "Andrew and I decided a long time ago children wouldn't fit into our lifestyle."

"Tell me about your lifestyle. Living in Whistler must be awesome."

"We love it," she says, her blue eyes shining. "Obviously, we do a lot of skiing and mountain biking. We've got a condo right on Blackcomb. We travel. It's a good life. What about you? What do you do?"

"I'm a writer. I've had a few novels published."

"Very cool," Alison says, but doesn't ask where she might be able to pick one up. Maybe she's not the historical romance type.

While they're catching each other up on husbands, weddings, careers, and all other notable events of the past two decades, a tattooed server with long dreadlocks brings them a platter of warm tortilla chips, guacamole, and grilled street corn.

"Hearing from you was really out of the blue," Alison says, reaching for a tortilla.

"I know. And I'm so glad you texted me today. I've thought about you so often over the years."

"Me, too."

"I guess the short version is I was going along in my life, pretending the Lycée didn't exist, trying never to think about it, and then I got the invitation to the hundredth birthday celebration, followed by a letter from Lille. I figured it must be time to face it and hopefully get some closure."

"How is Lille?"

"She died."

Alison's expression changes instantly. "How?"

"Breast cancer. Her mom found the letter on her computer and sent it to me." Kersti reaches into her handbag and pulls it out. "Here."

Alison reads the letter and then wordlessly hands it back to Kersti.

"I went to see Deirdre in Boston," Kersti says. "It turns out Cressida left a suicide note."

She waits for a reaction from Alison, but there's nothing.

"Deirdre and I aren't convinced Cressida is the one who wrote it, though," Kersti continues. "I went to New York to talk to Magnus—"

"Foley?"

"Yes. And then I spoke to Mrs. Fithern—"

"You're on quite a mission."

"Well, I'm also getting a lot of good material for a new book," Kersti says. "If I could just connect that missing ledger to what happened to Cressida—"

"How is Mrs. Fithern?" Alison interrupts.

"She remarried and has four daughters. She seems happy."

"Why did you call her?"

"To find out what she knew," Kersti says. "She was at Huber that night. She was housemother, remember?"

"So?"

"Magnus went to see her. He told her about the affair."

"Did she talk to Cressida?"

"She says she didn't," Kersti says skeptically. "She says she felt sorry for her, that Charles was the predator. She also told me Cressida was pregnant."

Kersti lets her bombshell land and then adds, "Mr. Fithern told her after Cressida fell."

"What a mess," Alison says. "I can't believe she told you all that."

"They both think Cressida jumped," Kersti says. "Which frankly I find rather convenient."

Alison dips the corner of a tortilla chip into the guacamole and nibbles on it.

"I'm going to Lausanne next month," Kersti says. "I was asked to speak as one of the One Hundred Women of the Lycée."

Alison laughs out loud. "What an honor."

"Well, I'm also going to be moral support for Cressida's mother,"

Kersti adds, playing down the reunion. "She's going to talk to Bueche about opening an investigation—"

"Bueche," Alison repeats, her tone full of disdain.

"Why are you so bitter about the Lycée?"

When Alison doesn't respond, Kersti says, "You weren't even friends with Cressida at the end. You seemed pretty happy there. Your whole life revolved around sports, which you love. You were the star of every team—"

"Thank God for sports," Alison says, and Kersti isn't sure if she's being facetious. "The skiing was good," she adds offhandedly.

"Remember Mahler?" Kersti says, rolling up her taco into a tight cigar. "*What are you doing, you silly twits? Three hits, you ugly spinsters!*"

"Give the ball to Alison, *schwachköpfe*!"

They giggle together at the memory, but Alison's mood has clearly sunk. There's a shadow over her eyes, a distance that wasn't there before. "I don't see the point of reopening an investigation," she says. "It's not like anyone is going to remember anything. Whatever happened to Cressida, only Cressida knows. You're going to have to make up an ending for your next book."

"I don't believe that," Kersti says. "Someone knows something."

"And you think they're going to share it with you?"

"I think Deirdre should reopen an investigation, that's all. She deserves to know the truth. Something isn't right and frankly I don't buy Mrs. Fithern's story."

"Are you hoping to prove Cressida jumped or that someone pushed her?"

"I'm not hoping to prove one thing or another," Kersti says. "But I think we can all agree that Cressida didn't fall off her balcony by accident. I did my part to move on and accept the Lycée's story, but

I know too much now. I want to know what happened to Cressida and I think I can get a hell of a lot closer to it in Lausanne."

Alison is staring at her, unmoved. She hasn't touched her tacos. Kersti has a strange feeling she knows something she's not saying.

"Anyway, look," Kersti says, trying to switch gears. "The main reason I contacted you is because Rafaella and Noa will be there and I thought it would be fun for us all to reconnect—"

"I can't go," Alison says.

"Because you have other commitments, or because you *can't*?"

"I just can't."

Kersti decides to leave it alone. Alison is one of those people who look really healthy on the outside—she's active and robust and outdoorsy—but underneath that rosy-cheeked façade is something starkly different, something dark and moody. That long-ago confession about her compulsive masturbating was no isolated quirk, Kersti thinks. There's a disconnect between who she presents to the world and who she really is, or whatever it is she's guarding.

"You haven't asked me about Cressida," Kersti says.

"Is she alive?"

"Yes."

"I didn't think she was a good person," Alison admits. "I still don't. She was a sociopath, if you ask me."

Kersti's hand instinctively goes to her belly and she wonders with a sickening feeling if Alison is right, and if such things are genetic.

CHAPTER 26

LAUSANNE—May 1998

"Here," Cressida says, spritzing Kersti's modest cleavage with her Chanel No. 5. It's the night of the spring Charity Ball. Lille, Noa, Raf, and Kersti are getting ready in Cressida's room. She's got the best dresses, jewelry, and makeup to choose from, as well as the most space, it being a corner room. Alison is out of their inner circle now. She hangs out with the athletic girls.

"I think you need a necklace," Raf says, giving Kersti a once-over.

Cressida nods and whips a stunning double strand of pearls from her underwear drawer. She puts it around Kersti's neck, fastens the clasp, and smiles approvingly. "Perfect," she says, her breath smelling of watermelon bubble gum. Kersti has noticed lately that Cressida is smoking a lot less and chewing gum instead. Mr. Fithern is an outspoken antismoker.

Kersti is wearing one of Cressida's dresses, a royal blue raw-silk strapless with a bell skirt that makes her feel a bit like Joan Collins. Noa says it's good with her eyes and Kersti has to admit, it does match them perfectly. It fits well, too.

She likes what she sees, until Cressida slides up behind her and dwarfs her. She's wearing a black strapless dress that pushes her breasts up and cinches her waist to the size of a wrist, with a ruffle at the bottom that barely covers her behind. She wears no jewelry, but doesn't need it. Her hair is wild, its springy coils bouncing on the slope of her pale shoulders. She's spectacular.

She scrunches her hair and shakes it out, smacks her lips twice, turns this way and that, thrusts out her breasts. "I hope Charlie likes my dress," she murmurs, uncharacteristically insecure.

"Isn't Magnus your date?" Kersti reminds her, and Cressida gives her a look.

Arndt Schultz invited Kersti to be his date, but she turned him down. He's popular at school but ugly; she didn't want to have to spend the night fending him off or being responsible for his good time. They decided as a group—Lille, Noa, Raf, and Kersti—not to go with dates, and to enjoy their last Charity Ball together.

Only Cressida is going with Magnus; he insisted. She's a bit peeved about it, complaining she just wants to hang out with the girls, but Kersti knows Mr. Fithern is the one Cressida wants to be with.

"You look gorgeous, Kersti," Lille says. "You're a Scandinavian goddess."

"Baltic," Kersti corrects, already starting to evaporate next to Cressida.

The ball is in the banquet hall of the sprawling Chateau D'Ouchy hotel, a turreted castle with a gray stone façade and orange-shingled tower on the banks of Lake Geneva. It's black-tie and open bar, even for the students. Cressida hands Kersti a vodka and orange juice. They're outside on the Lakeside Terrace, where it's easier to spike their drinks. They each have their own flasks to make the notoriously weak drinks stronger.

"Doesn't he look hot tonight?" Cressida says, admiring Mr. Fithern from a distance.

He's standing at the bar with Mrs. Fithern, talking to two other English teachers. He does look good in his tux, with his dark hair gelled and spiked out, edgier than he usually wears it. He glances over at Cressida a couple of times and holds her in his gaze.

Lille stumbles over, already drunk. Her bleached white hair is piled on top of her head in a frothy Marie Antoinette bun with loose wisps curling around her powdered face. She looks like an old-fashioned, sad-eyed doll. "Hello," she says, curtseying.

The sun hasn't even set behind the Alps and Lille is clearly not long for consciousness. She's never been able to hold her liquor well. Vodka nights usually end with her puking and blacking out. Tonight will be no different.

"Go easy, Grasshopper," Cressida says.

"I can't look Mrs. Fithern in the eyes," Lille slurs. "She called me over and Mr. F. was beside her and I had to bolt—"

"Don't say anything stupid," Cressida warns, her eyes flashing.

"I'm trying not to, but it's awkward. Aren't you uncomfortable?"

"No," Cressida responds. "Why should I be?"

"You could be a little more compassionate," Lille says, her eyes filling with tears. "She's her wife."

"*His* wife," Kersti says.

"Lille, you need to slow down," Cressida tells her, taking the drink out of her hand. "Take a break."

Lille snatches it back, spilling most of it on the front of her doll's dress. "Maybe *you* shouldn't be drinking," she huffs, and walks off.

"You know how much she loves Mrs. Fithern," Kersti reminds Cressida.

"So do I," Cressida says. "But I love *him* more."

She opens her clutch and retrieves her pack of cigarettes. She hands one to Kersti, lights both, and exhales over the railing. It's dusk and the sky is the color of salmon. The lake is dotted with rainbow-hued catamarans, behind which, east toward Vevey, the hilly vineyards of Lavaux stretch forever.

"I'm going to miss it here," Cressida says, her wistfulness catching Kersti off guard. "I've grown up here."

Kersti will miss it, too, she realizes, gazing out at the shoreline of Lac Léman. Will she even remember it in ten years? Or twenty? Will this picture of the Swiss Riviera, with the Alps rising in the distance out of its crystal blue bath, remain as bright and vivid in her memory as it does today? She tries to hold on to it, to impress each detail into her mind, but it's starting to sink in that what has turned out to be the happiest time of her life is coming to an end. She's going home soon. They all are.

She can't even imagine life without her best friends available to her at any moment, Hamidou's ubiquitous guidance, speaking French every day, traveling, mountains, Huber House and its decrepit third-floor bathroom. She can already feel the dread of having to be wrenched away from here and sent back to the place where she never felt right, or enough.

"At least you can stay here if you want to," Kersti tells Cressida, as a gentle breeze brings a layer of goose bumps to her bare shoulders. "You could live anywhere in the world. I'm the one who has to go back to Toronto."

Cressida turns, about to say something, but her gaze is hijacked, settling somewhere off in the direction of the ballroom. "That's her," she breathes, grabbing Kersti's arm. Her nails press into Kersti's skin and Kersti lets out a yelp. "In the pink Chanel suit. Oh my God. It's *her*."

"Who?"

"Amoryn Lashwood."

"Who?"

"Remember the old yearbook? She was in the picture with the two girls who got expelled. The one who bequeathed the ledger?"

As Kersti spots the woman in the pink suit talking to M. Bueche, she suddenly remembers. "Are you sure?" she says. "How can you tell?"

"She looks the same, only with shorter hair. I can't believe she's here. Let's go."

"Let's *go*?"

"Talk to her."

"About what?"

"About what happened," Cressida says impatiently. "Don't you want to know why her friends were expelled? And what was in that ledger?"

"You're going to accost a perfect stranger at the Charity Ball and ask her about a ledger from almost twenty years ago?"

"Why not?"

"Well, the better question is *why*."

"Something went down that year," Cressida says, her eyes shining with excitement. "I want to know what happened."

Kersti can tell that Cressida is drunk. She has that crazed look, which usually precedes some reckless, outrageous, and/or dangerous act, such as driving drunk or stealing a yearbook from the new library. She has another swig from her flask and pulls Kersti by the arm toward the ballroom, where Amoryn Lashwood is caught in Bueche's snare. They wait until he finally drifts away, schmoozing and hustling other helpless alumni for more donations.

Up close, Amoryn Lashwood is still very pretty. Kersti does a quick calculation and figures she must be in her early forties. Her skin is still relatively unlined, except for two deep vertical lines between her eyebrows, which make her look concerned or displeased. The pink suit *is* Chanel, Kersti can tell by the large gold buttons, which are the iconic C's, and she's extremely thin. Her hair is bobbed and so well sculpted even the lake winds don't move a strand.

They approach her and Cressida lightly touches her arm to get her attention. "Ms. Lashwood?"

The woman looks startled. "It's El-Bahz," she says, trying to place Cressida. "Mrs. El-Bahz. I haven't been Lashwood in years."

"I'm Cressida Strauss. This is Kersti. Class of '98."

Amoryn holds out her hand. A diamond ring the size of a cupcake gleams on her wedding finger. "Amoryn El-Bahz," she says. "As you already know."

"Class of '74," Cressida fills in.

"Yes. Correct." She seems even more confused by how much Cressida knows about her.

"Lashwood House is named after your grandfather, isn't it?" Cressida asks her, snatching a glass of champagne from one of the floating trays.

"He was a student in the late twenties, when they first started admitting boys," Amoryn says. "My father and his brothers also went. My uncle was a good friend of Monsieur Bueche. We have a very long history with the Lycée."

"Your year was the last year of the Helvetia Society," Cressida says. "And you were the president, right?"

The glowing petal pink of Amoryn's cheeks fades and she looks momentarily flustered. "That's true," she says, recovering her poise. "The last president, in fact. Tell me how you know so much about me. Certainly, there are more famous Lycée graduates than myself."

Kersti looks over at Cressida, wondering how she's going to proceed.

"Harzenmoser told us about your friends getting expelled for vandalizing the statue—"

"Harzenmoser?" she murmurs, her voice a thin leaf, floating in the air. "I've never known her to talk to the students."

"She doesn't usually," Kersti says, her eyes bouncing back and forth between Cressida and Amoryn.

"And did she tell you what they wrote?"

"Of course not," Cressida says, with an exaggerated eye roll. "But you must know."

"Why are you so interested in all this?" Amoryn asks her, resting a pink tweed arm on one of her jutting hip bones.

Kersti shrinks back, embarrassed, as the conversation takes a turn for the awkward. Even she has no idea why Cressida is so obsessed with whatever it was those girls wrote on the statue and their resulting expulsions.

"I just can't imagine what could get two students expelled from the Lycée," Cressida says. "No one else has ever been expelled that I know of. Bueche would never willingly give up two tuitions, not over some spray paint on a statue. And Madame Hamidou was against it—"

"Madame Hamidou," Amoryn repeats, her tone ambiguous. "How is she? I don't see her here tonight."

"She hates these things," Cressida tells her. "She calls it the 'groveling for money' ball."

Amoryn laughs and then her smile quickly goes away. "I don't know what they wrote," she says. "It was gone by morning."

"It must have been pretty offensive," Cressida perseveres. "Or incriminating?"

Their eyes lock then and Kersti is sure something passes between them. Some understanding, some transmuted secret that requires no spoken acknowledgment. Kersti is baffled, lost.

"You bequeathed a ledger in the yearbook," Cressida goes on, holding Amoryn's gaze. "All your friends did. One of them mentioned the secrets in the ledger—"

"Usually students bequeath funny memories and inside jokes," Kersti interjects.

"Usually, yes," Amoryn agrees. "But we didn't." She no longer seems upset or offended by the ambush. If anything, she seems roused, perhaps a little intrigued by Cressida's curiosity and brazenness. "Our memories weren't very funny," she says, and then she holds up her champagne flute to signal the conversation is over. "Have a nice time at the ball, girls."

As soon as she's out of earshot, Cressida says, "Something happened that year."

"Maybe one of them was sleeping with a teacher," Kersti mutters, as Magnus appears before them, glassy-eyed and beautiful.

"Hello, my love," he says to Cressida, pulling her into his arms.

She lets him sway her side to side in a silent slow dance, but her back is stiff and her face turns away from him, no doubt searching for Mr. Fithern.

CHAPTER 27

HERTFORDSHIRE—June 2016

The train glides swiftly through Edgware, North London, where the suburban landscape suddenly turns to woodlands at the border of Hertfordshire.

"Fifteen minutes to St. Alden's," Jay says, studying the app on his phone.

They boarded a Thameslink train at St. Pancras station, after having spent two days in London. They stayed at the Soho, a stylish boutique hotel on Richmond Mews, between the Tottenham Court and Leicester Square tube stations. The location was perfect, central enough to allow for as much sightseeing as they could cram into forty-eight hours. They took a double-decker bus ride, waved hello to Big Ben, made pit stops at Trafalgar Square, Kensington Palace, and Hyde Park. They went to Harrods and bought two Harrods of London onesies and two Burberry playsuits. Jay was thrilled Kersti was too pregnant to shop for clothes for herself; he couldn't stop converting the cost of everything to Canadian dollars. *This burger is thirty-five Canadian dollars! This latte is $15! This onesie is $120! Wi-Fi is $40 a night!*

They had dinner at a tourist trap pub in Covent Garden where the food was horrible and overpriced—(*my fish and chips were $40!!*)—and then they enjoyed a rain-soaked walk through Leicester

Square and down Shaftesbury Avenue to Piccadilly Circus. When they got back to the room, their hands were black from the soot in the air. The tap water turned gray as they scrubbed their hands, and neither of them could get clean in the shower. "Even my snot is black," Jay complained.

After managing to also cram in a brief visit to the National Portrait Gallery, see a play in the West End, and gorge on curry at Masala's in Earl's Court—which left her chest aflame for hours—Kersti was ready to move on.

She gazes out the window as the English countryside flies by, with her hand resting comfortably on her belly. She's nineteen weeks pregnant with twin boys, a revelation that still has her reeling.

The first Kuusk boys of their generation. Kersti saw them at her eighteen-week ultrasound. At first, they were adorably curled up against each other, sleeping head-to-toe in an upside-down spoon; and then they got restless and moved, and there they were: two distinct and irrefutable penises.

Kersti was more shocked than anything else. She was certain she was having girls. Jay wept with joy, staring dumbfounded at the screen. "My sons. My sons," he kept repeating.

Kersti's first reaction was that her parents would be disappointed. The Kuusk women breed *girls*. They have daughters. She knew as she lay there watching those beautiful little kidney beans in her belly that she was being irrational, crazy; but the yearning to fit in with her family, to feel accepted by them, is a relentless thing, its choke hold seemingly indestructible. It robbed her of being able to fully experience that moment in the ultrasound room.

But then something happened that shocked her even more. When she told her parents, they were ecstatic. Her father actually cried. Her mother danced her around the living room.

"Finally!" Paavo thundered. "One of my children is giving me a grandson!"

"Two," Kersti said.

"Two grandsons!" he cheered. "Palju õnne!"

They pulled out the vodka and toasted the good news in filmy water glasses. Her father slapped Jay on the back and kissed Kersti three times on her cheeks. "Terviseks!"

"Grandsons," Paavo whispered, his eyes watery and his cheeks flushed. "I had given up. Turns out Jay's Jew sperm is good for something!"

Kersti glanced over at Jay and laughed nervously. For the first time ever, *not* following that narrow Kuusk path has given her some value within the family.

"You're *too* happy they're happy," Jay said in the car on the way home. "You weren't this happy when we found out the sex."

"I know," she admitted. "But you know how my dad makes me feel. It's just . . . for once I've done something he's proud of. For once."

Jay sighed. "I'm glad my Jew sperm could help," he said, and then dropped it.

It's a thirty minute-ride to St. Alden's, where the St. Alden's School for Boys is cozily nestled beside one of the oldest abbeys in England. Kersti's been doing research and, as it turns out, Mr. Fithern hasn't done too badly for himself. St. Alden's School has one of the best reputations in the country. Their website's wordy "Ethos" promises to "provide an excellent education whereby young men will achieve the highest standard of academic success and develop character and self-discipline."

They must not have known when they hired Mr. Fithern that he was fleeing a scandal in Switzerland, and that he was completely devoid of both character and self-discipline. He obviously fooled them, just like he fooled everyone at the Lycée.

As the train moves deeper into Hertfordshire, Kersti stares out the window at the rolling green hills, with its hamlets of Tudor cottages, weeping willows, and patches of purple anemones. A lovely brook shimmers alongside their train, as though rushing valiantly to keep up with it. The sun is shining for the first time since they landed at Heathrow, transforming the scenery from the wet gray blur of London into a bright, colorful postcard.

"You know," Jay says. "We could just spend our time chilling and exploring. We don't have to visit that teacher—"

"Yes, we do."

"Why?"

She looks at him as though he's gone mad. "Because Cressida is literally a part of me now," she says. "I have to do this for her, Jay. I have to do this for all of us."

When they arrive at the Inn at London Colney, a restored red-brick coach house next to the Colne River, Kersti wanders the grounds while the sun is still shining, figuring it might be her only opportunity to take in the view before the sky turns dark and opens up and the damp chill returns to the air.

The inn faces a Tudor-style public house across the river, accessible only by a honey-colored stone footbridge canopied by willow trees and oaks blooming with catkins. Kersti heads off toward the bridge while Jay goes inside to check them in. She stands there for a little while, staring down at the rippling water, listening to the orchestra of birds. She notices a small owl staring at her from the branch of an oak tree, his round eyes fixed on her intently, his body perfectly still.

She peers down into the river, which is a significant drop. She thinks about Cressida tumbling from her balcony onto concrete and a wave of nausea pushes its way up into her throat. She's so close to Lausanne now. In another two days, she'll be pulling into the Gare, just as she did a little over twenty years ago. Only this time she'll be with Jay, not her mother. Now she's a grown woman, a success on all fronts, no one's shadow anymore. The babies move inside her and it feels like flapping butterflies. It still surprises her, the force of their sudden movements, how strong they already are.

After a two-hour nap, Kersti and Jay have supper at the inn, in its traditional wood-beamed pub with planked floors, paneled wood walls, and knotty pine tables sturdy enough to endure centuries of pint-slamming. They both order the shepherd's pie.

"I know we've talked about this," Jay says, drawing closer to her. "But now that we're actually here, are you sure you want to go see this creep tomorrow?"

"I need to see him," she says. "I want answers."

"You think he has them?"

"I think he has some," she says. "At the very least, I want him to know I have his dirty little love notes. I want him to remember what he did, and know that I know. I want to see his face when he reads them in front of me."

"He's not the one who pushed her, though," Jay says. "He wasn't there. That much you know for sure."

"Doesn't matter. If it hadn't been for their affair, Cressida wouldn't have wound up a vegetable for life. The fact is she was sixteen when it started. Regardless of how selfish or callous she was, she was still impressionable. He was the adult, and he took advantage of her—"

"And you're going to make him pay?"

"No one else did," Kersti says. "Look around at this charming little village. He's teaching at one of the most prestigious schools in England. It's a storybook. Tell me how he's ever paid for what he did?"

"I'm not disputing the fact that he's a douchebag. I'm just saying I don't want you to come away from this more upset or unsatisfied than you already are."

"It seems to me like he got off scot-free," she says. "I want to let him know I'm still out there and *I* know, and I'll never forget, even if he has. Besides," she adds, "I want to ask him flat out if he thinks his ex-wife might have pushed Cressida off her balcony."

"He's not going to tell you."

"Not with words," she says. "But he'll have a tell."

The next morning, Kersti leaves Jay sleeping in the lumpy four-poster bed and goes downstairs for a delicious English breakfast of eggs and bacon in the shaded courtyard. The sun is shining, though it's weaving in and out of the clouds, not quite sure if it's going to stay. A late spring breeze curls around as it passes through the courtyard, carrying with it the sweet fragrance of phlox from the inn's garden. Kersti gazes distractedly at the footbridge, which she can see from where she's sitting, her mind on Mr. Fithern.

You may not remember me, but I was Cressida's best friend at the Lycée. . . .

She checks her phone for the time.

"More tea?" the server asks her.

"No, thank you," Kersti says, lifting her new unwieldy body out of the chair. "Can you tell me what bus I take to get to the St. Alden's School?"

"It's just up the London Road a few miles," she says. "I can ask Nigel to drive you. We've got a car."

"That would be great," Kersti says. "I appreciate it."

St. Alden's is much the same as London Colney—a secluded, picturesque English village of weeping willows and hobbit-style cottages clustered around its most precious jewel, the ancient abbey. The abbey itself sits imperiously on a hilltop, where it has watched over the tranquil village since the eleventh century. Its long nave inclines up toward the sky, like it's proudly thrusting out its chin. The pomp and magnificence of the building, with its two turrets, central cross tower, and fabled setting, is breathtaking.

She walks along the hill toward the sprawling campus of St. Alden's School, which faces the abbey on the west side. She easily finds the main building, a great stone and redbrick castle with white dormer windows and the words ST. ALDEN'S SCHOOL MAIN ENTRANCE carved into its façade. In the front office, she tells the secretary she's a former student of Mr. Fithern visiting from Canada and asks if there would be an appropriate time to see him today.

"Mr. Fithern's on the field all morning for PE," the secretary says. "He'll be there till morning break. Best to wait out by the cricket pitch for him." She points out the window to a vast field behind them. "See out past the rugby field?"

"I'll find it. Cheers."

Kersti strolls the grounds, not in any rush. She still has an hour before he's done. She's nervous and excited, still can't quite believe she's here and about to see Mr. Fithern. The Lycée legend and likely link to Cressida's tragic ending.

When she reaches the cricket pitch, she sits down on one of the teak benches on the sidelines and scans the field. She spots him immediately, wearing Dockers and a light blue button-down, holding a clipboard and calling out to the boys who are running around in white uniforms. How anticlimactic, she thinks. She remembers his spiky black hair and Doc Martens boots from back in the nineties, and realizes what a disappointment aging is, what a status leveler. The sex symbol of her youth is now a balding cricket coach in Dockers.

He notices her sitting there and does a double take. She can tell he's trying to place her—he's squinting and straining—and then a shadow of recognition comes over his face and his lips form a pencil-thin line. He remembers her. Their eyes lock and he holds up both hands, letting her know he'll be another ten minutes. Then he turns away, back to his cricket game, his mind probably racing. She watches him with his students, not surprised by how much they seem to like him. He has an easy way about him, he always did, and Kersti can see how well he relates to boys. She can hear them from where she's sitting, bantering, teasing, arguing.

"Leadbetter's just been in to bat, Mr. F.! How's he up again?"

"Wait till they've bowled out and then you'll be up."

"Mr. F. I've been twelfth man since the beginning of the innings!"

"Wide ball!"

"Mr. F., that wasn't a bloody wide ball!"

"Peters, get your head out of your arse and bowl!"

Kersti doesn't have a clue what's going on, but it looks like a cross between baseball and lawn bowling. The game finally wraps up and the boys all stampede off the field. Mr. Fithern approaches Kersti, his expression wary and serious.

"You were at the Lycée in Lausanne," he says, as she stands up to greet him. She can see up close his teeth are a bit yellow. She used to think he looked like Sid Vicious, which seems absurd to her now.

"Kersti Kuusk," she says. "I was Cressida Strauss's best friend."

He flinches at the mention of Cressida's name. Kersti can't quite read him, but guesses a lot of shit must be churning behind his impassive face—guilt, embarrassment, discomfort, curiosity. Or maybe he's contemplating having her removed from the grounds. "You've traveled to England to see *me*?" he asks, sounding quite stupefied. "After all these years?"

"I'm actually on my way to Lausanne for their centennial."

He doesn't acknowledge either her pregnancy or the Lycée's birthday.

"I really felt I needed to see you," she tells him, as straightforward as she can put it.

"I'm, uh, shocked, to say the least," he stutters. "You've rather caught me off guard."

"Well, that was the point."

"It's not easy to disappear these days, is it?" he says, laughing awkwardly. "Bloody LinkedIn."

"Not everyone wants to disappear." She looks around. "You seem to have done very well. This place is magical."

"I've been very lucky."

"Yes," she says. "You have."

He rocks back on his heels, watching her. He has a nervous energy, like an animal in a trap. Maybe he thinks she's here to blackmail him.

"Can I ask you something?" she says.

"I imagine that's why you're here."

"Did you ever really love her?"

He exhales a long breath. "I was young," he says. "I married too young and too hastily. I was a kid myself—"

"You were almost thirty. Cressida was sixteen."

"She was no ordinary sixteen. But that's not the point, obviously. It was a mistake. A terrible mistake, one I shall never be able to undo or make amends for."

"You never went to see her."

"I hardly think that would have been appropriate," he says, running a hand through what's left of his thinning hair. "I was busy sorting out the mess I'd made of my marriage, my job. I'd hurt enough people, ruined enough lives. I wasn't about to go to America and inflict more pain on poor Cressida and her family."

"You never answered my question. Did you love her?"

"I thought I did. I really did."

"Mrs. Fithern told me you thought Cressida jumped."

"Mrs. Fithern?"

"Your ex. Mrs. Brains-Chowne."

"You spoke to Annie?"

Kersti nods, watching his pupils spread into black pools.

"She said you thought Cressida tried to kill herself," Kersti says. "To punish you because you didn't want the baby."

Mr. Fithern turns gray, the color draining so quickly from his skin he looks like a cadaver. He glances nervously out to the field, making sure no players are straggling around within earshot.

"What do you want from me, Kersti?" he says. "It was a lifetime ago. I fucked up, I was young and I fucked up. I hurt people. But I've tried to move on and be a better man—"

"Cressida doesn't get to move on."

"I didn't push her off that balcony!"

"Do you think your ex-wife might have?"

He takes a step back, flabbergasted. "*That's* what you're here for?" he says. "Oh, good God, no. Of course not. Absolutely not."

"Why not?"

"Annie?" he cries. "*Annie?* Really? Never."

"So you really do think Cressida jumped?"

"I thought it was possible at the time, yes. She was a little . . .

she was a very troubled girl, you had to have known that. She had a drinking problem. I wasn't the first one to come along and cause damage. I found her like that."

"But Mrs. Fithern had to be angry," Kersti says. "You humiliated her at the school where she was adored by everyone! We both know how much she adored Cressida, and she was the housemother on duty. How could she not have gone to her room to confront her? You do know that Magnus Foley told her about your affair that night?"

"Yes, but Annie already knew. *She knew.* The way a wife knows. It wasn't a shock hearing it from Magnus Foley. He didn't trigger some rage that made her run up to Cressida's room and throw her off the balcony. That's ludicrous."

"She may have suspected about the affair," Kersti perseveres. "But she didn't know that any of the students knew. She found out from Magnus that night that everyone at the Lycée was about to find out."

"She's barely a meter and a half!" he cries. "How could she possibly throw Cressida off a balcony?"

"Cressida was wasted. It would have been easy to shove her—"

"Exactly, Kersti. Cressida was wasted. She was reckless, careless, and she had a death wish at the best of times. She could have jumped, or she could have fallen by accident like they said. Hell, for all we know, she may have been standing on that railing like a tightrope walker. That's the kind of girl she was, Kersti. Or have you forgotten?"

Kersti remembers the car accident with Magnus. Remembers her leaning over her balcony railing and shouting, "I'm the queen of the world!"

"I still don't understand why everyone was so quick to rule out a crime," Kersti says. "She had hurt so many people, your wife most of all. And what a coincidence Mrs. Fithern was the teacher on duty that night—"

"Kersti, I don't know who or what has planted this seed in your head after all this time, but Annie wouldn't kill a mosquito if it was sucking her blood."

"The timing of Cressida's fall prevented the scandal from erupting, and it also took care of the baby—"

"I think you should go," he says.

"Are you protecting Mrs. Fithern because you still feel guilty about what you did?"

He shakes his head. "I won't stand here and have us both attacked," he says. "I have to get back. Is there something else you want from me?"

"One more thing," she says.

His shoulders slump.

"Cressida's mother gave me these," she says, taking the letters from her handbag. "We're going to pursue this. Deirdre may file criminal and civil charges for sexual abuse—"

"What are they?"

"I can only imagine the things Cressida must have written back to you," Kersti says. "Actually, I can't, but I do know that if Mrs. Fithern had ever found them . . . if she'd ever read them . . ."

She hands him the notes and watches him read the first one, waiting for his shocked reaction, for the horror and shame to rush to his face as it all comes back to him. He reads the next one and another after that, until he's read them all. His expression remains blank, bewildered. No tell.

He looks up at Kersti and says, "I don't understand. Who are they from?"

"Cressida's mother kept them. You've got to admit, they're very disturbing. In the wrong hands, you can see they're incriminating. You were going to leave your wife; the gossip would have destroyed her. These could be evidence if there's ever an investigation—"

"Evidence of what?"

Kersti is beginning to lose hope that he might reveal some useful bombshell, some admission that, yes, Mrs. Fithern *was* angry. In fact, she was so enraged she threatened to kill them both, or something dramatic and prophetic like that.

"I never wrote any of this," he says. "That's not my writing. Nor my, er, style."

"To C from C? Please. She told me what you were like. I saw the bruises. Who else could it be?"

"I've no idea who the hell wrote these. It's not my handwriting. I'd take a test if I thought it would assuage you, but I don't think anything will."

"Who else could possibly have sent her these?"

"Magnus?"

"They're from C. You're the only C—"

"I'm sorry, Kersti. I can see you're still in a lot of pain, you've had no closure, I can understand that. But I'm as baffled as you. Cressida obviously had other lovers. I didn't write those letters. Do whatever you want with them."

Not what Kersti was hoping to hear. She looks hard into his eyes, searching for that elusive tell that might betray him, something to reveal he's lying, but there's nothing other than genuine bewilderment. He doesn't seem the least bit concerned about what she might do with these letters. Unless he's the world's best bluffer.

"Maybe you should let it go," he says. "If the Lycée wants something covered up, it'll bloody stay covered up."

They stare at each other for a few tense moments before he turns and walks off.

As she leaves the field, her heart is pumping. She's excited, vibrating with adrenaline. She may not have heard what she wanted to hear today but the mystery is only deepening. *Who the hell is C?*

She looks back once as Mr. Fithern disappears into one of the buildings and then she quickens her pace, almost running to get back to Jay and tell him her news.

She's going to officially abandon *The Jewel of Reval* and write this story, wherever it takes her. She can already feel that creative euphoria kicking in. It's been there all along, percolating in her mind, teasing her, but until now she's felt an obligation to finish the Estonian novel. No more. This story is demanding to be birthed. And it's not just Cressida's story; it's Kersti's story, too.

CHAPTER 28

LAUSANNE—June 1998

A few weeks after the Charity Ball, Lille and Kersti are lying on Cressida's bed, watching her straighten her hair—an arduous, painstaking process that she's doing merely to kill time. The calendar beside her mirror has red X's on every day, counting down to graduation.

The door is open and Mme. Hamidou walks past with the mail. As usual, Angela Zumpt is trailing after her like a loyal dog. She's Hamidou's pet, always telling on people who smoke in their rooms or stay up past curfew. Acting like she's been specially appointed to enforce the house rules.

"Cress-ee-da," Hamidou says. "A package for you." She tosses a padded manila envelope onto the bed and disappears, Angela at her heels.

"Probably more bubble gum from Deirdre," Cressida mutters, ignoring the package.

"You don't look like you," Kersti says, as one-half of Cressida's usually untamed hair lies flat and smooth against her perfect skull. The room smells of singed hair.

"Good," she says. "Maybe Magnus will hate it."

"You're going to see him tonight?"

Cressida sets the hot iron down on the edge of her sink. "I have to tell him," she says, her lips making a pretty pout.

"You're going to tell him about Mr. Fithern?"

"I'm going to tell him there's someone else. I won't mention Mr. Fithern. But I can't keep doing this."

"But where can it go with Mr. F.?" Lille says, trying to be the voice of reason. "There's no future."

Cressida's pout explodes into a wide smile. "Charlie and I are going to travel around Europe this summer," she confesses. "He's leaving her."

"He's leaving Mrs. F.?" Lille cries, horrified. "To be with *you*? But you're his student—"

"He's in love with me. He's going to tell her as soon as school ends."

"What about his job?"

"He can teach anywhere."

"You can't break up a marriage—"

"It's already done," Cressida says. "Besides, he was never in love with her."

"Yes, he was," Lille argues. "She was the smartest woman he ever met."

"That was before he met me," Cressida boasts. "Now he gets beauty and brains."

"He moved here to teach with her," Lille says. "Of course he loved her."

"Like a best mate or a little sister," Cressida clarifies, probably quoting Mr. Fithern verbatim. "It was never passionate. Not like what we have."

Cressida turns her back to them and resumes straightening her hair. The iron makes a *ssssss* sound as it fries her curls into submission.

"Do you ever think about what you're doing to her?" Kersti asks Cressida.

"Who? Mrs. Fithern?"

"Yes."

"No."

"How can you not? Don't you love her?"

"Yes, but I told you, I love him more. And I love *me* more," she says. "If Charlie and I are meant to be together, which we are, why should I let her have him? So that we can all be miserable? Just because it's the right thing?"

"Yes!"

"That's absurd," she says. "I'm not going to live my life by default. They're not meant for each other or else he never would have fallen in love with me. I'm setting her free. She'll be happier with someone else. Her soul mate is out there."

"So you're doing her a favor," Lille quips.

"I'm doing what needs to be done. For all of us."

"Even Magnus," Kersti says, not that it makes any difference anymore. Kersti is going home in just a few weeks, probably never to see him again.

"I don't love him anymore."

"He really loves you, you know," Lille says, her voice breaking.

"It's just a trivial high school thing between us."

"*He* doesn't think so," Kersti says, reaching across the bed for the package.

"He'll figure it out eventually."

"Why don't you just finish the year?" Lille says. "Let him think the long-distance thing is the reason it's ending."

"I can't keep pretending," Cressida says. "It's making me resent him."

"He's going to be crushed," Lille murmurs.

"I have no control over how Magnus feels," Cressida responds coolly. The same thing she said to Kersti almost three years ago. Kersti has to wonder if it's the victory over another woman—a beloved teacher no less—along with the inevitable upheaval of the Lycée's complacent, embryonic world, that gives Cressida the real rush, or does she actually love Mr. Fithern?

Not long ago, Cressida asked Kersti if she was a bad person for always expecting to get her way. Kersti wouldn't answer any differently today. The truth is, Cressida genuinely believes she's doing the right thing. She knows no other way but to follow that intuitive voice inside her, whether it resides in her heart or her gut or the most spoiled, damaged part of her brain. Whatever it is, she's following something instinctual, the only compass she's ever known. How can that make her bad?

Kersti glances down and checks the postmark on Cressida's package. "It's from Brussels," she says, looking up. "A. El-Bahz—"

Cressida drops her hot iron in the sink and grabs the package out of Kersti's hands. "It's from Amoryn Lashwood—"

Kersti jumps off the bed and stands behind Cressida as she attacks the envelope with scissors. "Holy shit," she gasps, holding up a leather book the size of a diary. "It's the ledger."

CHAPTER 29

LAUSANNE—June 2016

Lausanne is like a dream. Walking up Rue Marterey toward the Lycée, Kersti experiences a visceral sense of nostalgia. Although most of the shops have changed, it could be 1995. Everything comes back to her at once—the snippets of singsong Swiss French, the Migros grocery store on the corner, the patisserie windows beckoning her inside with their artful *fruïts Charlotte* and *St. Honorés.* Lausanne is a feeling for her, distinct and timeless, as much as it is a place.

"I need one of those," she says, pointing to the window of a patisserie. Jay follows her inside and she orders two cheese tartlets. "One for each of the boys," she explains. They've started referring to the babies as "the boys."

Jay orders an apricot tart and they continue walking toward Avenue de Béthusy, which will take them to the Lycée.

They arrived last night by train. Flying would have been quicker and easier, but Kersti insisted on taking the Eurostar to Paris and then the TGV to Lausanne. She tried to convince Jay that traveling through Europe by train was part of the experience, the only way to do it. "Easy for the person exempt from schlepping luggage to say," he countered.

This morning, after gorging on fresh baked croissants with Hero strawberry jam and Suchard hot chocolate—her favorite

Swiss brands, which she's never been able to find in Toronto—they decided to walk from their hotel to the school, stopping as necessary so Kersti could either rest, pee, eat, or show Jay the sights. Their first stop was Place St. François to see the church, and then on to Rue de Bourg for a Coca and a pizza at Chez Mario, where Kersti celebrated her sixteenth birthday. Even the graffiti on the walls was still there, and she was able to show Jay where she and Cressida and Lille had scribbled their names.

As they continue strolling hand in hand toward the Lycée, Kersti's memories are becoming more intense. Not just concrete memories or linear recollections, but sensory memories. The grape soda smell of lupine flowers, the glacier blue of the lake from her window, the feel of cobblestone beneath her shoes.

"I'm feeling really sentimental," she says.

"It's probably your hormones."

"Mm."

It's easier for her not to try to explain it. It was here in Lausanne, at the most impressionable age in a girl's life, that she first felt everything meaningful, worthwhile, life altering. Enchantment. Desire. Acceptance. Belonging. Connection. Loss.

She became who she is *here*, in the absence of her family and their expectations; in relation to Cressida; when she lost her virginity to someone who didn't love her back. And in that moment when she found out her best friend, equal parts soul mate and nemesis, had fallen from her balcony.

"You crying?" Jay asks, touching her wet cheek.

"Being here is just bringing up so much. . . ."

He pulls her close and they walk along, his arm around her waist, her head resting on his shoulder.

Deirdre is waiting for them in the Lycée garden when they

arrive. It takes Kersti a moment to recognize the woman sitting next to her on the bench, and then she cries out, "Madame Hamidou!"

Hamidou looks toward Kersti, lifts her sunglasses, and says, "Mon Dieu! Mademoiselle Kuusk!"

She springs to her feet and holds out her arms. They hug tightly and Kersti is flooded with affection. "You're still here!" she exclaims.

"What else can I do?" Hamidou says. "I'm an old lady. I've been living off campus at 14 Béthusy, but I miss Huber House. I'm going to move back here in September."

Her short hair is completely white now. She's more petite than Kersti remembers, and a little frailer, but otherwise the same. Her chocolate brown eyes are twinkling with pleasure as she looks Kersti up and down and hugs her again.

"And what's in here?" Hamidou asks, touching Kersti's pregnant belly.

"Twin boys," Kersti announces.

"Congratulations," she says, beaming.

"Twin boys?" Deirdre squeals, jumping to her feet and embracing Kersti. "Why didn't you tell me?"

"I waited to tell you in person," she says. "We just found out."

Kersti remembers Jay, standing quietly behind her, and gently pulls him forward. "This is my husband, Jay."

Hamidou pumps his hand and Deirdre throws her arms around him. Whether he likes it or not, they have a powerful bond now, a lifelong connection. It still feels surreal to Kersti. Jay's sperm and Cressida's eggs growing inside *her* body.

"I'm going for a walk," Jay tells her. "I'll meet you at the hotel later." He waves good-bye to them and saunters off toward the garden.

"I was just showing Madame Hamidou some pictures of Sloane," Deirdre says.

"She look exactly like Cress-ee-da," Hamidou says, her eyes glistening with tears. "It's like looking at an *esprit*." The lines in her face sink deeper into themselves and she suddenly looks ancient, mournful.

"Sloane will be here Saturday for the ceremony."

"I can't wait to meet her," Hamidou says, brightening, forcing a smile. She still has that gap between her front teeth.

A young girl of about fourteen or fifteen approaches them. She's lovely, with long dark hair and licorice black eyes. "Bonjour, Madame Hamidou," she says.

"Bonjour, Amandine." Hamidou introduces the girl to Kersti and Deirdre. "Amandine is one of our top students," she says. "She's getting the maths award on Saturday. She's the first sophomore ever to receive it."

"Congratulations," Kersti says, envying the girl's youth, her brightness, all the promise that lies ahead like rolling Swiss hills.

"Right now Amandine and I have a science class to get to," Hamidou says. "A plus tard."

When they're alone, Deirdre links her arm in Kersti's. "I found out something interesting," she says.

"What time are we speaking to Monsieur Bueche?"

"Now," she says. "But listen to me. I did a little snooping."

Kersti lets Deirdre lead her up the path toward Bueche's office. "I had my lawyer look into Cressida's police investigation," she says. "It turns out the lead detective was Gavin Lashwood."

"Lashwood?" Kersti repeats. "That doesn't make any sense. Aren't the Lashwoods American?"

"Gavin Lashwood graduated from the Lycée in 1959," she explains. "*The same year as Bueche.*"

"They were good friends," Kersti says, remembering something

Amoryn Lashwood said at the Charity Ball years ago. "Bueche and Amoryn Lashwood's uncle were friends at the Lycée—"

"Bueche went on to *université* here and then started teaching at the Lycée. Gavin Lashwood married a Swiss girl and stayed in Lausanne. He became a gendarme for the Vaud police."

"So he was the detective who investigated Cressida's accident? Have you spoken to him?"

"He died," Deirdre says. "Lung cancer two years ago."

"He must have covered something up for Bueche," Kersti says. "It's too much of a coincidence."

Deirdre stops suddenly and faces Kersti. Her expression changes without any warning. "I should have done something years ago," she says, her voice trembling. "I should have demanded an investigation right after it happened."

"Deirdre, you were in shock—"

"I didn't even go to Lausanne," she says. "I didn't ask any questions. Not even about the note or how quickly they wrapped up the investigation—"

"You were dealing with Cressida back home."

"I didn't want to know," she admits. "That's the truth, Kersti. I was too scared to know the truth. And now it's probably too late."

"Whatever Bueche and Harzenmoser covered up, we can find out."

Deirdre nods, sniffling. She puts on her Chanel sunglasses, the large lenses covering most of her face. "I failed her," she says, as they continue on to Bueche's office.

"Everyone did."

M. Bueche is one of those ageless men who could be in their fifties or sixties. If Kersti didn't know, she never would have guessed seventy-four. He still has all his hair, dyed a dark chestnut brown and smoothed back with gel, and good white teeth that may or not be real. He always dressed well, favoring ascots and pocket squares with his blazers. A man for whom the word *debonair* was invented.

"Madame Strauss," he says solemnly, shaking Deirdre's hand. "Kersti, welcome back. And congratulations on being one of our One Hundred Women."

His English is perfect. There's no trace of a French or German accent. Kersti realizes she has no idea where he's from. She always thought of him as being generically European.

"How's Cressida?" he asks Deirdre, sitting down at his desk.

"She's basically a vegetable," Deirdre responds tersely. "So I'm not sure how to answer your question."

"I'm sorry," he says contritely. "It must be hard for you."

The French windows behind Bueche are wide open and Kersti has a perfect view of the back garden and vast green lawn that leads to the tennis courts. Lausanne in June is a thing of beauty, something Kersti had almost forgotten.

There's an antique cuckoo clock on the wall, alongside framed photographs of Bueche with faculty from eras past, including several with Mme. Harzenmoser. Kersti recognizes one of him with M. Mahler, holding up a trophy.

"What happened to Monsieur Mahler?" Kersti asks, staring at the picture.

"Mahler? He retired years ago. He's eighty-five and in fine form. He visits occasionally. Comes to cheer on the teams."

"And Madame Harzenmoser?"

"She's in a home nearby," he says. "She may be at the ceremony tomorrow, if she's well enough."

Kersti notices a photograph on Bueche's desk of him with his wife, children, and grandchildren at Ouchy. Something else Kersti never knew about him. He has a family. When you're a teenager, you really don't think about the grown-ups around you as having a life. You don't think about who they are as people. How old they are. Do they have kids. What do they do outside school. These things never crossed Kersti's mind about any of the teachers at the Lycée, perhaps other than the Fitherns.

"That's why we wanted to speak with you," Deirdre says. "Kersti and I have been revisiting Cressida's fall."

"Revisiting it?"

"Asking ourselves questions we should have asked when it happened."

When Bueche doesn't say anything, she continues. "We're both convinced it wasn't an accident."

Bueche leans back in his chair, his gaze unflinching. He has dark brown eyes—intelligent, incisive—and Kersti considers he must have been quite handsome back in the nineties.

"Madame Strauss," he says, in his deep velvet voice. "It was almost twenty years ago."

"Yes," Deirdre acknowledges. "But we have new information."

"New information about what?"

"About the circumstances surrounding her fall."

Kersti watches him carefully. If he's the least bit uncomfortable, she can't tell. His demeanor is calm. Relaxed, even.

"Did you know Cressida was having an affair with her history teacher?" Deirdre asks him. "Charles Fithern?"

"I remember hearing something about it after the fact. After both of the Fitherns resigned."

"Did anyone ever question the fact that Mrs. Fithern was the teacher on duty at Huber House the night my daughter fell?"

"Madame Strauss," he says. "We didn't know anything about the affair then. Of course we spoke to Mrs. Fithern that morning. We asked her what she'd seen, what she'd heard, if anything unusual had happened the night before—"

"And what did she tell you?"

"From what I remember, there was nothing unusual."

"Did she tell you Cressida's boyfriend, Magnus Foley, was at Huber House that night?" Kersti asks him. "That he went there to see Mrs. Fithern? And that he told her about the affair?"

The expression on M. Bueche's suntanned face turns grim.

"Did any students ever mention seeing Magnus that night?" Kersti asks.

"Not that I recall."

"Did anyone—either you or the police—ever question the students?" Deirdre interjects, her voice rising.

"I'm sure we did," Bueche responds, a fleck of defensiveness coming into his tone. "It's hard to remember after all this time, but I'm sure the police spoke to the students."

"The police never spoke to *me*," Kersti says. "Or Lille. Lille is the one who saw Magnus leaving Huber that night."

"I guess the police were satisfied that Cressida's fall was accidental," he reasons. "Cressida was very intoxicated. I remember she had a very high blood alcohol level—"

"And when you found the suicide note?" Deirdre produces the note from inside her purse and shoves it at him.

"I found no such note," he says in defense. "Your husband found it."

"And what happened then?"

"Monsieur Strauss asked me why the note hadn't been found sooner."

"Why hadn't it?"

"It was hidden in one of Cressida's books. Your husband found it when he was packing her things. It wasn't deliberate on the school's part to keep it a secret."

"How could the police not have found it, Monsieur Bueche? Didn't they search her room?" Kersti asks him. "Why didn't they bother to look for evidence? Why didn't they ever interview *us*?"

"I can't speak to what the police did or didn't do—"

"Can't you?" Deirdre says fiercely. "Wasn't the detective your best friend?"

"Our friendship would never have interfered with a case," Bueche says hotly. "I take offense to that. As I'm sure Gavin would have."

"Cressida was pregnant," Kersti says. "The baby was Mr. Fithern's, which is a motive in itself. Mrs. Fithern also had opportunity—"

"Cressida was pregnant?"

"Why wasn't a proper investigation conducted?" Deirdre wants to know. "Your friend Gavin didn't turn up any information, it seems. Not the affair, not the note, not the pregnancy. He must not have been a very good detective."

"Madame Strauss—"

"Why was the case closed so quickly?"

"I understand how unpleasant this must be for you—"

"*Unpleasant?*" Deirdre repeats, her lips curling into a sneer. "I lost my daughter, Monsieur Bueche. She would have been better off dead! It was a lot more than 'unpleasant.'"

"It was a tragedy," he agrees, placating her. "A terrible tragedy. Madame Harzenmoser and I brought in the police at once and gave them everything they needed to conduct their investigation. We opened up the school to them. *Whatever they needed.* But if Detective Lashwood ruled it an accident, it wasn't our place to disagree or challenge him."

"He ruled it an accident by nine o'clock in the morning?" Kersti says. "How is that even possible?"

"Are you accusing me of something?"

"Yes," Deirdre responds, straightening her back. "Of persuading your friend to say it was an accident and shut the whole investigation down as quickly as possible."

"There was plenty of evidence to warrant a proper investigation," Kersti adds. "But that would have been terrible publicity for the Lycée. It would have damaged your reputation."

"Of course it would have," says Bueche. "But I wouldn't have stood in the way of an investigation. I don't have that kind of pull with the police."

"We know how important the Lycée's reputation is."

"The students matter far more—"

"Monsieur Bueche," Deirdre implores softly. "You didn't want talk of suicide or extramarital affairs with students or the whiff of a possible crime to go public, so you asked your school chum to cover it up. At least tell us the truth. It's not a crime.

"I'm accountable, too," Deirdre continues. "I stood by and allowed it to be covered up. I let you and Madame Harzenmoser do nothing because I was protecting Cressida's reputation—"

"Mrs. Strauss," Bueche says, still cool and composed. "The truth is the gendarmes did search Cressida's room that morning. What they found was a half-empty bottle of vodka. She'd been smoking outside on her balcony. Besides that she'd had that car accident a couple of years before—"

"How did the police know about her car accident?"

"I think it was Madame Hamidou who told them when she was questioned."

"Why? It had nothing to do with anything. Why would she tell them about that?"

"She was trying to be helpful, I suppose," he says. "It showed Cressida had a history of reckless behavior and heavy drinking.

The police made their ruling based on the facts they had at the time. Did they probe enough?" He shrugs, cocks his head to the side. "Perhaps not. But I assumed they did the best they could with what they found. The suicide note came later. We didn't see any point in reopening an investigation because of the note. Who would it have served? Certainly not you or your family, Madame Strauss. Not our students." He pauses for a moment, seeming to gather his thoughts and carefully choose his next words. "I assure you that nothing I ever did was with the intent to conceal anything or protect anyone."

He stands up and comes around to the other side of the desk. "Why bring it all back up now?" he asks Deirdre, his voice softening. "Is there a point? What can be done, really?"

"If someone pushed my daughter, I want to know. At the very least, I want it acknowledged."

"It's not going to be easy after all this time," he says. "But I'll support whatever you decide. If it's what you need, I'll help any way I can. Is there something you want me to do?"

"I'll let you know," Deirdre says, standing up. "I just want to say that you did Cressida a huge disservice by impeding a proper investigation. As did I."

"Nothing was done intentionally."

"Thank you for your time, Monsieur Bueche."

Deirdre tucks her purse under her arm and hurries out of the office. Kersti notices the forgotten suicide note on Bueche's desk and grabs it.

On her way out, she remembers something and stops. "Monsieur Bueche?" she says, turning back to him. "Why did you expel those two girls in 1974?"

"I beg your pardon?" he says, confused.

"Amoryn Lashwood's friends were expelled in '74. I know it was for vandalism, but it doesn't make any sense."

"Do you know what they wrote?"

"No. But it was just a couple of words on the statue—"

"The matter was very grave."

"Students have committed far worse offenses and not been expelled," Kersti points out. "Cressida included."

"Those girls were also doing drugs and causing trouble. Madame Hamidou felt very strongly they had to be expelled and the Helvetia Society meetings banned."

"Madame Hamidou did?"

"Oh yes, she was quite passionate about it," he recalls. "She thought it was best for the school and I had to agree. It doesn't happen often that we agree, I assure you. But she convinced me it was the right thing to do for the Lycée."

CHAPTER 30

LAUSANNE—June 1998

Cressida holds the leather ledger in the palm of her hands with great reverence, as though it's some sacred text, the Bible or one of the Vedas. It's brown with embossed gold letters on the cover that say LEDGER. It reminds Kersti of her father's old bookkeeping ledgers when she was a kid. He used to sit in the den after supper with a cup of vodka and piles of receipts and invoices, and enter numbers into columns. He'd have a black pen and a red pen, and there were always a lot of red numbers on the pages.

Cressida opens it slowly, her fingers noticeably trembling. On the first page, tucked deep into the fold, there's an old photograph, square with a white border and the date in typeface. April 1974.

Cressida pulls it out. It's a picture of the Helvetia statue, flanked on either side like sentinels by two long-haired teenage girls, their solemn faces backlit by the pale moon, their hands placed defiantly on their hips. The statue has a helmet of black hair spray-painted atop, which, Kersti thinks, must have been a bitch to clean and restore in a single night. There's a word spray-painted on the Swiss cross of her shield, but it's impossible to read in the dark, grainy picture. The engraved plaque at Helvetia's feet is also defaced. Certain words in the slogan, which they can't read but know by heart—"Preparing Young Women to Become Citizens of the World"—are crossed out and scrawled over with other words, also illegible.

Cressida turns it over and discovers a handwritten note on the back.

> Do with this ledger what you wish. I've got no objections whatever you decide, only personal regrets. Amoryn El-Bahz.

"What does she mean by that?" Kersti asks her.

"I don't know," Cressida answers, but her voice has a strange tremor. "There must be something in here. . . ."

Lille is silent.

"What did they write on the statue?" Kersti says, holding the picture right up to her nose. "Can you see at all?"

"No. Can you?"

Neither Kersti nor Lille can make out the spray-painted words in the picture.

"Why would she send this to you?" Lille asks Cressida.

"I guess because I asked her about it."

"Why would they expel those girls for spray-painting a couple of words on the stupid statue?"

No one responds. Cressida opens the ledger, handling the thin yellow pages carefully between her fingers.

September 18, 1973. 23:00. Frei House.
Minutes:

Present:	Amoryn Lashwood—President
	Brooke Middlewood—Vice President
	Tatiana Greenberg—Secretary
	Caris Yaren

Fernanda Manzanares
Karen Kim
Donna Murthy

Agenda:
Initiation/ Pledge Night. Sept 30
Dinner for new Taps. [Beside which various restaurant options were scribbled]
Autumn Charitable Events:
Lycée's own Battle of the Sexes?
"Watergate" Ball ?

The dinner bell rings while the three of them still have their noses buried in the ledger, before they've even managed to get beyond the first page.

"Bring it to the dining hall," Kersti says.

"Are you crazy?" Cressida snaps. "I don't want everyone to see it."

"Who cares?"

"I have to go through it page by page."

"There's a lot," Lille says. "All the minutes from every meeting—"

"She wouldn't have sent this to me if there wasn't something worth finding in it," Cressida says.

"Check the very last page," Kersti says, growing excited at the possibility of discovering some potentially epochal secret.

Cressida quickly turns to the back page, searching for whatever shocking secret she believes lies within its hallowed pages. It's dated April 4, 1974. It says only *Easter Cuckoo Festival, Sunday Ap 14*.

The rest of the page is blank.

"Mesdemoiselles!" Hamidou shouts from the hall. "*Souper!*"

Cressida slaps the ledger shut. "Meet me back in my room after study hall," she tells them.

"I've got an AP tutorial," Lille says. "I'll come here straight after."

"I've got a volleyball match at Aiglon," Kersti says. "Playoffs."

"Then we'll meet after lights-out."

"Aren't you sneaking out to see Magnus?"

"I'll wait for you," she says impatiently. "Just come to my room as soon as you can. I'll have found something by then."

Something. That voluptuous secret, with its claws already in their flesh. What is it Amoryn Lashwood wants Cressida to know? And why Cressida? Simply because she was the one audacious enough to ask?

It's all Kersti can think about as Cressida shoves the ledger under her duvet and they file out of the room silently, giddy, conspiratorial.

On the dinner chalkboard downstairs, *Charcuterie.*

"Cold cuts," Lille mutters. They groan and split up, heading off with resignation to their assigned tables.

As Kersti rolls a cold ham slice around a *cornichon,* making a wet slimy cigar that she dips in hot mustard, her mind goes back to the ledger and the scandal they might uncover inside it. She wonders if Cressida is somehow connected to it. Why else would Amoryn write a note like that to her? *Do with this ledger what you wish.*

Kersti's excitement begins to turn to unease, a languidly creeping fear with tendrils reaching into every part of her body. She doesn't know why but she feels an ambiguous sense of dread. There's a voice in her head telling her that Cressida is somehow mixed up in something bad. Why else would she be so inexplicably consumed with what happened to those girls unless she had a personal, vested stake in it?

Kersti looks across the dining room and finds Cressida. Her heart surges. In spite of everything that's happened over the last four years, she knows they're kindred spirits. They always have been.

Their friendship isn't something Kersti ever sought or had to work hard for; it simply *was*, from day one, when they shared chopes and secrets. Cressida is the one person who's always understood Kersti, who never judged her or expected anything from her other than for her to simply be Kersti. Cressida's done hurtful things, she's made mistakes, but her love for Kersti has never been in question.

Their eyes lock. Kersti smiles but Cressida's expression is remote. She doesn't smile back.

CHAPTER 31

LAUSANNE—June 2016

Over braised lamb shanks at the Brasserie Lausanne-Moudon with Jay, Kersti rehashes her conversation with M. Bueche. "It doesn't make sense," she says, brooding. "Madame Hamidou told us she fought Bueche to keep those girls from getting expelled. Why would she lie?"

"I'm sure it's meaningless," Jay says, stabbing a potato with his fork.

"And why would she tell the police about Cressida's car accident? It was ancient history at that point. The Hamidou I remember would have protected Cressida. Not thrown her under the bus."

"Sounds like she wanted them to know Cressida had a history."

"Why, though?"

"So the investigation would wrap up quicker? Maybe it was the best way she could think to protect Cressida and the school."

"You're probably right," Kersti says. "She adored Cressida . . . more than anyone else in that school. She would have done anything for her, as any mother would."

Kersti thinks about it for a moment and then realizes Bueche almost had her. "It's Bueche who's lying," she says decisively. "His friend was the detective on the case. He's the one who covered it up, not Hamidou. He's trying to throw me off."

"Why do you think?"

"I'm sure it has something to do with the two girls who were expelled," Kersti says. "Cressida must have found something in the ledger. What if Bueche has it?"

"You'll never get your hands on it, Kerst. And now's not the time to be playing Scooby-Doo."

"I'm not playing Scooby-Doo," she mutters indignantly.

"We're having twins soon," he reminds her. "Prioritize."

"Something happened to Cressida and it was covered up. I want to know what."

"Then let Deirdre figure it out. Surely she can afford to hire a lawyer or a private investigator."

"We're here, though—"

"We're here because you've been chosen one of the Hundred Women of the Lycée."

After dinner, they go back to the hotel in silence. Jay heads up to the room while Kersti goes to the lobby lounge to wait for Noa and Rafaella. She orders a ginger ale and texts Deirdre.

Need to talk to you tomorrow. Convo with Bueche troubled me. FYI you forgot the note in his office. I've got it.

When she looks up from her phone, she spots Noa coming through the door, smiling and waving boisterously, two long braids swinging out behind her. She's wearing a loose poncho shirt, torn jeans, and Havaianas flip-flops. She looks plump and happy. She hugs Kersti hard.

"Don't crush the boys!" Kersti teases.

"Hello in there!" Noa says, crouching down so she's eye level with Kersti's belly. "Leuk je te ontmoeten!"

"You still look sixteen," Kersti tells her, fibbing to make her feel good.

"You look very well yourself," Noa says.

They sit down and Noa pulls out her phone to share photos of her kids—four apple-cheeked blonds, the spitting image of Noa's younger self.

"This is all I've got for the moment," Kersti says, pulling out her eighteen-week sonogram picture.

"I'm so happy for you," Noa says. "I have a lot of friends who went through the same thing with not such happy endings."

"We're grateful," Kersti says, withholding the bit about Cressida's eggs.

Rafaella shows up a few minutes later in a DVF wrap dress that accentuates her new fake breasts and her tiny waist. Her hair is slicked back in a ponytail, her lips inflated with collagen, her skin waxy and wrinkle-free. As with Deirdre, all the work she's had done has rendered her age a blur, contingent upon the angle at which you catch her or the lighting in the room.

"Bonjour!" she sings, hugging and air-kissing both of them. "Holy shit! Look at us."

"We're grown-ups."

"Speak for yourself," Raf says, smiling. Lipstick on her two front teeth.

They spend the first hour catching up in much greater depth than Facebook can accommodate. As Kersti gleaned, Noa is a full-time mom—hands-on, attentive, endlessly involved in her kids' lives. She bakes her own bread and forbids screens, choosing instead to fully engage with them when they're home. By her account, she's always at their schools—volunteering, fund-raising, being the class parent, going on the class trips. And in her small amount of free time, she's usually crusading to make the world a better place for them.

Raf, for all her wealth and privilege, doesn't seem to have made much of her life. She has no permanent address, no real career aside from a social column she writes for a Paris daily, no current or significant past relationship.

"Are you happy?" Noa asks Raf, leaning across the table.

"What does that mean, anyway?"

"Are you fulfilled, content? Comfortable with yourself?"

"Of course not." Raf laughs. "Are you?"

"Yes," Noa responds.

"And you, Kersti?"

"Yes," Kersti says. And in this moment, she is.

They sit in silence for a few moments, happy to be reunited even though they're a lifetime away from who they were at the Lycée.

"I saw Madame Hamidou today," Kersti tells them. "She doesn't live at Huber anymore."

"Really? I can't picture her not living there."

"Maybe she got married," Raf says.

"She wasn't wearing a ring—"

"She's asexual," Noa says. "She's married to the Lycée."

"She's moving back to Huber in the fall."

"Which proves my point," Noa says smugly.

Kersti suddenly gets that fluttering butterfly sensation in her belly. She shifts in her chair and lets out a surprised giggle. "The babies are on the move," she says.

"I miss that," Noa laments. "Seeing you like this makes me want to have another one."

"Four isn't enough?" Raf says.

"Nils and I have always talked about having six."

"Six?" Raf rolls her eyes. "Are you going to send them all to boarding school?"

"Of course not," Noa says, sounding offended. "I was only sent to the Lycée as a matter of safety. Because of my brother's kidnapping."

"Are you implying the rest of us were sent there because our parents didn't want us?"

"I'm not implying anything."

"It's true, though," Raf says. "That's why we were all so fucked up. Look at Cress."

"I prefer not to," Noa says.

"I think she tried to kill herself," Raf blurts. "No way she fell off that balcony by accident. What do you think, Kerst?"

Kersti thinks about it for a split second and then decides to tell them everything, right from the beginning. "Lille wrote to me before she died," she begins.

Raf and Noa fall silent. She's got their full attention now. She tells them about Lille's letter, her first meeting with Deirdre, their suspicions that someone might have pushed Cressida off her balcony. The subsequent conversations with Magnus, the Fitherns, M. Bueche. The half-assed police investigation. Cressida's pregnancy.

"He got her pregnant?" Noa cries.

"Wait. What if Bueche and Mrs. Fithern were having an affair?" Raf says excitedly. "Maybe Mrs. Fithern pushed Cressida and Bueche covered it up to protect her?"

"That's ridiculous," Noa says.

"Plus it doesn't explain the ledger—"

"Maybe the ledger has nothing to do with Cressida's fall," Raf says. "Or with those girls getting expelled."

"I agree," Noa says. "If anyone pushed Cressida off her balcony it was because she was sleeping with Mr. Fithern."

"Here's the suicide note," Kersti says, retrieving it from her purse. She hands it to Raf first, who reads it and makes a strange face, and then to Noa.

I will miß you. Im sorry

Noa looks up, frowning. "Who wrote this?" she asks.

"Cressida, supposedly."

"No. It wasn't Cressida."

"How do you know?"

"This is an *eszett*."

"A what?"

"*Eszett*. A 'sharp *s*.'" Noa points to the misspelling of the word *miss*, which Kersti always figured was a drunken scribble. "It says 'I will "miß" you,' the old German way."

"Are you sure?"

"It's the *eszett*," Noa states. "Only the German alphabet has that letter. Before '96, the *eszett* was always used instead of *ss*. Words like *dass* and *strass* were spelled with a sharp *s*, just like in Cressida's note."

"So the person who write the note was German?"

"Yes."

"It could just be a messy double *s*. Cress was drunk—"

"It's an *eszett*."

"Isn't Bueche German?" Raf says.

"No. Swiss French."

"Mahler was German," Kersti says. And it hits her like the kaleidoscope of blindness that precedes a migraine. Could Bueche be covering up for Mahler?

The next day, Kersti takes a taxi up to the Lycée and waits outside the chemistry lab for Mme. Hamidou. When she finally emerges in her lab coat and protective goggles, Kersti pulls her aside and asks if they can speak.

"Bien sur," she says, stuffing the goggles in her pocket.

They go outside into the sunshine, where a crowd of young smokers has gathered between classes. "They still allow smoking?" Kersti says, incredulous.

"It's Europe," Hamidou responds, lighting up a trademark Gauloises.

Kersti takes a few steps back and waves away the smoke. It would be bad enough if she weren't pregnant.

"Oh, Mon Dieu," Hamidou says, hiding the cigarette behind her back. "I'm sorry. Come."

They move away from the smokers and Hamidou throws her free arm around Kersti's shoulders. "It's so good to see you," she says. "Your year was one of my favorites. Such a special group of girls."

"I saw Rafaella and Noa last night," Kersti tells her.

"I'm looking forward to seeing them tomorrow."

"Madame?" Kersti says, not sure how to bring up what she wants to say. "I don't think Cressida fell off her balcony by accident, and neither does Deirdre. Bueche's friend was the detective in charge of the investigation. The case was closed too quickly—"

"Bueche may be an ass, but he would never cover up a crime."

"How can you be so sure?" Kersti asks her. "Wouldn't he do just about anything to protect the Lycée's reputation?"

"And its bank account."

"Exactly."

"Oui, mais quand meme . . ."

"Deirdre wants to reopen the investigation. Too many things don't add up."

"Like what?"

"There was a ledger," Kersti says. "I think Cressida discovered something in it that had to do with Monsieur Mahler and those expulsions in 1974. It went missing the day she fell—"

"Monsieur Mahler?" Hamidou says. "What could he possibly have to do with anything?"

"I have my suspicions. But . . . well, Bueche said *you* were the one who wanted those girls expelled, not him. I don't believe him, but I just wanted to check with you. . . . I think he's still trying to cover something up."

Hamidou sucks on her cigarette. "I can't imagine why he would say I'm the one who wanted them expelled. *C'est ridicule.*"

"That's what I thought. I just wanted to be sure."

"What is Deirdre going to do?"

"Go to the police, I guess."

"And what can they do now?"

Kersti shrugs. "Order a proper investigation, I hope. There's enough new evidence to warrant it."

Hamidou sighs and crushes her cigarette under her heel. "Tragique," she murmurs. "Of all my girls to have wound up this way, why Cressida?"

"Did you know she was pregnant?"

Hamidou stops. She looks straight at Kersti. "You mean when she was thirteen? She told you about the abortion?"

"No. When she fell."

Hamidou clears her throat. "She was pregnant again?"

"With Mr. Fithern's baby."

Her eyes close for a moment as she takes it in. She looks upset. "I did not," she manages. "This is the first I hear of it."

Kersti rolls onto her back and stretches.

She tucks her feet between Jay's legs, which are warm and soft under the duvet. She's piecing together a dream from last night—

she dreamed she was lost in a forest, calling out for her mother. When she was a little girl, Anni used to tell her about the swamp forest in Soomaa, just outside of Tallinn. Soomaa meant "bog land" and its many walking trails wound through the peat bogs and bog pools surrounded by dunes, the ground carpeted with mushrooms and berries. In some places, her mother told her, the thickness of the peat layer could be as tall as *four daddies*. Back then Kersti's father was like a giant to her; four times his height reached the sky. Anni's favorite trail was the Riisa because you had to walk under a giant wood wishbone to enter it. In winter, they would snowshoe or ski through the towering pines, cold and free. Kersti always wanted to go. She imagined the Soomaa forest was enchanted, magical.

"What are you thinking about?" Jay asks her.

"Estonia. I want to take the boys there one day."

"Of course we will."

Next week is June 23, Jaanipäev—the night of the Estonian summer solstice—and all she can think about is celebrating with her family. Sitting around the bonfire watching her nieces run wild, knowing that in a couple of years, her sons will be running with them.

"Maybe my parents could come to Estonia with us," she says, snuggling closer to Jay.

"They haven't been back in fifty years," he reminds her. "They'll never go back."

"I think they would."

"What for?" Jay says. "For all intents and purposes, they still live in Estonia."

"Toronto isn't Tallinn."

"Geographically, no," he says. "But that doesn't matter to them. What they love about Estonia is exactly what they've created in Toronto. It's their world. Their culture, their language, their people. Their family."

Kersti thinks about this in the context of Lausanne. Maybe Jay's right. Maybe all that sentimentality and nostalgia she feels has more to do with her memories of the experience and the people with whom she shared it. Which reminds her the Lycée is one hundred years old today.

She's been practicing her speech; she fell asleep last night rehearsing it in her head. *It's an honor and a privilege to stand up here as one of the One Hundred Women of the Lycée. I would not be here speaking about my literary career had it not been for the foundation I received as a student in the early nineties, particularly from my English teacher—*

"You nervous for today?" he asks, knowing exactly where her mind has gone.

"A bit."

"I'm proud of you," he says. "It blows my mind how you never give up on anything. You got us pregnant when I was ready to quit. You believed enough for the both of us."

"You're right about that."

He kisses the top of her head and rubs her belly. "Babe," he says. "I've been thinking. I'd like to name the boys after my Bubbe Chana and Zadie Hyman. They were really special to me."

"You want to name our sons Chana and Hyman?"

"No. I was thinking Chase and Hayden," he says, clearly bracing for a fight. "I've been pretty flexible with all the Estonian stuff, with the donor. But this is something I really want and it means a lot to me. I know the names aren't Estonian—"

"I love them."

"You do?"

"Chase and Hayden," she says, testing out the way they sound. "They're kind of perfect."

"They're not Estonian."

"I know that, and I don't care. Let's be honest, the babies aren't really Estonian, are they?"

"Really?" he says, sitting up.

"Maybe their middle names could be Nuut and Jaagup?" she jokes.

"Chase Nuut and Hayden Jaagup," he says. "I could live with that."

"Or maybe Chase Jaagup and Hayden Nutt?"

"I like that, too," he says, lying back down.

"Do you think we'll be a normal family?" she asks him.

"Of course not."

"What about happy?"

"I think it's definitely a possibility," he says pragmatically. And then, upon further reflection, he says, "Yes. Happiness is most certainly on the horizon for us."

The phone rings on Kersti's bedside table and they look at each other. Who would be calling their hotel? She reaches for it with a slight palpitation of dread.

"Mrs. Wax? There's something here for you at the front desk."

Jay is looking at her mouthing, *Who is it?*

"There's something for me downstairs," she whispers.

Kersti slides her legs out and hoists herself up off the bed, something that's becoming increasingly difficult. "I'll be right back," she says.

"I'll go down for you," Jay offers.

"It's fine, I'm also going to grab breakfast. The boys need a croissant immediately."

She bends over and kisses him, throws on one of her maternity sundresses, and heads down to the lobby. The man at the front desk hands her a blank envelope. "Who left this for me?" Kersti asks him.

"I don't know, Madame. It was left here late last night." He looks down at a logbook and then back at Kersti. "It was just after midnight."

Kersti thanks him and takes the envelope. On her way back to the elevator, she looks inside. There are two Polaroid pictures and a note. She removes one of the pictures and stops short.

With shaking hands, she shoves it back into the envelope and rushes over to the front desk. "Who was working last night when this was delivered?" she asks. "Can you look that up?"

"It was Afzal. He starts at five p.m. today."

"Can you have him call my cell phone as soon as he's in?"

"Bien sur, Madame."

Kersti stands in the middle of the lobby for a few moments, waiting for her heartbeat to slow down. Wondering who's left this for her. *And why?*

She goes back up to her room with the envelope in hand, having completely forgotten about breakfast.

"What is it?" Jay asks her. "Did you bring me a croissant?"

She wordlessly hands him the envelope.

"I don't have my glasses—"

"You don't need them," she says. "Look inside."

He opens the envelope and dumps out the contents. "Shit," he mutters, looking at the pictures. "Who left this?"

"I don't know."

"Do you know who this is?"

"No idea," she says, looking at a young naked girl, staring into the camera with a vacant expression. Haunted eyes. Hair spread out on the pillow beneath her. Breasts bare and one hand attempting to cover the patch of black pubic hair between her legs. The Polaroid looks old, possibly from the late seventies or early eighties. Kersti can tell the room is in Huber House but not much else.

"And this one?" Jay holds up the second Polaroid.

"It's Cressida," she murmurs, tears springing to her eyes.

Cressida naked. Her legs spread open, her face defiant, seductive. Posing like she wasn't the victim, which is exactly how she would have acted.

Thinking about you is written on the Polaroid in black marker. Across her body.

"That's not her room," Kersti says. "It's a room in Huber House, but not hers. That wasn't her bed—"

"Whose was it?"

"I don't know."

"What the hell was going on at that school?" Jay asks, putting on his reading glasses. "Nothing like this ever happened to you, did it?"

"No. No. Absolutely not. This is . . . I'm shocked."

"Did any of the male teachers have access to your dorm?"

"Bueche, I guess. Maybe all of them. I don't know."

She wonders now if Mahler used to sneak in and visit certain girls, the ones he'd had access to since they were little, who'd been boarding since elementary school.

"Maybe Hamidou knew," Kersti says, with a wave of despair. "Maybe she was part of covering it up."

"This is one of those sexually explicit notes," Jay says, handing it to her.

"I can't read it," Kersti says, getting up and going over to her laptop.

"What are you doing?"

"Looking something up."

She types "Mahler Bobsled '52 Olympics." His name pops up immediately. Friedrich Mahler. "Shit."

"What?"

"I couldn't remember his name. It's Friedrich."

"Who?"

"The coach. He's German. I thought it might be him but his name doesn't start with *C*—"

"What if *C* was just a code name?"

"What if it was Mr. Fithern?" she says, pacing around the room. "His name is Charles. It makes the most sense. Maybe he's just a damn good actor and he fooled me—"

"Kersti, please sit down. You're making me nervous."

She sits reluctantly, still trying to fit the pieces together.

"What does this all mean?" he asks her, reaching for her hand.

"Cressida was obsessed with those girls who were expelled in '74," Kersti says. "I never understood why, but she must have suspected they'd been sexually abused, just like she was being abused."

"She probably figured out that whatever they spray-painted on the statue of Helvetia incriminated their abuser."

"And got them expelled," she adds. "Cressida was determined to get to the bottom of it . . . right up until she fell."

"Who do you think left this for you?"

"Another of the victims."

"Someone who's here for the Lycée's hundredth birthday."

"Why give it to me, though?"

"They couldn't tell you at the front desk who left it?"

"I'm waiting to hear."

Kersti tosses the Polaroids and the note on the bed, feeling as sad for Cressida as she is confused. "I'm guessing there's a lot more incriminating evidence in that ledger," she says.

"Maybe Cressida was going to give it to someone."

"And someone stopped her."

"Are you going to tell Deirdre?"

Kersti lies back and stares miserably up at the ceiling. "How can I not?"

"You don't even know who it was."

"Someone who was there since the seventies," Kersti says. "Whose name starts with C. Or doesn't. You think I remember any of the teachers' names?"

"And German."

"Maybe."

"We'll start researching after your speech. All that information must be at the school—"

"My speech?" she cries. "Are you fucking kidding me? I can't stand up there and talk about the Lycée's hundredth birthday."

"You're not. You're talking about *you*. This is an honor."

"No, not anymore. I don't want anything to do with this school."

She reaches for the Polaroid of Cressida, drawn to it as though to a car accident. She stares into Cressida's frozen eyes and sees there, beneath the mask of defiance, a brokenness as plain and straightforward as her beauty. Maybe she *was* the suicide type after all, Kersti reflects.

And then she notices something. On the very edge of the bedside table, of which only the corner is visible, there's a pack of cigarettes. Kersti recognizes the navy blue box without having to see the brand. *Gauloises.*

"Look at this," Kersti says, grabbing the note. "It's not the same handwriting as the other *C* love notes. This one is *from* Cressida, not to her." And she reads it out loud.

> C, Thinking of you every minute. Your fingers inside me, mine inside you.
>
> C

Kersti lets the note slip out of her hand. Jay picks it up and stares at it. "How did we miss that?" he says, his skin flushing deep red. "It's a woman."

"Yes," she says. "It's Hamidou."

"Please welcome one of our One Hundred Women of the Lycée, best-selling author and soon to be mother of twins, Kersti Kuusk-Wax."

Kersti rises amid the applause. She decided to wear her strapless black empire sundress and ballet flats. Less chance of tripping and falling on her face. Turns out it was the right call because the sun is blazing hot today. She can already see the redness flaring up on her shoulders.

It was Jay who convinced her to come and give the speech as planned. In the end, she agreed. Not because she wants to be part of the celebration, but because she wants to confront Hamidou.

Kersti should have put it together a long time ago. Hamidou had everything to lose, everything to hide. She was the one who'd wanted those girls expelled, just like Bueche said. He hadn't lied about that. Even telling the police about Cressida's car accident was a way for Hamidou to plant the seed of an alcohol-related accident; it gave the police precedence.

Cressida must have threatened Hamidou the night she got the ledger. Assuming there was incriminating proof of the abuse in it, she probably warned Hamidou she was going to go to Bueche and Harzenmoser with it. Hamidou must have panicked. How could she not? She was a small slip of a woman, but she was athletic and strong. She had remarkable energy. Fueled with fear and rage, who's to say she couldn't have pushed a drunken eighteen-year-old off her balcony? And then faked a suicide note?

All this is going through Kersti's mind as she makes her way across the lawn to the podium. She hasn't seen Hamidou yet. She looked for her earlier, heart pounding, palms sweating, and was secretly relieved not to have found her.

"Bonjour," she says, her voice a tremor. "Thank you, Monsieur Bueche."

She looks out into the crowd and sees Jay, Noa, and Raf, front and center, beaming at her supportively. A few rows back, she spots Hamidou. Their eyes lock. Hamidou smiles and waves. Kersti holds on to the podium and lowers her eyes. She's sweating. Trickles of water rolling down her back, clinging to the modal fabric of her dress. I know what you are, she thinks.

The audience is silent, waiting. Kersti forces a smile and draws a breath. Her heartburn is killing her. The boys are fluttering wildly inside her belly, probably feeling her stress, reacting to her nervous energy. "It's an honor and a privilege to stand up here as one of the One Hundred Women of the Lycée," she begins. "I would not be here speaking about my literary career had it not been for the foundation I received as a student in the nineties."

She looks up from her notes and connects with Jay. He looks worried.

"My English teacher at the Lycée, Mrs. Fithern, used to tell me I had an unpolished diamond," Kersti continues. "She always said, 'You must polish your diamond.' She encouraged me to read. She'd say, 'Writers read, luv.' She suggested I write a short story and I did and it was terrible and all she said was, 'Keep polishing that diamond, luv.'"

The audience chuckles.

"I didn't have the confidence back then to even think I could be a writer when I grew up," Kersti says. "I knew I enjoyed writing, but it was here, at the Lycée, that I first discovered I actually had something worth pursuing."

She's struggling to stay focused; her mind keeps going off on tangents. Hamidou. The naked Polaroids. Cressida's eyes. The dirty note. Who left it for her? And why *now*?

"But I didn't just learn to write here," Kersti plods on. "I also learned to observe and to absorb. We were exposed to so many extraordinary places and experiences, which helped to shape me and pave the way for a lifetime of wanting to create extraordinary places and experiences. I'll never forget visiting Shakespeare's birth house in Stratford-Upon-Avon, and then seeing *Romeo and Juliet* at the Royal Shakespeare Theatre. Who gets to do that?"

A few people applaud. "I was a kid from Toronto," she says, glancing up and accidentally making eye contact with Hamidou again. *Child molester. Murderer.* Are you still a murderer if you take away someone's life without actually ending it? Kersti looks away, but as she's about to resume her speech, she notices someone standing behind the last row, over by the path to the tennis courts.

Alison Rumsky.

Kersti's mind starts racing. What is she doing here? She wasn't supposed to come. Said she couldn't. And then all at once, the puzzle pieces slide into place. When they met for lunch in Toronto,

Kersti mentioned the ledger, how she was trying to connect it to what happened to Cressida. Alison never asked what the ledger was, didn't show the least bit of curiosity. It was like *she knew.*

It never occurred to Kersti at the time that there was no reason for Alison to know about the ledger. She wasn't even friends with them when Amoryn Lashwood sent it to Cressida. And yet she knew about it. Who told her?

It's starting to make sense now. Her resentment toward the Lycée. Her wound, her darkness. *I can't go.*

Alison was one of Hamidou's victims.

CHAPTER 32

LAUSANNE—June 1998

Volleyball is torture. All Kersti wants to do is get back to Huber House and read the ledger with Cressida, but it's like each game is unfolding in slow motion. Usually Alison's deadly hitting makes quick work of the other teams. They've been the undefeated Vaud champions three years in a row, but tonight the Aiglon team has stepped it up and is challenging them on every point. Now they're in a third game tiebreaker.

Kersti is still second setter. She's spent most of the time on the bench tonight, which makes waiting all the more excruciating. All she can do is watch and keep checking the time. M. Mahler is pacing the sideline, pumping his fist in the air, shouting at the team in German. *Set. Set! Zree hits. Ovah! Du idioten! Set to Alison. Set to Alison, Dummköpfe! Time out! Time out! What are you doing, imbeciles?* With his old-fashioned uniform and overused whistle, his cartoonish accent and wiry, white hair sticking out of every possible socket—head, nose, ears—Mahler has become something of a celebrity, renowned throughout the canton for his boisterous Germanic slurs and his impeccable record.

At around nine thirty, Alison finally spikes the game-winning ball. They all jump to their feet, cheering—Kersti because now she can finally get back to Huber House—and line up to shake hands with their opponents. Mahler is happy. He kisses Alison and swings her around. "Glückwunsch, mein Meister!" he cries. No longer imbeciles, now they're his champions.

On the bus ride back to the Lycée, Kersti sits beside Alison. Neither of them says much. Kersti is thinking about the ledger, not wanting Cressida and Lille to look through it without her. Alison is staring out the window with a sad face, even though they've just won the championship.

"You okay?" Kersti asks her.

"Sure," Alison says, not turning her head.

"Are you looking forward to graduating?"

Alison lets out a strange laugh.

"You've probably got athletic scholarships everywhere," Kersti says, trying to engage her.

"I'm going to UBC for volleyball."

"Cool."

Alison doesn't ask Kersti where she's going next year, which is fine because Kersti doesn't know. Instead she says, "Is Cressida still sleeping with Mr. Fithern?" Completely out of nowhere.

"They're traveling together this summer," Kersti blurts, almost gleefully. "He's leaving Mrs. Fithern."

Alison shakes her head in disgust. Her face turns pink, even her freckles. She slumps down in her seat, turns back to the window, and doesn't say another word. As though Kersti is somehow at fault.

By the time Kersti reaches Cressida's room, it's well after ten and Lille is the one she finds sitting on the bed. "Where's Cressida?"

"I don't know," Lille says quietly, her voice faraway. She seems preoccupied. "I just got here."

"Are you okay?" Kersti asks her. "You seem spacey."

"Komiko said she just saw Cress on the second floor. She was leaving."

"Leaving?"

Kersti rushes over to the balcony and pushes open the doors just as Cressida is crossing the lawn, almost languidly, as if she's out for a stroll in her own garden. Even in the dark, Kersti is able to make out the shadow of her lithe body gliding on the grass. The wild tangle of hair blowing out behind her like a cape, the gazelle legs that are not quite concealed by her knee-length white cotton skirt.

She watches Cressida approach the iron gates, which are supposed to keep them safely locked inside the campus, and her chest flames with anger. Cressida was supposed to wait for them to read the ledger. Kersti stays out on the balcony until Cressida vanishes in the darkness—off to break Magnus's heart—and when she comes back inside the room, Lille is gone.

She decides to look for the ledger herself. She walks over to Cressida's bed and pulls back the duvet, but the book isn't there. Cressida must have moved it. Kersti does a swift scan around the room and then starts opening drawers, lifting the mattress, checking under the bed. She sifts through Cressida's school bag, the papers on her desk, her closet.

She must have taken it with her, which makes no sense. Why would she have done that? Kersti tidies Cressida's room, making sure it looks exactly the way she found it, and then shuffles dejectedly back to her room. She changes out of her sweaty volleyball uniform and without even showering or brushing her teeth, falls into bed wearing a T-shirt and boxer shorts. She lies there for a long time, waiting. She'll wait as long as she has to until she hears Cressida's door, and then she'll charge in there and demand to see that ledger.

She stares up at her sloped ceiling, seething and restless. Her window is open and she can hear Mme. Hamidou talking on the second floor with the other on-duty teacher, whose voice Kersti recognizes as Mrs. Fithern's. Mrs. Fithern has to board here all week, which means Mr. Fithern is home alone. Will Cressida pay him a visit after she leaves Magnus's place? Will they celebrate her new freedom?

It always lines up for Cressida. No matter what she does, it invariably works out for her. And as Kersti lies here simmering, she begins to imagine her life without Cressida—an inevitable reality as the school year draws to a close.

Maybe it won't be such a bad thing, she considers. It goes without saying she'll miss her. She'll miss confiding in her, she'll miss her pep talks, their laughter, their antics, her unconditional love. What she won't miss is the perpetual hum of inadequacy she feels whenever she's in Cressida's presence. Or that throbbing sense of injustice that never has a voice. *Why does everything work out for her? Why don't the rules apply to her? Why did she get away with it?*

Kersti knows Cressida will always want her in her life, even just to know Kersti is there in some corner of the world, her reliable little beacon of ordinary; a connection to normalcy. She'll anticipate Kersti's postcards from Toronto and find them comforting, particularly while she's jet-setting around the world, handing off lovers like relay batons. "Oh, it's from my best friend," she'll tell her Spanish bullfighter lover. She'll treasure Kersti's lame postcards of the CN Tower and the Hockey Hall of Fame as though they're novelties, just like Kersti's boring life will also be a novelty. But maybe the long-distance friendship—which is not much of a friendship at all—will prove vastly healthier for Kersti's self-esteem.

CHAPTER 33

LAUSANNE—June 2016

Kersti somehow manages to finish her speech. It's a good thing she prepared notes. As she returns to her seat, she realizes she has absolutely no recollection of what she's just said. "You were great," Jay whispers.

Noa leans over and squeezes her knee. "Good job."

Kersti turns around to look at Alison. They acknowledge one another. Kersti mouths, *Do you want to talk?*

Alison nods and points toward the tennis courts.

"I have to pee," Kersti tells Jay. "I'll be back."

She gets out of her chair again and squeezes through the aisle. As she comes to the end of the row, she realizes the person whose legs she's climbing over belong to Angela Zumpt. "Hi, Angela," she says.

Angela is noticeably heavier and has a few more wrinkles and gray hairs, but otherwise she hasn't changed much. For today's ceremony, she's wearing serviceable chino pants and a yellow button-down. There are beads of sweat on her forehead.

"Hello, Kersti," Angela mutters, without really looking at her.

Kersti escapes and finds Alison at the tennis courts.

"What are you doing here?" Kersti asks her, wasting no time on small talk.

"I have to tell you something."

"Alison, I think I know what you're going to say."

"I don't think you do," she says, shaking her head, her red hair swinging. "I know something that might . . . well, it might help you get some closure."

"Alison—"

"Mrs. Fithern didn't have anything to do with Cressida's accident," she says, her freckled cheeks turning pink and splotchy. "This is hard to say—"

"Alison," Kersti interrupts. "Did you come here to tell me about Hamidou?"

Her pink splotches turn bright red, flaring up all over her neck and chest.

"I've seen the Polaroids," Kersti says.

"What are you talking about?" Alison asks. "What Polaroids?"

"Of Cressida naked in Hamidou's bed, for one," Kersti says, lowering her voice. "And a very disturbing note from Cressida to Hamidou."

"Who gave that to you?"

"I have no idea," Kersti says. "I thought maybe you—"

"No. I've never told anyone. I never let her take my picture."

"So it did happen to you?"

"It started when I was eight," she says, her tone flat. "In third grade. She came to my room one night and got into my bed. She told me she loved me like a daughter and offered to snuggle with me."

"You don't have to tell me—"

"I said yes, of course. I loved her, too. And the first few times, that's all she did. Snuggle me. I felt so cared for, so loved. I was lonely at the Lycée and her coming to me at nighttime and lying down with me, it meant the world to me."

Kersti sits down on the bench feeling hot and tired. Alison sits down beside her.

"She used to scratch my back and hum songs to me," Alison remembers. "I would fall asleep like that, feeling so content. And then one night, she was scratching my back and her hand slid around to my chest. She fondled me for a while and I honestly didn't know what to make of it. I was confused. I don't remember being traumatized at all, not at the time. That came later. At the time, I just remember thinking that maybe that was how European moms snuggled."

Alison looks up at the sky, squinting into the sun. "Anyway, it went on for years. She would masturbate me and then I would do it to her. I thought I was the only one."

"Did you ever try to tell someone?" Kersti asks, not wanting to offend her. Knowing she's out of her depth.

"No," Alison answers. "I loved her. It was very confusing. I dreaded her visits, but part of me didn't want it to stop. It was really the only affection I got. At some point I clued into the fact that it was wrong. I was ashamed. I thought it was my fault. I never would have told anyone. In fact, until I got together with you in Toronto, the plan was to basically take it to my grave."

"What happened?"

Alison shrugs, looks away. "I guess you got me thinking about what happened to Cressida," she says. "You got inside my head."

"Did you know it was also happening to her?"

"I never knew for sure," she says. "Until the night she fell."

"What happened?"

"She stopped in my room when I was getting ready for volleyball," Alison remembers. "She was very cryptic. She told me she had proof of what was happening. She never used Hamidou's name, but she showed me a ledger. I don't know what was in it, but she told me she was going to bury it somewhere until she could give it to Bueche and Harzenmoser."

"Bury it?"

"Hamidou used to go through our things," Alison says. "I'd come back to my room and I could tell she'd been in there. She would leave little clues. We had no privacy. I'm sure Cressida was paranoid. Plus, she was always very dramatic."

"So she knew it was happening to you, but you didn't know it was happening to her?" Kersti clarifies.

"I guess so."

"No one else besides Cressida ever said anything to you about Hamidou?"

"God, no. It was like an unspoken rule for us, I guess. No one ever asked me and I never asked anyone."

"What about Lille?"

"I always figured if it was happening to anyone else, it was probably Lille. She was so damaged. But I never had the courage to bring it up."

"That must be what she was going to tell me in her letter," Kersti says, thinking about how Lille's fifth point had been left blank. "She never finished."

"I don't blame her," Alison says. "Especially Lille. She had so much shame."

"I wonder if Cressida went to every girl who she knew was being abused by Hamidou and told all of them about the ledger?" Kersti says, thinking out loud, suddenly remembering the look on Lille's face when she burst into Cressida's room after volleyball that night. What if Cressida had already showed Lille the ledger and told her of her plan to go forward with it?

"Alison, didn't you think Cressida's fall might have had something to do with the sexual abuse?" Kersti asks her. "I mean it happened the night she told you she was going to Bueche with proof—"

Alison looks away guiltily. Her body sags, her eyes cloud over. "The mind does extraordinary things to cope," she says softly. "You wouldn't believe the lies I've told myself, the denial, the rationalizations, the blind spots. I had to find a way to function and I did."

In a way, Kersti understands that. Hasn't she done exactly the same thing all this time?

"The guilt finally got me," Alison says. "That's why I came here."

She looks away for a moment and Kersti can tell she's struggling to hold back tears. She's not the type to let anyone see her be vulnerable. "I'm also going to tell the school about Hamidou," she says, her discomfort palpable. "Which I should have done twenty years ago. I could have prevented—"

"Don't go there," Kersti says gently. "You can stop her now."

"I'm going to Bueche first," she says. "And if it turns out Hamidou did push Cressida, I'll do whatever I can to help Deirdre."

"Do *you* think Hamidou pushed Cressida?"

"No," Alison says. "I think Cressida tried to kill herself. And I *get* that."

"But Cressida was going to expose the whole thing—"

"You know what I think?" Alison interrupts. "I think Hamidou really loved Cressida. I think she was probably in love with her, and I don't think she could have pushed her off that balcony any more than I think she could have pushed me. She loved us, Kersti. That was the worst part of it. I know it's twisted, but she really loved us."

She stands up and Kersti has to shield her eyes from the sun to see her.

"So, no," Alison concludes. "I don't think Hamidou pushed Cressida, but I do believe she's one hundred percent responsible for what happened to her. And for that she has to pay."

After the ceremony, when everyone starts to mingle around the grounds and sip champagne, Kersti makes a beeline for Bueche.

"Excellent speech," he says, popping a petit four in his mouth. "We're very proud of you. You've represented the Lycée very well. Madame Harzenmoser wasn't up to being here today, but she asked me to give you her regards and congratulate you."

"Monsieur Bueche," Kersti says urgently. "Something is about to come out that will destroy the Lycée's reputation."

She can see the panic darken his eyes. A vein starts to pulsate down the middle of his forehead.

"What did those girls spray-paint on the statue in '74?" she asks him.

"This is hardly the time—"

"I know about Hamidou," Kersti says, glaring at him.

"I don't know what you're talking about," he responds.

"What did they write on the statue of Helvetia?" she repeats. "Did it directly implicate Hamidou?"

"No," he says, looking around nervously, sweat dribbling down both sides of his face. He pulls his handkerchief out of the breast pocket of his blazer and pats his skin.

He's always known, she realizes. Known and turned a blind eye to protect the school.

"They added some words to our motto," he admits. "They wrote: 'Molesting young women to become fucked-up citizens of the world.'"

"They were expelled for *that*?"

"It was very disrespectful and vulgar," he whispers, still looking around him like a frightened animal. "And they were doing drugs—"

"You didn't bother to ask them why they did it?" Kersti says accusingly. "You weren't concerned they were trying to tell you something?"

"Hamidou felt they were troublemakers—"

"So you got rid of them and kept Hamidou."

"There was nothing in the world to suggest Madame Hamidou was doing anything inappropriate," he says. "The students adored her! I have to trust the members of my faculty—"

"But you're not at all surprised by what I'm telling you, are you?"

He averts his dark eyes and leads her by the elbow farther away from the minglers.

"You suspected, didn't you?" she presses, when they're hidden behind a tree.

"Madame Harzenmoser occasionally used to roam the dorms late at night," he confesses. "Over the years, on more than one occasion, she observed Madame Hamidou leaving some of the students' rooms."

"Harzenmoser told you that?"

"Yes, but we decided to give her the benefit of the doubt," he explains. "The students loved her, as you know. We both felt strongly that if she were doing anything untoward, the students in question would come forward. No one ever did, so we surmised she was just offering comfort. Maternal comfort. Or perhaps the girls were sick when she visited them—"

His voice falls off and he withers visibly under Kersti's hard stare.

"You *knew*," Kersti hisses. "You both knew and you let it go on. You didn't even fire her!"

"We didn't know. She is beloved here—"

"She's been molesting students for four decades!"

"We never knew that," he repeats, his voice climbing. "No one in forty years ever came forward! Certainly we would have dismissed her and pressed charges if anyone had ever spoken up. You can't expect us to have fired her without grounds."

"But the vandalism? *Those* girls came forward! And Hamidou's late night visits to students' rooms?" Kersti reminds him. "My God, shouldn't you have investigated?"

"It was a different world back then," he tells her. "It was not the topic du jour like it is now. Even when you were students in the nineties, no one knew or understood anything about such matters."

"And what about the past twenty years?" she fires back.

"We've never had a complaint."

"Did you ever suspect she had something to do with Cressida's fall?" Kersti pursues. "Is that why you had your friend close the investigation so quickly?"

"Of course not—"

"As soon as I tell Deirdre what Hamidou did to Cressida, she's going to demand a new investigation. *Be prepared.*"

She leaves Bueche standing there, stunned, and goes off in search of Jay.

"Where do you keep disappearing?" he asks, coming toward her.

"I was talking to Bueche," she says. "I'm sorry."

"What the hell is going on?"

"I have to talk to Deirdre," she tells him. "I have to tell her."

"Kerst, it's like a hundred degrees out here," he says. "You're getting worked up, you haven't eaten since breakfast . . ."

"There's nothing to worry about, Babe."

"We've worked so hard for this," he says, placing his hands on her stomach. "For *them*. First we flew to the UK, then we took a train here. You're speaking to all these people and getting stressed and emotional. I agreed to come here to celebrate this hundred-year anniversary thing. Not to follow you around while you play detective."

"I'm not playing detective," she says. "You want me to eat? I'll eat."

She grabs a handful of cheese tarts from a passing tray and devours them all, realizing she's actually starving. "Look, why don't you go back to the hotel."

"No way. Not without you."

"Just wait for me at the hotel," she says calmly. "I'm going to talk to Deirdre, and then I'd like to hang out with Noa, Raf, and Alison for a few hours. I came here to see them, too."

"What about Hamidou?"

"Hamidou is Deirdre's problem," Kersti says. "She can handle it however she wants. I'm just going to tell her what I know and give her the Polaroids."

"Promise?"

"Of course."

He pulls her into his arms and holds her. "You've got my sons in there," he reminds her.

"I know."

"What time will you be back at the hotel?"

"We're grabbing a bite at the Pont Bessières," she says. "No later than eleven?"

He nods reluctantly. "Any idea yet who sent you the Polaroids?" he asks her.

"Not yet." She looks at her watch. "It's not quite four. I'm still waiting for the guy at the front desk to call me."

"Behave," he tells her, and disappears across the lawn.

Kersti spots Alison sitting by herself on the front stoop of Huber House. "I'm hiding," Alison confides. "I'm afraid to bump into Hamidou right now. I saw her sitting there in the audience—it was just the back of her head—and I started shaking and I wanted to throw up."

"Bueche knows," Kersti says.

Alison turns to her. "You told him? Or he already knew?"

"I told him, but I think he knew."

"Fucker," she mutters. "Of course he did. I feel like going up to that podium and telling everyone right now."

Kersti imagines how that would go down. *May I have your attention please? I'd like to let everyone know that our treasured Madame Hamidou has been sexually abusing her students for forty years, me included. If it's happened to any of you out there, please put up your hand! Dozens of hands shooting into the air. Oh, and Monsieur Bueche and Madame Harzenmoser have known all along but they covered it up to protect the school's reputation. Happy 100th birthday, Lycée. Enjoy yourselves, everyone!*

"I could never do it though," Alison admits. "I couldn't even tell you up till today. It's so fucking humiliating."

"You have nothing to feel humiliated about."

"I *let* her," Alison says. "Even when I was old enough to know better. I loved her."

"As a mother."

"Who knows anymore?"

Kersti puts her arm around Alison, but Alison quickly squirms away. "I'm fine," she says stiffly.

"So what's your plan?" Kersti asks her.

"I guess on Monday morning I'll go see Bueche," she says. "I'll tell him everything that happened. Maybe you could let Deirdre know and ask her if she'd like to join me? Power in numbers."

"Of course," Kersti says. "I want to tell her first, though. I was just about to go and find her."

"If Deirdre presses criminal charges for sexual abuse, that's fine. But I don't want any part of a civil suit. I'll help, but I'm not interested in suing or getting any money out of this."

"What do you want then?"

"I want Hamidou fired," Alison responds. "I want the students to be safe. I want everyone at the school to know what she's done and what she is. I want her to be publicly shamed and disgraced and I want to be the one to do it. I don't want any more regrets."

"Regrets," Kersi murmurs. "You know, when Cressida and I were friends I thought she had the most charmed life. I would look at her and think how lucky she was to be so beautiful and revered and completely exempt from the rules the rest of us had to follow."

"You didn't know what was going on."

"I was so jealous of her," Kersti confesses. "There was never a moment when I wasn't jealous. I don't think I even realized it at the time. I was constantly comparing myself to her; always bitter about how easily everything came to her. I thought *she* was the one who made me feel worthless and inadequate."

Kersti lets out a sad laugh. "But then I also blamed my family for making me feel worthless and inadequate. And then I blamed not being able to get pregnant. Notice a theme here?"

"You've always felt inadequate?"

"Turns out I didn't need Cressida for that," Kersti acknowledges out loud, probably for the first time. "But I always held her accountable anyway."

"You seem more than adequate to me."

"Thanks," Kersti says. "But I'm still always focusing on what's wrong with me. What I didn't do, what I didn't say. What I can't be. Cress was always trying to get me to see what I had to offer.

I'm the one who took her beauty and her magic and twisted them into something threatening and diminishing. Not the other way around."

"You were a teenager."

"I'm not anymore. And I've been doing this my whole life."

"You're doing it now," Alison says. "You're still talking about what's wrong with you. There's a lot right about you, too."

Kersti nods, trying to absorb that. "I don't want regrets anymore, either," she says.

They sit there for a while, the sun still blazing above them, the spicy scent of dianthus hanging thick in the air. It isn't until Kersti's phone rings that she remembers she's expecting the call.

"This is Afzal from the Chateau D'Ouchy."

"Yes, thank you for calling," Kersti says. "Someone left a package for me last night?"

"Yes, she didn't leave her name."

"*She?*"

"Yes. A woman."

Kersti's heart is pounding. Her whole body feels like it's vibrating, or maybe it's the babies. "This may sound bizarre," she says, "but can you describe her?"

Poor Afzal is silent on the other end. He probably speaks to dozens if not hundreds of people a day behind that front desk. "It's hard to remember," he finally says. "She didn't say much."

"Was she American?"

"Oh no. She spoke French. Swiss French."

"Was she old? Did she have short hair?"

"She was older, maybe forty?" he says. "I didn't see her hair. She wore a hat."

"A baseball cap?"

Alison is looking at her strangely.

"Yes," Afzal says. "It might have been blue. Or brown?"

"Anything else?" Kersti asks, desperate.

"I'm sorry, Madame. She handed it to me and left immediately."

Kersti thanks him and hangs up, discouraged. She's not one step closer to figuring out who gave her the Polaroids. Alison is watching her, but doesn't ask any questions.

"I have to find Deirdre before she leaves," Kersti says.

The chairs have been removed and the crowd is thinning on the back lawn. Kersti scans the grounds looking for Deirdre. She sees Bueche, talking with some alumni, his smile forced and his charm cranked up at full volume. He must be sweating on the inside, Kersti thinks. Praying that whatever happens with Hamidou happens after today's celebration, behind closed doors.

Someone offers Kersti a glass of champagne, which she waves away, annoyed. She could use a glass of water and some food, though, so she sets off in the direction of the buffet—an enticing spread of all her favorite Swiss pastries. She stops when her eyes land on Deirdre and Mme. Hamidou, huddled together in deep conversation, with little Sloane by their side.

Kersti forgot Sloane was going to be here. Beautiful, precocious Sloane, the spitting image of Cressida with her mane of curls, loose and wild, and her exquisite features. She's got a pastry in the palm of each hand and a wide grin on her face. Hamidou playfully tugs on a coil of her hair and she giggles.

Kersti takes a couple of steps back, a wave of revulsion rising up inside her. Part of her wants to flee; another part wants to ambush Hamidou and snatch Sloane away. She realizes she can't speak to Deirdre now, not with Sloane here.

"Kersti?"

She spins around. Noa and Raf are standing there, looking sunburnt and wilted. "You okay?" Noa asks her.

Kersti looks back at Hamidou and Sloane, standing side by side. Hamidou's fingers are still twirling the little girl's hair. "I have to get out of here," Kersti says, and she rushes away from the Lycée garden as fast as her chafing pregnant legs will take her.

CHAPTER 34

LAUSANNE—June 1998

Kersti wakes up with the sun shining directly in her eyes. There are noises outside her door, which is probably what woke her. Banging, yelling. She sits up and waits. She hears someone say her name. *Where's Kersti? Is she in her room?*

And then she hears wailing in the background. She jumps out of bed just as someone throws open the door. It's Mme. Hamidou. Her face is as white as the bedsheets, her eyes swollen and ringed with red. She comes to Kersti and takes both Kersti's hands in hers. Her body is trembling violently. Kersti can feel it just holding her hands. Hamidou can hardly look her in the eyes.

"What is it?" Kersti whispers, expecting to be told her parents are dead.

"It's Cressida," she says softly.

"What?"

"Something's happened—"

"*What?*" Kersti starts shaking. Her heart is in her throat, pulsating.

"She fell."

"Fell?" Kersti is confused. "Where?"

"From her balcony."

"Is she alive?" Kersti cries, trying to understand if it's a matter of broken legs or a broken back or—

"Yes, but it doesn't look good," Hamidou says, her voice quivering. "She . . . if she lives, I don't know if she'll ever be the same."

If she lives?

Kersti collapses on the edge of her bed, struggling to breathe. She can't find her voice to ask more questions. Mme. Hamidou must be in her own private hell—Cressida is like her daughter. *Fell from her balcony on the fourth floor.*

Everything comes rushing into Kersti's mind at once, a random blur. *What time did Cressida get home last night? Is she alive? How the hell did she fall over the railing?*

"Did she jump?" Kersti asks Hamidou, suddenly remembering something Cressida said the night Noa's boyfriend tried to kill himself. *Anyone who doesn't die didn't really mean to.*

"Of course not," Hamidou responds, horrified.

Kersti has to see. She runs from her room, ignoring Hamidou's imploring screams for her to come back; ignoring the other Huber House girls, who are huddled together on every floor, some crying, others shell-shocked. Lille, Alison, Nastia, Komiko, Angela. She notices Mrs. Fithern, sobbing quietly into her hands in the staff lounge on the second floor. Kersti races downstairs to the main floor, out the front door, and around back, where Cressida would have landed. Half-expecting to find her there, her beautiful body broken, mangled. But Cressida is gone. Her body has been removed and all that's left is her blood, splattered like red graffiti on the cement. The police are clustered around the spot where she landed.

Mme. Harzenmoser and M. Bueche must have taken care of everything before they woke the students, just like they did with the vandalized statue twenty years ago. They called the ambulance, the police, the house supervisors.

"Kersti!" Hamidou is running toward her. "Come here, *mon amour*," she cries, enveloping Kersti in her thin arm and leading her away. "You shouldn't see this."

"Where is she?" Kersti manages, her voice strangled.

"They've taken her to the hospital," Hamidou says, rubbing Kersti's back.

Kerst breaks away and heads back to Huber. She runs up the stairs and locks herself in a stall in the third-floor bathroom. Why didn't she go to Cressida last night at dinner when she had that dread feeling in her gut? Why didn't she go over to her and hug her and tell her it would be okay? Why didn't she tell her she loved her? She knew Cressida was troubled. *In trouble.* She could see it in her face, in the grim set of her mouth and the melancholy look in her eyes. Instead, Kersti did nothing.

She just went off to her volleyball tournament without saying a word, without offering a shred of comfort to her. Why hadn't she hugged her at least? And then, when she got back to school and saw Cressida leaving campus to go meet Magnus, she was resentful, spiteful. She assumed the worst about why Cressida hadn't shown her the ledger. She ransacked Cressida's room looking for it and then lay in her bed all night contemplating life without Cressida; how that might be a good thing for her.

If only she had called out to her from the balcony and begged her to come back. Why didn't she? Cressida might have come back. For Kersti, she might have.

Kersti pulls her knees tight into her chest. She feels hollow inside. Maybe this is partly her fault. All her wishing that Cressida would get what was coming to her—a consequence, some disciplinary action, a punishment of any kind—has finally come to fruition. Wasn't she always secretly hoping Cressida would get in trouble just once, to balance things out? Wouldn't that have meant the world was just a little bit fair?

Kersti has always wanted life to be fair. She thought Cressida having to pay for even one of her transgressions would make it so; would appease her. How many times had she silently, secretly wished for her best friend to be taught a lesson?

She never meant for something like this to happen. She never wanted her prayers to be answered in such an irrevocable, cataclysmic way. If Cressida dies, she'll never forgive herself.

Someone bangs on the door. "Kersti? *Ouvre la porte!*" It's Hamidou.

"Is she still alive?" Kersti wants to know.

"They're doing everything they can to save her."

Kersti knows it's a lie. Cressida can't be saved.

CHAPTER 35

LAUSANNE—June 2016

The Café le Petit Pont Bessières used to be a loud, bustling place filled with convivial, chain-smoking students pounding back chopes of beer before heading out to the bars. Tonight it's a different vibe altogether. Maybe it's the new smoking laws or maybe it's just Kersti's mood, but the loud din and party atmosphere she remembers is far more subdued and there are only a handful of old men at the other tables.

After a long discussion about Noa's planned trip to Africa to adopt a Sudanese refugee, the looming threat of Ebola in Europe, and the alarming revelation that asteroids are going to crash into earth at some point, Kersti politely excuses herself to go to the washroom. She scrubs her hands and splashes water on her face and then stands there by herself, savoring the quiet. Noa has become a crusader, which is noble and exhausting at the same time. Rafaella called her a "cause" junkie.

Raf is the opposite. She seems to care about very little, only opening her mouth to complain or make negative comments. Her spaetzle tasted like rubber, the wine was cheap, the speeches at the ceremony today were interminable, Paris has lost its magic, the Western world has stopped valuing women, which is why she "chooses" to be alone, and on and on.

Kersti takes a breath and wills herself to go back out there.

"We should do something radical," Noa is saying, with a mouthful of gelato.

"We're talking about Hamidou," Raf tells Kersti.

"We should call a TV news station and expose the whole thing," Noa says excitedly. "I've done that before."

"You can't do that," Alison says. "It's not just Hamidou you'd be destroying. There were victims."

They all fall silent. Kersti and Alison told them everything about Hamidou earlier in the evening. Noa was appropriately shocked and outraged, but all Raf said was, "Why am I not surprised?"

"Did she ever try anything with you?" Kersti asked her.

"Are you kidding?" Raf responded. "I literally would have beaten the crap out of her and told everyone in school."

"No you wouldn't have," Alison said softly, and Raf turned red and shut up.

Noa tops up Raf's wineglass and then refills her own. Alison doesn't drink so she's keeping Kersti company in her pregnancy-imposed sobriety.

"We should all go to Hamidou's place together," Noa continues. "The four of us. Right now. To confront her."

"I'm not going to her place," Alison says wearily.

"Don't you want to look her in her beady eyes and tell her that you know?" Noa says, with an intensity that makes Kersti squirm. "Don't you want to see her face when you tell her you're going to talk to Bueche and the police?"

Kersti almost shouts yes, realizing it's exactly what *she* wants to do, but she stays quiet.

"Hamidou knows who has the ledger," Noa concludes. "I guarantee it."

"You think she'd tell me?" Alison says.

"She'll have nothing left to lose."

"What if she flees the country?" Raf says. "I would if I was a child molester about to get caught."

Alison and Kersti look at each other. What if they've both come all this way and Hamidou manages to slip away? Hamidou is sly. She may have seen Alison at the ceremony today and already figured out they know.

"You can make a civil claim against the school, you know," Raf mentions to Alison. "Bueche would love that."

"I don't care about the money."

"There's been a ton of civil suits against former boarding school teachers," Noa says. "I read an article that said at least a dozen schools in the UK have had teachers convicted for child abuse." She finishes her gelato and washes it down with red wine. "The system is broken," she adds, in a grating, dramatic tone. "I just never imagined it was happening at the Lycée. And Hamidou! She loved us so much—"

"People harm people they love all the time," Raf mutters. "That's what families do."

"The system needs to be fixed," Noa rants. "And it must start with the class system. These allegations are being reported at the most elite schools."

Kersti tunes her out and prepares to make her exit. The pregnancy excuse is always universally accepted.

"I just can't believe Bueche ignored what those girls spray-painted on the statue," Alison says. "He just scrubbed Helvetia clean and got rid of the *girls* instead—"

In the middle of Alison talking, it hits Kersti like a bolt. "Holy shit," she blurts.

"What?"

"The statue," she says. "Helvetia."

"What about it?"

When Kersti went to Boston, Cressida tried to say the word *statue*. It was totally random and out of the blue. Kersti assumed she was just remembering something from her time at the Lycée, but what if she'd been trying to convey something to Kersti about it? Maybe she didn't even know what, just that there *was* something. Somewhere in her psyche. What if she remembered?

"I think I know where the ledger is," Kersti says. "I should have clued in when Alison told me Cressida buried it."

"She buried it?" Raf says. "Why the hell would she do that?"

"Hamidou used to go through our things," Alison tells her.

"I bet you anything the ledger is buried by the statue," Kersti says.

They pile out of the cab with shovels, flashlights, and gardening gloves from the Brico+Loisirs, giggling in spite of themselves. It feels a lot like the old days as they sneak across the school grounds in the dark, heading round back.

"Kersti, you just sit and let us do all the work," Noa says.

"I'm fine," Kersti tells them, excited to start digging. "She wouldn't have buried it too deep or too far from the statue. Remember, she was planning to come right back for it."

Kersti walks around the statue, trying to get inside Cressida's head. She would have been in a rush, not a lot of time to make a plan or demarcate her spot. She knew she would need it again in a matter of days. She would have shoved it somewhere she could easily remember.

"I wish we had vodka and smokes," Raf says, kicking off her shoes. "I'm not quite drunk enough for this to be fun."

"It's not supposed to be fun," Alison mutters, already on her knees, digging ferociously behind Helvetia.

"All right," Raf concedes. "Then at least bearable."

Kersti thinks about where Brooke Middlewood and Tatiana Greenberg—the two girls who were expelled—were standing in the photograph Cressida discovered inside the ledger. They were on either side of Helvetia, two sentinels with long hair and broken spirits, valiantly trying to send a message. Kersti kneels down and starts digging to the left of the statue.

"At least it's a nice night," Noa says.

"Are we crazy?" Alison asks, looking up from her pile of dirt.

"Batshit," Kersti says. "If Jay knew I was doing this . . ."

"What are we hoping to find in this ledger anyway?" Raf asks.

"Cressida," Kersti answers. "We're trying to find part of Cressida."

Kersti knows on some level they already have all the evidence they need. She knows the ledger will contain more evidence of some kind and that it's probably superfluous at this point, unnecessary to make or break an investigation. But it belonged to Cressida. It was the catalyst that propelled her to speak up—for herself and for all the other girls Hamidou abused. She went to each one of them that night and told them she had the ledger and that she was going to put an end to the abuse. Whatever secrets it held, it obviously gave Cressida the courage and the ammunition she'd been waiting for to finally break her silence. Maybe all she ever needed was the support of someone like Amoryn Lashwood, who gave her the reassurance that she wasn't alone—that it was a horrific legacy that needed to stop. Ledger in hand, Cressida decided she would be the one to do it. She was that brave.

The ledger has become, for Kersti, the symbol of that bravery; the reminder of what she loved so much about Cressida.

"Oh!" A small cry from Alison on the other side of the statue. "There's something here!"

Kersti crawls over, not giving a shit about her modal sundress, and starts digging right beside Alison. She can feel something hard.

"Move," Alison says, and yanks it out of the earth like a weed. It's wrapped in a plastic Migros bag.

"I don't fucking believe it," Raf says.

"O mijn God," Noa breathes.

Alison hands it to Kersti. Kersti removes it from the bag and holds it the same way Cressida held it all those years ago, with reverence, incredulity.

The ledger. It's exactly as Kersti remembered it, only now it has an even more pungent smell of mold and dampness and dirt. She starts to go through it page by page, as Cressida would have done. She imagines Cressida holding it, just like she's holding it now, reading every line of every page, looking for that secret.

She's aware of Noa holding a flashlight over her shoulder, Raf's wine breath behind her. The first thing she finds is the photograph of the statue with the two girls on either side of it. "Those are the girls who got expelled," she says.

"I can't read what they spray-painted—"

"Read the back."

Do with this ledger what you wish. I've got no objections whatever you decide, only personal regrets. Amoryn El-Bahz.

The other girls are dead silent as Kersti continues turning the pages, scanning the entries for something noteworthy. September, October, November, December. It all seems fairly innocuous.

December 3, 1973. 23:00. Frei House.

Minutes:

Present:	Amoryn Lashwood, President
	Brooke Middlewood, Vice President
	Tatiana Greenberg, Secretary
	Caris Yaren
	Fernanda Manzanares
	Karen Kim
	Donna Murthy

Agenda:

Candlelight Descent. Dec 19.

HS XMAS dinner. (Café Pont Bessières.) Dec 15?

1974 Charitable Events:

Winter Olympics—Funds to Orphanage Lousanna—5 votes.
International Women's Club of Lausanne—2 votes

"There's nothing interesting," Raf says, with disappointment.

But when Kersti turns the page, she discovers another Polaroid jammed into the spine of the book. "It's Amoryn Lashwood," she murmurs, her voice a whisper. She removes it and has a hard time looking at young Amoryn naked in Hamidou's bed, her expression frightened and confused.

On the next page, another Polaroid. "Cressida," Alison says, turning away. The picture is similar to the one that was left for Kersti at the hotel; the pose might be slightly different, but it's the same bed, the same angle of her body.

There are at least half a dozen of them. Stuffed between the pages, photos of Cressida, compromised in every possible way. Naked, wearing underwear, touching herself.

Alison sits down on the base of the statue, her face in her hands.

Noa and Raf are standing on either side of Kersti, both of them now shining their flashlights on the journal. They're sniffling. Kersti can't bring herself to look at them. She turns another page.

"Oh God!" Noa cries.

Kersti slaps the ledger shut before the image can burn itself into her brain.

"What?" Alison asks from where she's sitting. "What is it?"

"Nothing," Kersti says. "Just more of the same."

She doesn't have the heart to tell her it's a photograph of Hamidou—explicit, grotesque. Something Kersti wishes she could unsee, the incontrovertible evidence that would have ended Hamidou's career and destroyed her life if anyone had ever gotten hold of it.

Alison, clearly traumatized, is the first to leave. Raf and Noa decide to go for a drink at a nearby brasserie, and Kersti begs off, telling them she's exhausted.

She walks a few blocks by herself, needing to clear her head. She's not exhausted at all. That was a lie. She's charged with adrenaline. At the corner of Rue Centrale, she flags a passing cab and impulsively tells him to take her to 14 Rue Béthusy.

Hamidou's apartment is in one of those early seventies buildings with a white stucco façade and frosted green balconies. It probably looked futuristic in 1972 and now looks like something out of *The Jetsons*. Kersti dials Hamidou's apartment code, surprising her. She buzzes her in and Kersti rides up in the elevator feeling strangely calm, almost possessed.

"Kersti," Hamidou says, opening the door. "What a surprise."

She's wearing a navy velour robe that exposes her thin white legs. There's a package of Gauloises sticking out of the pocket. Kersti's skin crawls imagining Hamidou dropping her robe for Cressida, revealing that scrawny, boyish body. She tries to get the image out of her head.

Amoryn, Alison, Lille. How many others? How many were there over forty years?

Kersti steps inside the apartment. It reeks of smoke. There are Persian rugs on the linoleum floor, some mismatched antique chairs, and two lamps made of silver samovars sitting on a carved mahogany sideboard, none of which suit the dated apartment, with its Formica kitchenette, low ceilings, and vertical blinds. A clunky old air conditioner rattles from a picture window overlooking the back courtyard.

"What brings you here so late?" Hamidou asks her. "Is something wrong?"

"Yes, something's wrong," Kersti says.

"I was just about to my brush my teeth—"

"I found the ledger."

Hamidou's left eye twitches. "What ledger?" she asks, trying to sound offhand.

"You know what ledger," Kersti tells her. "How many girls were there?"

"What are you talking about?" Hamidou says, tightening the sash of her robe around her narrow waist.

"I've seen pictures," Kersti tells her, not recognizing the cold, threatening tone of her own voice. "I know about Amoryn, Alison, Cressida, Lille. I've read your disgusting letters to Cressida. I know what those girls spray-painted on the statue and why you got them expelled."

"I don't know what you are talking about," Hamidou says softly, unfazed.

"I've seen *you*," Kersti tells her. "Naked. I've got the Polaroid."

Hamidou is quiet, probably trying to figure out her next play.

"There's no point denying anything," Kersti says wearily. "Alison's already come forward. There's too much evidence."

Hamidou sits down on her couch. She crosses her legs, rests her hands on her lap. "What did Alison tell you?"

"That you sexually abused her and many others. I told you, I've seen all the Polaroids."

"Did she tell you she loved me?" Hamidou says.

"As a matter of fact, she did."

"So then. How do you come to call it abuse?"

Kersti sits down on the armchair facing Hamidou. "They were kids," she says, disgusted. "You were an adult. That's the very definition of abuse."

"I disagree."

Kersti shakes her head. "You disagree?" she repeats, incredulous.

"I'm not the one who instigated the affairs."

"The *affairs*?"

"That's what they were," Hamidou says, her tone unrepentant. "I loved each and every one of them, and they loved me in return."

"Like a mother!" Kersti points out. "Not like a lover."

"That's where you're wrong," Hamidou responds calmly. "We *were* lovers, Kersti. All my relationships were mutual and consensual. They wanted me as much as I them."

"Alison was eight!" Kersti cries. "You manipulated and brainwashed them. They grew up confusing maternal love with sex. They were lonely. We all were. We missed our families, we felt abandoned, we were vulnerable. And that's when you preyed on them."

"I did no such thing," she says, indignant. "If they felt attracted to me and they expressed it, I merely responded. Perhaps I shouldn't have—"

"Perhaps you shouldn't have?" Kersti cries.

"I suppose I could have turned them away," she reflects. "But I didn't want to hurt them any more than they were already hurting. They were all so sensitive and eager to please."

"You're sick."

"I was in love with all of them. They were my lovers. I didn't just 'abuse' random students; otherwise it would have happened to you. I had relationships when I had feelings for someone."

"Children!"

"They were not children," Hamidou argues. "Cressida, Lille, Alison. They all had old souls. They were wise on a level you would not understand. The spirit has no age, Kersti. Society labels us with a number. Fourteen. Forty. Sixty. But the soul has no age."

Kersti doesn't even know how to respond.

"You see? Love is ageless, too," Hamidou continues. "Should I have deprived us all of that passion? Of the physical experiences we shared? I chose not to. I chose to express my love for them, and to let them express their love for me."

She pauses and closes her eyes, and then utters wistfully, "Cressida most of all."

"I can't hear this—"

"I can see how uncomfortable it makes you," Hamidou acknowledges. "But Cressida was the great love of my life. And she felt the same way."

"I doubt that."

"We should have been together forever," she murmurs, her eyes watering.

"She was pregnant with Mr. Fithern's baby," Kersti says. "Remember?"

Hamidou flinches.

"She was in love with him."

"She was not," Hamidou snaps. "She was using him."

"For what?"

"It doesn't matter," she says. "Fithern was meaningless to her. She loved *me*."

"You started abusing her when she was in grade two or three!"

Hamidou purses her lips.

"I know you know it was wrong," Kersti says, leaning forward. "You had two students expelled for attempting to speak up."

"They were troublemakers, those two."

"I'm sure they were." Kersti has some water. "Alison doesn't think she was your girlfriend. She thinks you ruined her life and she's going to ruin yours now."

"Alison has narrow views about age and sexuality."

"How many were there?"

"What is it you want from me?" Hamidou asks her. "I understand you are going to tell Bueche and I will lose my job."

"You'll go to jail is what will happen."

"Jail?" she says. "Because of what Alison is going to tell them? Because of a photograph of me that could have been taken by anyone?"

"Because you pushed Cressida off her balcony."

At this, Hamidou's eyes turn black. "You think I pushed Cressida?" she says, her voice trembling. "I loved her more than—"

She jumps up and starts to pace. "I loved her. I would never have harmed her! Never."

"The day Amoryn Lashwood sent Cressida the ledger," Kersti says, "Cressida told Alison—and probably some of your other victims—that she was going to show it to Bueche. Did she tell you, too? Did she threaten you?"

"She did not."

"Bullshit."

"I could never hurt her—"

Kersti almost believes her. *Almost.* "Someone left something for me at my hotel today," she says. "A dirty note and a couple of Polaroids in an envelope. One of them is of Cressida, which is very strange. How would someone wind up with a picture *you* took of Cressida?"

Hamidou sighs.

"There's someone else in Lausanne right now who has evidence against you," Kersti continues. "Do you know who it could be? And why they would give it to me?"

Even as Kersti asks the question, she can see the horror registering on Hamidou's face, clouding her eyes.

"Why me?" Kersti repeats. "Why now?"

Hamidou is shaking her head. Something is dawning on her—the shock of having been sabotaged by someone, or the realization that her entire life is about to blow up.

And then a key turns in the lock and the front door swings open.

CHAPTER 36

BOSTON—July 2001

Kersti follows the home care nurse down the hall with a terrible feeling of dread. Cressida has massive brain damage and very little awareness, Deirdre warned her in preparation for this visit. It's the first time since Cressida fell that Deirdre has allowed Kersti to see her, although her acquiescence has come with plenty of warnings. *She's not the Cressida you knew. There's very little brain function. Expect the worst.*

Kersti just wants to see her. The last time they were together was in the dining room at Huber House, right after Cressida got the ledger from Amoryn. No one could have predicted the catastrophe that lay ahead, the complete derailment of life as they knew it. It's three years later and Kersti still isn't over it. In spite of her best efforts, she hasn't quite managed to move on or fill that void. Cressida, of course, will never move on.

Now just a few feet away from that long-overdue reunion, Kersti is terrified. She's done some research on the Internet about vegetative states, trying to find the most optimistic information and best-case scenarios. Though most victims show no outward signs of awareness, some do recover an "inner voice." Kersti desperately wants to believe this will be the case for Cressida; that she might still be in there.

The nurse opens the door and the first thing Kersti notices is how bright the room is. The blinds are wide open with sunlight pouring in, as though its rays might miraculously restore Cressida's health. An adjustable hospital bed is set up in the middle of the room with one of those sliding tables and a bedpan on the floor. The TV is on—a soap opera—which Deirdre is watching. Cressida lies there, absent.

Cressida. The sight of her like this is almost more than Kersti can handle. She forces a smile, which feels overwrought and inappropriate.

"Kersti," Deirdre says, noticing her in the doorway. "Come in."

Kersti approaches the bed. She's brought Villars chocolate bars and Ovomaltine, which she found at the Swissbäkers in Boston. They were Cressida's favorites.

"You can set those down on the table, Kersti."

Kersti does as she's told and musters the courage to look at Cressida, really *look* at her. Her first thought is, No one is there. She's gone. Remarkably, she's still gorgeous. A living ghost, ethereal and far, far away. Deirdre is obviously still tending diligently to her appearance. Her hair is freshly washed—Kersti can smell the expensive shampoo—and she's wearing makeup. Maybe Deirdre did this for Kersti's benefit. It's something she would do; fix her up like a doll to make a good impression. Maybe she does it every day.

"Hey, Cress," Kersti says trepidatiously, reaching for her limp hand.

Cressida's eyes follow the sound of Kersti's voice. She blinks and stares up at Kersti's face.

"Wipe her chin, will you?" Deirdre says. "There's a cloth right there."

Kersti reaches for the cloth and wipes her best friend's chin. And just like that, tears start rolling down Cressida's cheeks.

"She's crying," Kersti says, feeling her own tears beginning to form.

"This must be too painful for her," Deirdre says, jostling Kersti aside. "This wasn't a good idea. I had a feeling—"

"She recognizes me," Kersti says.

Cressida's tears are still flowing freely, though not a sound escapes her lovely lips.

"She doesn't want to be seen like this," Deirdre surmises, wiping her daughter's tears. "She wouldn't want any pity."

Kersti isn't sure how Deirdre knows this. Who can possibly know what's inside Cressida's locked mind?

"You have to leave now, Kersti."

"Can I come back?" Kersti asks, as Deirdre steers her brusquely out of the room.

"I hope so," Deirdre says. "I'll be in touch, dear."

But Kersti knows she won't be. And as she steps outside onto Beacon, she breaks down and cries. She's not sure what's worse—being thrown out by Deirdre, or seeing what's become of Cressida. She's not sure she'll ever recover from either.

When she finally manages to collect herself, she pulls out her map of Boston and starts heading toward Charles Street, where Aleks is waiting for her at a coffee shop. She walks quickly, wanting to get as far away from what just happened as she can. All she can think is, Why did the sight of her make Cressida cry?

CHAPTER 37

LAUSANNE—June 2016

Kersti turns to see who it is. It takes her a moment to recognize the woman stepping inside the apartment and then her heart stops. It's Angela Zumpt.

"Hello again, Kersti."

"What are you doing here?" Kersti manages, frozen on the couch.

"I live here," Angela responds, as though it should be the obvious assumption. "With my wife."

Shocked, Kersti turns back to Hamidou. "You've known the whole time who sent me those Polaroids, didn't you?"

"The same person who pushed Cressida," Hamidou states. "The one I thought loved me most."

Kersti looks back and forth between Angela and Hamidou.

"I told you every relationship I ever had was mutual," Hamidou continues, her tone smug. "Angela is thirty-six. Surely you can't think I'm abusing her?"

Angela is standing in the foyer, filling the entire space with her height and breadth, making no move to come any closer. Blocking any possibility of a smooth and hasty exit for Kersti.

"If that's true," Kersti says, "why did she give me pictures that prove you're a child molester?"

Hamidou turns her dark, accusing eyes on Angela. "You must

have known when you did this that we would both lose everything?"

"I've already lost you," Angela says, her tone flat.

"How can you say that?"

"I'd rather us be locked up than have you move back to the Lycée to be with Amandine."

Kersti rides out a wave of nausea, remembering the young girl from the other day.

"You did this to punish me?" Hamidou murmurs, incredulous.

"I did it to stop you from being with Amandine," Angela says, sulking, sounding like a child. "When you told me Kersti was in Lausanne asking questions about Cressida, I just thought—"

"You thought you would ruin both our lives? Over a student? Do you know how many others there have been?"

Angela looks down at the floor. She's still in the doorway, hasn't budged since she arrived.

"Mon Dieu," Hamidou rails. "You know what I have to do now, don't you?"

"I don't care."

"You don't care? Did you think any of this through? Do you even understand?"

"You love Amandine," Angela says, her voice breaking. "You haven't loved anyone like this since Cressida."

They both fall silent at the mention of Cressida, staring at each other defiantly, neither of them so much as flinching. Kersti watches numbly, transfixed, finally piecing it all together. "Is that why you pushed Cressida?" she asks Angela. "Out of jealousy?"

Angela says nothing. Her expression is blank, her blue eyes strangely vacant, as though all hope has gone out of them.

"Angela and I have an unspoken arrangement," Hamidou says, reaching for a cigarette.

Kersti holds her breath, bracing for the truth. Her heart is pounding so hard it feels like the room is shaking. She instinctively places her hands on her belly and looks over at Angela, fixated on her body barricading the door.

"Cressida never threatened me with the ledger," Hamidou says. "Angela is the one she went to."

Kersti stares at Angela. It makes sense now. Cressida went to each and every one of Hamidou's victims—Lille, Alison, and Angela—and told them what she was going to do.

"She came to my room at study hall," Angela recalls, sitting down on a green velvet armchair by the door. "She said she had something that would make us free. She said Claudine would never harm another girl again."

She shakes her head, looking as bewildered and confused as she must have looked to Cressida back then. "I told her Claudine had never hurt me and that we were in love, but she laughed at me and handed me the Polaroid photograph of herself in Claudine's bed. I asked her where she got it. She told me she took it from Claudine's room and that she had others. *Keep it,* she said. *There are plenty more where this came from.*"

At the other end of the room, Hamidou lights a Gauloises off the one she's already smoking and fills the air with more of that pungent smell.

"It made me very angry," Angela says. "I went to Claudine's room and I looked in her drawers and I found more pictures." She looks over at Hamidou, her face and neck splotchy. "And their love notes, as well."

"I loved all of you," Hamidou interjects softly.

"Cressida told me she was going to speak to Bueche," Angela resumes. "She was going to tell him about my relationship with Claudine. I asked her how she knew about us and she said she used to sit on the stairs and wait for me to come out of Claudine's room."

Kersti remembers the night they caught Angela creeping around on the second floor. Cressida must have known why Angela was there. It breaks her heart to imagine Cressida huddled on the stairwell in her nightgown, waiting to see who would tiptoe out of Hamidou's room each night. Had she been jealous? Or merely gathering evidence?

"I warned her not to go to Bueche," Angela says, her voice rising. "She knew it would destroy Claudine's life, but she didn't care."

Kersti is very still, doesn't dare speak. Angela is watching Kersti watch the door. She must be aware of Kersti's discomfort because she gets up, folds her arms across her chest, and plants herself in front of the door again before continuing with her story.

"She went out that night and I waited for her in her room," Angela says, never taking her eyes off Kersti. "She came back very drunk. After curfew, of course. Claudine never made Cressida follow the rules. Isn't that right, Claudine?"

Hamidou doesn't answer and Kersti realizes she's witnessing the bitter end of their sick relationship.

"Cressida was drinking from a bottle of vodka. I asked her to give me the photographs but she said she buried them somewhere and I would never find them. She went outside on the balcony to smoke. I followed her."

Kersti sinks into the couch, reeling.

"I was trying to protect you," Angela tells Hamidou, tears springing to her eyes. "I love you, Claude. I've always loved you and I thought you loved me. Why else would we still be together?"

"Why? Because you've been holding me hostage for almost twenty years."

"I have not—"

"We both know the implication has always been very clear. That's why you kept my pictures of Cressida. So I wouldn't leave you."

"But you were planning to leave me anyway, weren't you?" Angela says, sounding hurt and resigned.

"So you gave Kersti those photographs to punish me?"

When Angela doesn't respond, Hamidou turns to Kersti. "After she pushed Cressida, she came to me and confessed everything. I made her write a suicide note and I helped her cover it up."

"Didn't you think someone would figure out it wasn't Cressida's handwriting?" Kersti asks.

"But no one did," Hamidou responds. "As I knew they wouldn't."

"How?"

"Because I knew there would be no investigation," she explains. "Because I knew Bueche. It was quickly and quietly swept under the rug, as I knew it would be. As it always was."

"You helped her get away with trying to kill Cressida?" Kersti whispers, heartbroken. "I thought you loved her—"

"I did," Hamidou says, sounding remorseful for the first time all night. "But Angela had my pictures and my letters. She kept them locked someplace all these years so that if I ever decided to turn her in or leave her, she had leverage."

"Cressida didn't die," Angela points out, sounding disappointed.

"She may as well have," Hamidou says, looking very old and defeated. "You think pushing her off a balcony could stop me from loving her? All it did was bind you and me together like hostages. That's all we are now, Angela."

Kersti's phone starts vibrating in her purse. She ignores it but Angela and Hamidou suddenly look over at her with worried expressions. It occurs to Kersti that something has to be done now. One of them has confessed to attempted murder, the other to covering it up and to sexually abusing God knows how many girls.

They're both watching her, probably trying to decide what to do. If only Angela would get the hell away from the door and sit down on the couch. Kersti's phone starts up again, vibrating with calls and texts. She reaches for it and reads Jay's last text.

WHERE THE HELL ARE YOU?

She manages to type 14 Béthusy before Angela comes over and takes the phone right out of her hand. Kersti's not even sure the message was sent. She looks over at Hamidou, searching for that long-ago ally, but she's gone.

I'm in danger, Kersti thinks. The realization is like a punch in the throat. When she decided to stop by here tonight she didn't consider for a second that Hamidou—now in her late seventies—would pose any kind of threat to her safety. She hadn't counted on Angela Zumpt.

"My husband is on his way," Kersti mumbles, hardly able to breathe.

"What are you going to do, Kersti?" Hamidou asks her.

"I don't really have any options," Kersti says in a small voice. "Neither do you—"

"Claudine?" Angela says. "Was nun?"

"Ich weiß es nicht," Hamidou says.

Kersti doesn't like them speaking German. It makes her extremely anxious. She stands up, scheming how to get past Angela and out of the apartment.

"Where are the photographs Angela gave you?" Hamidou asks her.

"At my hotel," Kersti says, inching toward the door. "Everyone knows. I told Bueche, Deirdre, my husband—"

"Why did you come here then?" Hamidou wants to know. "If you already have everything you need?"

"I wanted you to look me in the eyes and admit it," Kersti says. "I wanted to hear you say that you're sorry. And I wanted you to know that *I* know, we all know."

"And that would give you what?" Hamidou says. "Peace of mind?"

"I don't know."

"Did it?"

Kersti looks away.

"Maybe you should have thought more about taking care of yourself and your baby," Angela says. "Instead of coming here to avenge Cressida. But she was good at that, wasn't she? Getting people to think about *her* and do things for *her.* Now look where it got you."

Angela is staring at her. Kersti can feel the fear twisting and tightening in her chest. She looks over at Hamidou, counting on her to still have some common sense left. "You have to know it's over," she says softly.

Hamidou lights another cigarette. She turns and looks out the window, not saying anything. Angela doesn't budge. Kersti swallows nervously, fighting back tears. She doesn't want them to know how scared she is.

"Your husband hasn't answered your text," Angela says, looking at Kersti's cell phone in her hand. "Perhaps he fell asleep?"

It's possible, Kersti thinks with a sinking heart. He's still jet-lagged. He thinks she's out with the girls reminiscing about old times.

"We might have time," Angela says to Hamidou. They start speaking German again. Kersti makes out the words Algeria, Paris. "Wir haben Zeit."

Kersti considers they could feasibly get away.

"Claudine," Angela says. "Tell me what to do."

Hamidou's eyes lock with Kersti's. She stubs out her cigarette and disappears into her bedroom without a word. Angela takes a step toward Kersti and Kersti backs away. All she can think about is Jay and their babies. What has she done? He warned her. He told her to stop playing detective and leave it to Deirdre, but she wouldn't listen. She kept bulldozing her way through the lives of everyone who ever knew Cressida. Bulldozing and bullying, doing whatever it took to get what she wanted. *Jäärapäine.* And for what? Justice for Cressida? Insatiable curiosity? A great story for her next book? Personal vindication?

Yes, Kersti thinks. It was for all those things. Somewhere along the way, she got hijacked by the adventure, by what she kept discovering about herself.

"Cressida only cared about Cressida," Angela says, stepping closer to her. Sounding almost childlike.

Did Cressida know she was in danger right before Angela pushed her? Did it unfold the way this moment is unfolding for Kersti?

"Angela, you're a victim in this," she says, trying to talk her off the ledge. "You were only a child when it started. You were hurt and confused. Nothing would happen to you now. It's *she* who should be locked up—"

"I am not a victim," Angela says. "I love her. She's my life."

Angela is towering over her now. Her eyes are bottomless pools of dark blue, implacable. Kersti eyes the door, but Angela's body is a wall.

Kersti's phone starts vibrating in Angela's hand. They both look down at it. Angela frowns. "Claudine?" she calls out.

An antique grandfather clock is ticking loudly in the corner of the room, measuring each agonizing minute, second, millisecond.

After a seemingly eternal moment, Hamidou's voice from the bedroom beckons Angela.

Angela doesn't move. Kersti stays equally still, not daring to show a fissure of weakness. She wants to grab Angela by the neck and shake her. Does she still think something can be done? That she can be saved?

Of course she does, Kersti realizes with a violent stab of dread. She lives in her own world, always has. She has no grasp on reality.

"Angela!" Hamidou calls again. "Komm hier!"

Angela's expression is eerily blank. There's nothing there. Not rage, not fear. Not even regret. Maybe she's only capable of one authentic emotion: love for Hamidou. Perhaps nothing else has ever mattered to her.

With one last glance, Angela robotically hands Kersti her phone and evacuates her sentry position at the door. She disappears into the bedroom, where she's been summoned, the victim of a lifelong brainwashing from which there is no possible return.

Kersti lets out a tremulous breath and checks the message from Jay.

Are you OK? In cab. On my way.

She doesn't care anymore if they run, if they get away. She just wants to be safe in Jay's arms. She wants to live. She lunges for the door and escapes the apartment.

The moment she steps outside, she sees the taxi pulling up to the curb. The door opens and Jay is rushing toward her. "What the hell?" he cries, pulling her into his arms and holding her. "What's going on? What are you doing here? I've been worried out of my fucking mind—"

Inside the cab, she tells the driver, "Gendarmerie, Place de La Gare 1."

As the driver is about to pull onto the road, they hear sirens. Kersti turns around to look out the window, certain the sirens are coming toward them. As they get louder and the ambulance and fire trucks turn the corner onto Béthusy, Kersti knows exactly what they're going to find—Hamidou and Angela's bodies on the concrete. Broken necks, twisted backs, pooling blood. Hostages in life and death. There's a tragic symmetry to it all, she thinks.

The babies move inside her—that wonderful flutter that reassures her more now than ever before—and she rubs her belly, communicating silently to them. *We're safe.*

CHAPTER 38

BOSTON—July 2016

Kersti follows Laylay down the hall, past Sloane's room to the one that smells like French perfume and vanilla diffuser and moisturizer. Déjà vu.

"She's grumpy today," Laylay warns.

Kersti takes a tentative step inside the room. Cressida is staring up at the ceiling with uninhabited eyes.

"Hey, Cress."

Cressida doesn't move. Kersti approaches and sits down on the edge of the adjustable bed. Cressida is pale today. Her hair is tied back in a bun and she's wearing mascara and plum-colored lipstick, but her cheeks don't have their usual glow. She smells of Lubriderm.

Deirdre hasn't told Cressida anything about what happened in Switzerland and she made it very clear that Kersti wasn't to say anything, either. "There's no point upsetting her now," Deirdre said, her tone a command.

Kersti isn't sure she agrees. Deirdre underestimates post-accident Cressida. Kersti suspects she knows and understands a lot more than Deirdre thinks and might possibly get some peace if she knew how things had ended in Lausanne.

"How are you?" Kersti asks Cressida.

Cressida blinks.

Kersti watches her for a long time, resisting the urge to tell her about Angela and Hamidou. Instead, she takes her hand, leans in very close, and whispers, "I'm so sorry."

Cressida doesn't react.

"I *know,*" Kersti adds, her voice full of compassion. "I know what happened to you."

Cressida squeezes Kersti's hand, hard. And then she turns her head away and stares out the picture window, leaving Kersti to wonder what's going through her mind. Do Kersti's words mean anything to her?

Maybe she'll die soon, Kersti thinks, feeling guilty for even entertaining it. But what kind of life is this for someone like Cressida? Surely, *she* must want it to end. And when it matters, Cressida gets her way.

Her life has already been too long. She once told Kersti that life was short. How could she have known that back then? Kersti assumed with typical adolescent hubris that life would go on forever. In her ignorance, she believed time was a given, disposable and abundant. Cressida, on the other hand, had an eerie intuitiveness and seemed to understand on some level that she had to grab everything she could while she was still cresting with promise, beauty, youth, vitality; while she was still desirable and fertile. Kersti was far more lackadaisical and thought everything would endure—her angst, her opportunities.

But the Lycée was a moment in time, as evanescent as their splendid youth and as anointed as the chance meeting of sperm and egg to create life. A precious, perilous moment where events converged and unfolded in perfect, divine alignment, right up until the moment Cressida fell.

The day of your arrival is fast approaching and I'm feeling very contemplative. I find myself looking back over this year and I'm absolutely certain that some divine power, along with my newfound tenacity and single-mindedness, orchestrated every moment of this journey.

Here's what I want you to know: you can't live life by default. I suffered so much because I allowed myself to be the passenger in my own life. I didn't think I deserved, or was allowed, to expect more. (And yet I see now that my decision to marry your father in the face of my family's disapproval was the first glimpse of grit and doggedness I'd ever shown. I suppose I had it in me all along.)

I told you when I first started writing this letter that everything I did to bring you forth made perfect sense to me at the time. And it still does. I hope it will to you one day. I loved you long before you were ever conceived. I loved the idea of you, the possibility of you, the promise you held for me. And when I realized that this love might never get a chance to express itself—that it could possibly perish inside me—I woke up. I instinctively knew that passivity and self-doubt wouldn't cut it anymore, and I finally began to act with resolve. I began to act, period.

Maybe I defied the universe, if that's even possible. Or maybe I answered a call, acting on pure instinct, as Cressida would have done. I miss her more now than before I knew her story. I've decided to remember her as someone noble, impossibly strong, a survivor. She's the reason you exist. Not just because we used her eggs but also because she showed me how to go after what I want. She taught me to stake my claim at all costs.

It took me a long time to muster the nerve, but you summoned me to fight, to do the inconceivable and be utterly dauntless about my ambition. The best part is, the harder I fought—not just for you, but also for the truth—the more I began to like myself.

I don't care what anyone thinks about my choices. How freeing that is to say and to actually mean it! Yes, what we did was madness, but you were created from an irrational and outlandish love. How can that not be right?

ACKNOWLEDGMENTS

First and foremost, a huge thank you to Billy Mernit, my Hollywood guru, mentor, writing instructor, and the man who helped bring this book to life. I credit you fully with the rebirth of my writing career, and for having re-ignited my passion and enthusiasm with your brilliant insights and your gift for understanding how to tell a damn good story. Every writer should have a Billy.

Thank you to my patient and tireless agent, Bev Slopen, who never gives up on me. You are my greatest champion and my best reality check, and I am so grateful that you took me under your wing when I showed up with my mom twenty years ago. We did it!

Thank you to Jennifer Barth, who changed everything when she welcomed me into the Harper Collins family. It's been a thrill and an honor to work with you. Thank you for taking such good care of this book.

Thank you to Jessie and Luke for always entertaining me, making me laugh (and cry), filling my days with joy, and letting Mama write when she needs to write. I am truly blessed.

A most special thank you to my "live-in" editor and self-described "co-author" of the book, Miguel. Your red 'X's and scribbles on my pages—*Embarrassing! Pathetic writing! Rewrite!*—never fail to take my books to the next level. And on top of always being my first and most brutally honest reader, thank you for picking up the kids and driving them all over the city and letting me be The Writer. I love you.

Finally, thank you to my mother, Marsheh, whom I miss every single moment of every single day. I wish you were here to hold and read this book, to come to all my readings, to give me the support you always gave me and to still be my number one fan. You knew I was a writer even before I did, reading and celebrating every word I ever wrote from the time I was four years old. I am a writer because of you. And I have to believe that there's a huge Indigo up there, and you still spend your days *schma-ing* through books, and you'll see mine there and read it, and I'll know.

ABOUT THE AUTHOR

JOANNA GOODMAN is the author of three previous novels. Originally from Montreal, Joanna now lives in Toronto with her husband and two children, and is the owner of the Canadian linen company Au Lit Fine Linens.